**The rugged, masculine and independent men
of America's West know the value of hard work,
honor and family. They may be ranchers, tycoons
or the guy next door, but they're all cowboys at heart.
Don't miss any of the books in this collection!**

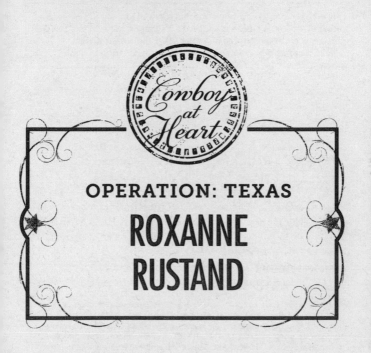

Cowboy
at
Heart

OPERATION: TEXAS

ROXANNE RUSTAND

HARLEQUIN®

entertain, enrich, inspire™

Recycling programs
for this product may
not exist in your area.

ISBN-13: 978-0-373-82606-3

OPERATION: TEXAS

ROXANNE RUSTAND

lives in the country with her husband and a menagerie of pets, many of whom find their way into her books. She works part-time as a registered dietitian at a psychiatric facility, but otherwise you'll find her writing at home in her jammies, surrounded by three dogs begging for treats, or out in the barn with the horses. Her favorite time of all is when her kids are home—though all three are now busy with college and jobs.

RT Book Reviews nominated her for a Career Achievement Award in 2005, and she won the magazine's award for Best Superromance of 2006.

She loves to hear from readers!
Her snail-mail address is P.O. Box 2550,
Cedar Rapids, IA 52406-2550.
You can also contact her at:
www.roxannerustand.com,
www.shoutlife.com/roxannerustand or at her blog,
where readers and writers talk about their pets, at
www.roxannerustand.blogspot.com.

Acknowledgments

Many thanks to the past and present Texans
who provided so much help with the research
for this book, including Peggy and Jim Phifer,
Betty Owen, Susan DeLay, Kathy Bennett and
especially the wonderful Superromance author
and Texan, K.N. Casper.

Thanks also to
Nancy and Dave Nicholson,
for their technical advice on weapons.

To Diane, Nancy and Jacquie
with deepest appreciation for our friendship.
And as always, to Larry, Brian, Emily, Andy,
Jenni and our little sweetheart Danielle,
because I love you all so much!

Chapter One

AT THE SOUND of a truck door slamming, Celia Remington grabbed her rifle and strode down the aisle of the barn, anger simmering through her veins.

Eight miles of rough ranch road led out to the highway, and another forty miles of pure desolation lay between here and the tiny town of Saguaro Springs, Texas. Visitors—the welcome kind—rarely stopped by.

The unwelcome kind came far too often.

But the truck parked outside wasn't Garcia's silver Ford, and the tall, broad-shouldered stranger sauntering toward her wasn't the cocky little bastard who'd delivered Garcia's threats in the past.

"Brady Coleman, ma'am."

The rifle lowered at her side, she stepped out into the bright March sunshine. "Who?"

"Sorry I'm late getting here. I was held up for a few days in El Paso."

This was the guy who'd called last week about a job? She'd been rushing outside to tend a difficult calving at the time, and hadn't even caught his name. "Today's fine. No problem."

Definitely no problem at all.

She'd held little hope that her advertisement in the county paper would garner any notice, much less bring her a capable ranch hand. The last two applicants had been stove-up old cowboys with missing teeth and a mind-numbing smell of bad whiskey, barely able to sit a horse.

Maybe there was something about this guy that was a little too…polished, for an ordinary ranch-hand, but his saddle-worn Levi's, black Resistol and scarred western boots were those of an experienced cowboy, and he appeared muscled and fit, young enough to put in a good day's work.

Best of all, he looked like he could take on someone in a fight, deck him, and be ready for more. Given the increasing numbers of late-night trespassers fording the Rio Grande and crossing her ranch, he'd be perfect.

"We'll be branding, fencing and moving cattle onto summer range soon. I do some horse training, but you won't be involved in that." She narrowed her gaze. "As the ad said, no drugs, no alcohol. Wages include a cabin and meals up at the house."

"Wages?"

Her heart sank. "You're not here about a job?"

Pulling back the lower hem of his denim jacket at an angle, he displayed a silver badge clipped to his belt. "Special Agent Coleman. DEA."

Startled, she stared at the badge.

"Agent Luis Mendoza talked to you several weeks ago. Remember?" he added in a voice gentle enough to reassure a small child.

His patronizing tone bit deep. "Of course I remember."

She'd called the DEA regional office several times and had been expecting the arrival of a female agent next weekend. This guy had to be for real, though, because no one around here knew about those calls.

Even so, his presence sent a shiver down her spine that had nothing to do with the slow grin deepening the dimples in his rugged face, or that strong jaw. He was living proof that the DEA had taken her seriously.

Finally.

Frowning, she surveyed the black Dodge Ram pickup parked at the edge of the fenced yard. A couple of dusty duffel bags were piled in the back, along with a well-worn roping saddle. "So where is she?"

"She?"

"The agent—the woman who was supposed to come out here. Did you bring her?"

He shrugged. "Change of plans. They sent me instead."

Remembering all that had happened at the ranch, her frustration grew. "But the DEA guy I talked to said—"

"He planned to request Agent Sara Hanrahan from the Dallas field office, but she's been transferred to Fargo."

Celia cradled the rifle in the crook of her arm and tugged off her buckskin gloves, slapped them against her thigh, and stuffed them in the hip pocket of her Levi's. "You can't get her anyway?"

"She's in the middle of a major case up north."

He folded his arms across his chest, appearing entirely too resolute, and she gave an exasperated sigh. "Look, I told people around here that I had a *cousin* coming to stay this spring. No one would have questioned her arrival. There isn't another female agent?"

"No one who is available for the next several months. You need an agent who isn't from this part of Texas—someone who can work undercover as a ranch hand won't be recognized. You also need someone with ranch experience, who can handle a horse and who's familiar with drug trafficking along the Rio Grande. So you got me."

He exuded confidence. Control. He probably dealt with bad guys seven days a week, and maybe he was exactly what she needed. But how was she going to explain away a guy like this one? He looked like Joe Hollywood, not a working cowboy.

Over his shoulder, she saw her two ranch hands watching them from the machine shed. Adan Calaveras lounged at the door, his young face filled with suspicion at the arrival of this newcomer. Old Vicente Marquez stood beside him, his gnarled, leathery hands propped on his hips.

As much a fixture on the ranch as the weathered buildings and the ancient saguaro cacti marching across the desolate landscape, Vicente had worked here since her grandfather's early years. Now, he mostly cooked meals, ran occasional errands and helped out in other ways when his arthritis wasn't acting up. Adan had drifted in just six months ago and never left.

Both of them were scowling at her latest "job applicant."

Adan finally gave an irritable jerk of his head and disappeared into the machine shed, but Vicente started walking toward the main barn.

"Please, come to my office," she said in a low voice. "Vicente is on his way, and this needs to be private."

Brady shot a swift, assessing glance at the older man. "You don't trust him?"

"With my life. But the fewer people who hear this, the better." She pivoted and led Coleman across the parking area to the back door of the sprawling adobe ranch house, then through the kitchen and down the hall to her office, where she shut the door behind them.

Coleman took off his hat and sunglasses and held them loosely at his side as he surveyed the room.

Getting a better look at him now, she was even more convinced that no one would ever buy the idea that he'd come here to ride fence, herd cattle, and pitch manure.

His warm brown eyes were intense, assessing, intelligent. His wide forehead, solid jaw and sensual lines of his mouth made him look like some up-and-coming newscaster for a major network, not a saddle-worn cowboy drifting from one ranch to the next.

"Nice," he said, running a hand over the carved back of one of the two horsehide-upholstered chairs placed in front of her desk. "Collect antiques?"

"We live with them, one generation to the next. My family has owned this ranch since the 1800s." Celia gave an impatient wave of her hand. "Look, we need to get down to business here, if you're going to stay. We can say that I hired you, but I'm not sure people will believe it."

He waited until she settled her rifle in the gun rack behind the desk and sat down, then he pulled up one of the chairs and sat, propping an elbow on the edge of the desk as he retrieved a small notebook from his shirt pocket.

"That's one option. Another is that I could be an old college boyfriend." His seductive voice lowered, and a teasing glint lit his dark eyes. "One who wants to hang around a while, hoping for a second chance."

A funny little flutter tickled her midsection as she tried to imagine a guy like this one begging for another chance with her. Not likely, but the vision was enticing and it took a moment to rein in her wayward thoughts.

"Skip *that* idea. Though," she added darkly, "I'm not so sure the first is any better. How much do you know about this kind of work?"

"I grew up on a ranch. I know my way around livestock, ma'am."

"Kind of a stretch, isn't it—ending up in the DEA?"

"Our ranch went under when I was fifteen. I didn't have money for college, so I spent four years in the Marines, then earned a couple of degrees in law enforcement and business." He gave her a patient smile. "I may be a little rusty, but I was on a horse before I could walk."

This wasn't ideal. But with a thirteen-year-old daughter, livestock and a ranch to protect, she had to take what she could get.

"You still look doubtful," he said with a low laugh. "If people ask, just say that I was in the area and called you just for old times' sake. You needed help, I was looking for a temporary job. The past relationship angle will give me more mobility, and more access to the locals. An ordinary ranch hand wouldn't get to town much, except for Saturday night."

She frowned at him. "I'll need to lie to people I've known all my life, and I don't even know if I can pull that off."

"Just don't say anything, then."

"You have *no* idea what this will do to the gossip mill around here. People will assume we're having an affair, and long after you leave, they'll be patting me on the hand and saying, 'I'm so sorry, dear—you must be heartbroken.'"

"Not if you say that you ordered me off your ranch after discovering I was a no-good, lying cheat. I won't be here long—a couple months at the most."

"Well…"

He took her hesitation as a yes and gave a nod of approval. "You'll need to give me regular paychecks, or your banker might realize that something's fishy. I'll cash them, and give the money back." A flash of amusement lit his eyes. "Just out of curiosity, what does a ranch hand make these days?"

She quoted the pitifully low wages she could afford right now, then jerked her chin toward three small cabins set back in the willows lining Cavalas Creek, a hundred yards west of the main house. "Last one on the right can be yours. It's small but clean, so if you have a wife or…um…someone who'd want to stop by…"

"Not married, no commitments."

A muscle ticked at the side of his jaw—a touchy subject, maybe? But surely a guy like this one would have no trouble finding Mrs. Right…or plenty of women who would settle for less than a wedding ring.

"Lucky, then," Celia said lightly. "Not many women find this area appealing."

But his single status wasn't so lucky. Not for Celia, anyway.

There was something about him that made her wish she'd thought to put on mascara and a better pair of jeans this morning, and the very last thing she needed was to start thinking with her heart. Never would she regret the birth of her beloved daughter, but she wouldn't risk making a foolish mistake again, either.

He searched her face. "What's kept you here? It's lonely. Isolated. And God knows, it must be hard work for a woman with just an old man and a boy to help out."

The sympathy and curiosity in his eyes rankled, and she had to take a steadying breath before answering. Over the years, too many people had assumed she would give up. She'd had to fight for respect and prove herself many times over, to her ranch hands, her customers and even the community.

"This place is my daughter's legacy—and for her children's children. It's our heritage, and I'm not a quitter."

Not like my mom was. On some of her worst days, when the hard work and struggle seemed almost insurmountable, Celia had only to remember her mom's breezy departure, on the arm of a rodeo cowboy, to feel renewed resolve. At the age of ten, she'd been devastated. At thirty-two, she was a far stronger woman than she might have been.

She watched him study his notebook. "When do you want to start?"

"Today." He tucked the notebook back into his pocket. "You reported an increase in late-night traffic across your land. Anything else since then?"

"Not anything specific…a prickly, uneasy feeling that I'm being watched, sometimes, when I go outside after dark. A few phone call hang-ups later at night." Situations for which she could provide no solid evidence, and which he'd probably attribute to paranoia.

He frowned. "You and your daughter need to stay close to home until this is over."

Celia felt a tremor of anger. At him, for assuming he could give her orders. At the drug traffickers who had changed her life in so many ways. "My daughter will, of course. But I've been dealing with this situation for a long time, and my ranch doesn't run itself."

"I don't want anyone here getting hurt." His eyes locked on hers, telegraphing exactly how serious he was. "Be careful. Report any unusual activity that you see or hear, but take no action yourself. Deal?"

She'd grown up hunting coyotes with her rifle, and had spent a lifetime wrangling cattle and training horses. For the past thirteen years, she'd managed this ranch and earned the grudging respect of the proud Mexican cowboys she employed, but she hadn't been able to stem the tide of drug runners crossing her land. Would there be even greater danger now? Higher risks for her family and workers?

She hesitated, then nodded. "Deal."

Feeling the firm confidence of Brady's handshake, more like that of an excutive than a cowboy, she hoped she hadn't made a big mistake by setting this all in motion.

"So where is this fine cowboy of yours?" Vicente waved an arthritic hand toward the empty chair at the kitchen table.

Across from him, Adan looked up from his plate loaded with Vicente's specialty—enchiladas and refried beans. "Big mistake," he said darkly. He chugged down his glass of milk and pushed away from the table. "Guys like him belong on some fancy dude ranch, not here. Where did you say you met him?"

"College. He and I dated a few times before I met Ethan. He needed a job, and he was willing to take this one short-term." The lie settled uneasily in her stomach as she forked up another bite of her salad and eyed the clock above the stove.

Adan followed her gaze and smirked. "He's probably lost."

After Brady had settled his meager possessions into his cabin, she'd pointed out a good buckskin in the corral and sent him up into the hills over the north ridge to check the fence line. Celia bit her lower lip. He'd been gone over four hours. "He'll be fine. We can set a plate of leftovers for him in the fridge."

Adan snorted. "Maybe he's taking a nice nap in the shade."

"Or maybe ole Buck dumped him off on some cholla." Vicente gave her a broad wink. "That would be fun, no?"

Celia winced at the memory of her own childhood experience with a cholla. In pain every step of the way, she'd had to lead her pony a good two miles home to the ranch.

The humiliation of being bucked off had surpassed having to bare her backside while her mother deftly tweezed out a few hundred cactus spines.

"Maybe he's out there frying like some burrito." Adan moved to the kitchen sink and rinsed his dishes, his swagger reminiscent of his former life. "*That* would be a big loss."

Through the windows to the west, the evening sun balanced on the tips of the Quitman Mountains, gilding the endless expanse of sand and sagebrush leading out into the desert.

She'd watched Brady catch and saddle the gelding, and his movements had been swift and sure. He'd swung up into the saddle with the grace of someone who'd spent a lifetime on horseback and headed for the rugged pastures, where sparse grama grass and greasewood fed her cattle.

If he'd run into trouble, the canyons and rocky ravines studded with prickly ash and soapberry trees could offer respite from the sun. Surely he was okay.

Even so, she gathered her own dishes and crossed the spacious kitchen to peer out the windows again. A beachball-size tumbleweed bounced across the yard. Mojo, her ten-month-old golden and border collie mix, slept in the shade of the ranch pickup.

"What's your problem?" She gave Adan a quelling stare. "Brady's big and strong, and he's going to make our lives easier. We need help, now that my grandfather's ill—at least for a few months."

"You told him about this new guy yet?" Adan shot back.

"I run this ranch now, Adan. It's my decision."

At the table, Vicente took a long swallow of his coffee and rose stiffly. "I'm going to mass as soon as I get this kitchen picked up. Anyone want to come along?"

"Count me in." Adan spun around and reached for his Resistol and a set of keys on the row of hooks in the entryway. "I'll get the truck started."

Vicente chortled as the boy slipped out the door and thundered down the wooden porch steps. "He's stir crazy as a bull in spring."

The old Mexican faithfully attended Saturday evening mass. Adan never joined him in church, but never missed a chance to head for town, either.

"Just try to bring him home with you, okay?" Celia warned. "Last time…"

"Yeah…he don't look for trouble, but it sure looks for him."

And last time, it had cost her fifty dollars and a lot of fast talking with the new sheriff, Ramon Quintero, down at the local jail.

From the first day Adan had shown up at her ranch, he'd reminded her of her late brother, who'd run wild and rebelled as a teenager…then died in a car wreck just as he was turning his life around. This eighteen-year-old had faced a lot of tough breaks, too, but he also had potential. She was doing her best to see he reached it.

"Well, do what you can to keep him out of trouble, okay?"

Nodding, Vicente gathered up the salsa bottle and other condiments from the table. "Heard from Lacey?"

"She called. She didn't sound all that happy about her bunkmates, and says she's really looking forward to coming home to her horse." Celia smiled at the thought of her thirteen-year-old daughter, who'd been so excited about the prospect of going off to scout camp over spring break—until the day she had to pack. "I don't think she has a lot in common with some of the city girls, but it's a good experience for her."

After helping him rinse the dishes and load them in the dishwasher, Celia shooed Vicente out the door and finished up the counters. At seven o'clock, she gave another worried glance out the windows.

The buckskin wasn't back in his corral, and the sun had slipped below the horizon. The temperature was already dropping. *Where are you, Brady?*

Surely Buck would have come home alone if Brady had fallen...unless the horse had stepped in a prairie dog hole and left his rider to come home on foot. And then, there was the possibility that he'd encountered someone unexpected.

And that could be fatal.

Grabbing her worn leather gloves from the bench by the back door, she stepped outside and whistled for Mojo as she strode to the corral by the barn. In ten minutes, she'd saddled her big bay mare, Duster, settled her Ruger .30-06 into its rifle scabbard on her saddle, and was headed up over the first ridge with the dog tagging along behind, its tongue lolling and tail waving.

At the top of the ridge, Celia pulled to a halt and lifted a pair of binoculars from her saddlebag.

Twenty thousand acres of Triple R sagebrush-strewn grassland spread out before her, reaching to the horizon in three directions.

Just a few miles to the north, her best grazing land faded into parched, high desert terrain. Two miles to the west lay the Rio Grande, and beyond it, Mexico.

She stood in her stirrups and slowly twisted, studying the barren landscape. No sign of a buckskin gelding…no sign of a man on foot. Lowering the binoculars, she urged Duster into a lope and headed down one slope and up the next until sweat lathered the mare's neck and the eastern sky darkened to the deep indigo of nightfall.

At the top of yet another low rise she stood in her stirrups and scanned the terrain once more, then slumped down in her saddle. The local cellular company offered poor reception at best. Out here, there weren't any cell towers for miles, so there hadn't been much reason to carry a phone. It would take a good hour to get home and call the Gelman County sheriff to request a search party.

And in the meantime, Brady Coleman could be somewhere out here. Bleeding to death. Unconscious. Easy prey for a pack of hungry coyotes or a mountain lion.

Uttering a quiet prayer under her breath, she reined her horse into a neat pivot and started for home.

Mojo rushed ahead, then veered off to the west and stood barking at the top of a small knoll. Her tail wagging furiously, she looked over her shoulder at Celia, her barks escalating.

Hope flooded through Celia as she reined the mare toward the knoll and urged her into a lope. At the top, she pulled to a halt. It didn't take long to see why Mojo was excited.

In the distance, she could make out the dirt road bordering the Triple R's western boundary. No one ever used it unless they were lost—or were high-tailing into the USA from the Mexican border.

Riding from the other direction, she hadn't seen this particular spot. But now, through the scraggly trees growing at the base of a rocky outcropping, she could see a dark vehicle. In its headlights were the silhouettes of a horse and several tall figures.

"Hush." She dismounted and quickly silenced the dog with a gentle hand on her shoulders, then moved her mare behind the knoll and ground—tied her out of sight.

THE OTHER HORSE fidgeted and danced sideways into the pool of light in front of the vehicle. Its coat flashed pale—buckskin?—before it moved away from the light.

"Buck?" Celia breathed, her senses sharpening. The cool evening air slid over her as she lowered herself to the ground and adjusted her binoculars.

The vehicle was clearly a dark SUV. Their faces were indiscernible, but the three broad-shouldered figures were probably male. Two of them gestured expansively, and after a few minutes, they climbed into the SUV, hauled it into a jerky, three-point turn, and headed north toward the county highway.

The third guy swung up into the saddle and headed south. And from the way he sat his horse, she no longer had any doubt about his identity.

She'd sent Brady out here to do a ranch hand's

job, and he sure hadn't said a word about meeting any of his "fellow agents" tonight. Maybe he *was* with the DEA—she'd seen his badge and accepted his obvious knowledge of her conversations with the local office—but that didn't mean he was honest.

Sometimes, the vast amount of money flowing through the bigger drug trafficking organizations was too great a lure for those sworn to stop it. Her thoughts flicked to Aubrey Booker, the previous county sheriff, who'd collected his salary and then tripled it with payoffs from drug traffickers who used Gelman County as a convenient trade route. Apparently, they hadn't been satisfied with his cooperation. Found dead in his living room with a bullet through the heart, he hadn't lived long enough to enjoy an early retirement.

Maybe she'd welcomed a man to the Triple R who was just as dangerous as the ones who crossed her land under the cover of night. A man who would now be living within sight of the main house...and thus know exactly when her young daughter and elderly grandfather were alone.

Celia whistled softly to Mojo as she gathered up her reins and eased into her saddle. She knew this land like she knew her own face. By the light of the half-moon above she could ride parallel to him, move faster and beat him home.

She brushed her fingertips against the reassuring weight of her rifle and scabbard, then urged Duster into a dead run.

And prayed that Brady wasn't what he seemed.

ADAN WATCHED THE old man cross the deserted street and trudge up the six steps to Saint Mary's. "Come with me," Vicente had urged him—as if *that* would ever happen. Any religion he'd ever had as a kid had been ground to dust long ago.

His mother had worked hard at two jobs after his dad split, and she had taken in a brood of his cousins when their parents were sentenced for running a meth lab. She'd never missed attending mass. Despite all that goodness in her life, she'd died in a hit-and-run accident with a lousy drunk at the wheel when Adan was fourteen.

His two sisters and cousins ended up living with another aunt and uncle. Adan ended up living on the street. And two years later, his sentence to one of the toughest detention centers in Texas had confirmed Adan's lack of belief. Maybe there was a God, but He sure as hell hadn't been watching Adan's back any time it counted.

Not when his mom lay bleeding to death on a street corner.

Not when another juvie secretly slipped a shiv made from a stolen table knife under Adan's bunk for safekeeping, just before inspection.

For that, Adan had spent the last four months of his sentence—until he turned eighteen—in solitary. Twenty-three hours a day in a windowless, six-by-ten cell, with one hour of exercising alone, had nearly driven him crazy.

But now he was free. *Free.* And there was no way he'd risk going back. Maybe a Saturday night in this one-dog town wasn't exciting, but at least he could feel the hot wind in his hair and do just what he wanted.

He sauntered down the empty sidewalk, still feeling—after nearly six months—almost light-headed as he looked at the cheerful scattering of lights glowing from houses huddled close to the two-block-long main drag. Colorful neon Corona and Miller beer signs hung in the windows of Juan's Cantina a few doors down, a place where you could buy a good Mexican dinner and two beers with a ten-dollar bill and still come out with enough change to buy a magazine in the little grocery store next door.

He'd done that for a while, anyway, until Juan's wife Trinidad had folded her arms over her massive bosom and demanded Adan's fake ID. One glance and she'd tossed it in the waste bin by the front door.

"You can come for the food," she announced, her dark eyes flashing and her mouth pulled in a grim line. "The rest, when you turn twenty-one."

The memory still rankled, but there was no other place open in town and Vicente's mass would last another forty-four minutes. Setting his jaw, Adan strode to the cantina and jerked the door open.

As usual, Juan was standing behind the bar, drying glassware with a striped bar towel. At the jangle of the bell hanging above the front door, his wife poked her head out of the kitchen and gave Adan a curt nod, then disappeared.

But everything—Juan, his wife, the gleaming bottles of liquor on the glass shelves behind the bar, and the pair of wiry cowboys hunched over a hand of poker—faded as Adan's eyes settled on the most beautiful girl he'd ever seen.

She was reading a book at one of the tables, with an untouched hamburger and glass of lemonade in front of her, her silky black hair shimmering down to her waist and her chin propped on a slender hand.

He didn't know one thing about fancy clothes, but the white dress she wore skimmed her slender figure and accented her smooth, golden skin, and probably cost more than he'd ever be able to make in a month.

From behind the bar, Juan winked and waved him toward a table near her. "What is it today, my friend? One of the best dinners this side of the border?"

"Nah. Just a Coke." Adan sauntered over to the old jukebox a few feet away from the girl and braced one arm high on its frame to study the listings. Embarrassment warmed the back of his neck as he tried to think up something to say to her.

On TV, it all looked so easy. A little flirting, some laughs and a girl would melt at a guy's feet. But he'd been off the streets during the years when most guys learned that stuff, and he didn't have a clue.

"Here you go." Juan crossed the room with a frosty glass of soda on a tray. He waggled one bushy eyebrow and shot a quick glance at the girl, then gave Adan a thumbs-up. "Say hello," he mouthed.

Adan gave the man a dollar and took the Coke. Thought hard about what to say as Juan headed for the bar. "Uh…nice night."

She kept reading for another few seconds. Then she sighed and lifted her gaze. Her dark eyes were huge, framed by long lashes, with an exotic tilt suggesting that she might not be pure Hispanic. Her pouty mouth was full and soft, and made him wonder what it would be like to kiss a pretty girl again after two long years.

But her expression couldn't have been more bored. "Are you talking to me, cowboy?"

Panic slid through him. "Um…yeah."

Her laughter was soft. Derisive. "Go play with your horses. Or go rope a cow, or something. I don't belong here, and I'm not staying long."

He'd felt awkward. Hopeful. Now his embarrassment changed to humiliation. Touching the brim of his hat, he moved past her to a table at the farthest corner of the room, where he could watch the old TV placed up on the wall.

It didn't take some city slicker to tell him he was nobody, but the pain of it still bit deep.

Chapter Two

BRADY RUBBED THE buckskin behind the ears, slipped off the bridle, and sent him on into the moonlit corral by the barn. The gelding jogged a few yards, then snuffled the dirt as he turned in a tight circle, dropped to the ground, and rolled.

Chuckling, Brady shouldered the bridle and turned to collect his saddle and blanket from the hitching rail in front of the barn.

Startled, he jerked to a halt.

Celia stood in his path with a rifle at her side like some otherworldly, avenging angel, her long, straight blond hair gleaming beneath the security light overhead and anger sparking in her eyes.

There was nothing fragile, however, about the set of her jaw or her aggressive stance. "You're back late," she said evenly. "Everything go okay?"

How had he missed hearing her approach? Four years of reconnaissance missions in the Marines and another six tracking suspects here in the States had honed his senses, keeping him wary and alert whether he was working or not.

"No problems." He met her gaze squarely. "There were some sections of fence down about a mile from here, though. Lost any cattle?"

"We'll do another count tomorrow." She studied him for a long moment, her eyes narrowed on his. "You don't have anything else to say?"

"I found a herd down in a draw, a couple miles north." Moving around her, he lifted the saddle and blanket from the hitching rail and stored them in the tack room just inside the barn. "I counted seventy-two cows and seventy calves, and they all looked healthy."

She stood waiting in the barn aisle when he stepped out of the tack room. *"And?"*

He'd grown up with a rancher's concern for cattle and predators and fence lines, but from the veiled intensity in her voice, it was pretty clear that she wasn't talking about coyotes. "I saw that herd of cattle…and a lot of wide-open land."

Those flint-gray eyes of hers flashed fire. "Pack your gear, Coleman, and get out of here."

Brady studied her, surprised at her anger. "Maybe you could tell me why you're upset. Fair enough?"

"It was getting late and you weren't home, so I saddled a horse and went looking. You met some people out there and it wasn't any 'oops, you missed the turn' kind of conversation with travelers—you seemed to know them pretty darn well. Now why would you be meeting anyone after dark in an isolated place like that? In these parts, with the Mexican border just a stone's throw away, that means just one thing to me."

She thought *he* was transporting drugs? After fixing the fence, he'd ridden another three miles looking for the most desolate, hidden location he could find near the road along the western perimeter of the ranch. Then he'd used his satellite-based phone to arrange a quick meeting with the two other agents on his team.

She'd not only followed him but had also been sharp enough to find him. He wouldn't underestimate her again.

He touched the brim of his hat. "You're wrong, Celia," he said quietly. "I'm one of the good guys, remember?"

"Then what were you doing out there?"

"I'm part of a team. I need to keep in touch—and with Adan and Vicente around, I figured it was better not to be too obvious about it."

"Really. You might have that badge, and a lot of fancy explanations, but none of that guarantees you're honest. I've run people like you off my land more times than I can count, and you won't be the last." Her mouth curled in disgust. "And just in case you get any crazy ideas, I wouldn't hesitate to pull this trigger. Texas has remarkably appropriate laws regarding self-defense."

He debated a split second, then reached for his back pocket.

Just that fast, she had her rifle raised to her shoulder. "Not so fast, Coleman. I'm beginning to like you less and less."

He slowly withdrew his billfold and set it on the hitching rail. "Photo ID. There's a business card behind it—call the number written on the back."

She gave it a contemptuous glance. "I'll call Luis at the DEA office—the guy who was *supposed* to send out a competent female agent who could do this job right."

"And that's his personal number." Brady retrieved his cell phone from his jacket pocket and set it next to his billfold. "Call him now, so we can get this straightened out."

Without taking her eyes off of him, she lowered the rifle, sidled over to retrieve the card and the phone, punched in the number, and frowned as she spoke to Luis. After several minutes of intense conversation, she ended the call and tossed the phone to Brady.

"Sorry." She gave a weary shrug. "I've learned to be careful. The sheriff and his deputies cover a huge area, and the nearest border patrol station is a good forty miles away. Out here, we have to stand on our own two feet."

For all that he didn't enjoy being at the wrong end of a weapon, he had to hand it to her—she knew how to take control of a difficult situation.

The contrast between her feminine, fine-boned body and that rifle was intriguing. A combination, he reminded himself, that he would need to ignore.

"Then we're all set?" he asked.

"Just one thing. This is going to be a difficult situation if you can't be more upfront with me."

He hesitated. Sure, she'd called in the DEA to request assistance a few weeks ago, but from the reports he'd read, her past wasn't pristine. There was a slim possibility that she wanted to divert suspicion from herself, or even sabotage a cohort.

Stranger things had happened—that case up in Fort Worth came to mind—and the last thing he'd wanted was to share any information that could jeopardize an entire operation.

An operation that could well be his last.

Obviously reading his hesitation, she gave a derisive laugh. "You sure haven't done your homework."

He had—on the bleak financial situation at the Triple R, and on Celia herself, clear back to her college days. That information alone had been enough to make him wary. "Why do you say that?"

"I've spent my life trying to keep this ranch in the black. Protecting it. Over the past few years, my dogs and I have run off more traffickers and illegals than you could count."

"Maybe you and I can make a difference."

"But you don't trust me, and I'm still not so sure

I can trust you." She gave a bitter laugh. "It was probably a waste of time to ever contact the DEA."

"No, it wasn't."

"I just don't think…"

"Consider it a chance to clear your name, then."

"What?"

"Your ranch is in financial trouble, and there've been cases where ranchers have cooperated with the drug runners just to keep their ranches afloat. So," he added after a long pause, "the agency did a background check."

"That's ridiculous! I haven't even had a parking ticket in the past ten years."

"We know," he said, watching her expression and body language, "about Ethan."

Her face paled as she stared at him, her eyes angry and accusing and hurt. There was a flicker of fear there, too, and that made him feel like a complete jerk. Her reaction was too raw, too open for anyone trying to hide secrets about the past. He'd bet his badge that she'd never been associated with the darker side of Ethan Dearborne's life.

"If you think I was involved in his party scene, then you're wrong," she said finally. She gave a bitter laugh. "I was a shy, innocent ranch girl, away at college in the big city. I had no idea about what he and his rich friends were doing for fun, until the day he died."

"He didn't just party, Celia. He sold drugs to support his habit."

"No. Maybe he made some mistakes, but he came from a good family. He was a nice guy, not some criminal."

"He also embezzled money from his parents' company."

"You're dead wrong. I think I'd like to hear everything else that you *think* you know about my past."

Brady shrugged. "Let's see…you went off to Texas A and M for college at eighteen. Rented an apartment a few blocks off campus with two gals from Lubbock. Started dating Ethan—a wealthy dude from out East—at the start of your freshman year, and your dad was upset about it."

She stared at him in disbelief. "Anything else?"

"You and your dad apparently had a falling out, because you didn't come home for Christmas that year." His gaze drifted toward the ceiling as he thought. "And Ethan must have gone home for the holidays without you, because you weren't there when he hit a little too much crack at a party and died. People around here believe you two actually eloped before then and that you kept your own name. There's no legal record of a marriage, though."

So casually related, yet those months had been the hardest she'd ever faced. Just before Christmas she'd found herself pregnant, and Ethan—a junior—hadn't been pleased. She'd been so in love with him, imagining them working things out and becoming a family.

"You finished most of your freshman year, though," Brady continued. "Until your dad was accidentally shot out in one of the pastures."

"An *accident?* I don't think so."

"That's what the report says."

"When I got home he was in a coma, and he died two days later. He never knew about the baby, and we never had a chance to make peace with each other." A familiar wave of sadness washed through her. "But worst of all, he was never able to tell anyone what happened that night, and there was never any evidence to prove it. I'll go to my grave believing that someone got away with murder."

"And since then, you've run this ranch on your own…with minimal help from two old men, and now Adan." Brady's voice took on a hint of admiration. "Close enough?"

So close that it made her skin crawl. "Just how much time did you spend snooping into my past?"

"Not me—several other special agents worked on it. We needed to know who we were dealing with, Celia."

"And were you satisfied?" she snapped. "Do you know what I read? What I eat for breakfast?"

"I don't know everything. I don't, for instance, know why you're not in contact with Ethan's parents. Does Lacey ever ask about them?"

Celia flinched. "That's not your business, Coleman. If you had to verify whether or not I was a good risk for your investigation here, fine. Beyond that, I want my privacy."

He had the grace to look uncomfortable, even though he'd probably spent an entire career poking into other people's histories without a second thought. Chagrined, she added softly, "I thought Ethan was the love of my life. Did your research tell you how this broke my heart? How scared I was, knowing my dad was so angry about my boyfriend—and how I never dared tell him I was pregnant? Lacey was born two months after he passed away."

"I'm sorry." Brady regarded her with somber eyes, then reached out to take her hand. His thumb massaged the tender inner flesh of her wrist—meant to comfort, surely, but instead the contact of his skin against hers sent sparks of awareness flying through her like miniature fireworks.

Embarrassed, hoping he hadn't noticed her response, she gently pulled her hand away.

"Ethan told his parents I was pregnant. They were sure thoughtful—sent ten thousand dollars for an abortion plus a nice little payoff, with a letter from a lawyer warning me to stay away from Ethan. They said they were filing a no-contact order so I couldn't ever talk to anyone in the family. I was just eighteen, and that legal stuff was scary." She shuddered. "I couldn't even imagine having an abortion, but the money helped bury my father a few months later."

"And now?"

"Lacey should know her grandparents, but the Dearbornes are cold, calculating people, and they wanted her dead rather than suffer the embarrassment of an illegitimate child in their midst. Maybe when she's older, I'll let them know...but I expect they'll just think I'm somehow after their money."

"I'm sorry, Celia."

"I don't need sympathy," she retorted. "I need my life to go on as it did before the drug smugglers showed up. I need my grandfather to get better, and I need to protect my daughter from the truth about her dad. What happened between me and the Dearborne family is old history."

For all of her bravado, she looked so fragile at that moment that he had to fight the impulse to offer her the shelter of his embrace, but he knew she would only jerk away. In the light of dawn, she'd probably be embarrassed and horrified at telling him so much.

"Look, I know this situation is hard. But just try to work with me, and by the time I leave in a few months, at least you'll all be safer. Deal?"

Wrapping her arms around herself, she ignored the offer of a handshake. "I have a daughter here. A couple of old men who couldn't hit the side of a barn with a shotgun if they were twenty feet away—and a hothead of a kid who could try to play hero and get himself killed if there was trouble. I want to keep my family safe, so tell me what's going to happen. I have to know."

From the set of her jaw, he knew she meant every word. And despite his resolution to keep everything on a professional level, his admiration for her grew.

He considered his words. "I can tell you just this much—we're building a multiagency investigation of a major new player in drug trafficking. We plan to track shipments back to their initial arrival in Mexico, and follow them to their destinations in the U.S. It's going to take a while to set this up, but it's a chance to take down some big players and a network with tentacles reaching throughout the United States."

"How can that be? There aren't endless parades of drug runners through here—these people are on *foot.* How much can one of them carry—maybe eighty pounds at the most?"

He allowed himself a satisfied smile. "The organization uses multiple routes—but this one is newer, and probably the most isolated. They aren't expecting much attention here. They'll be more careless."

"I hope so, because people like that have taken a lot away from me, and I'd like to see them all rot in hell." She leveled a long, steady look at him. "Please believe that I had nothing to do with Ethan's…activities. Ever. But most of all, promise you won't say anything to Lacey about him. She doesn't know the truth—and I want her to believe only good things about her late father."

"When this is over I'll ask the office to shred my background file on you, and she'll never hear a word from me about your past. I'll keep all of you safe, Celia. You have my word."

He just hoped he could keep it.

CELIA RESTED HER forehead against the door of her grandfather's bedroom and willed the tension out of her spine before tapping on the frame. "Hey, are you okay?"

After a moment, she heard bedsprings creak and the snap of a bedside lamp switch, and instantly regretted her visit. It was only ten o'clock now, and he'd always been a night owl, but lately he'd taken to just sitting in his darkened room with his hands folded in his lap and his face a mask of silent grief.

She opened the door a few inches and peered inside to find him sitting up in bed, fumbling for the glasses he kept on his nightstand. "I'm sorry—did I wake you up?"

"No, no…come in. I always have time for my Grace. Are the kids in bed yet?"

Her heart turned over at the gentle smile wreathing his leathery face as he relived his memories, and at the fine tremor of hands that were once strong, tanned and capable, but now lay on the covers like fallen birds.

His Parkinson's had been coming on slowly for

over a decade. Fifty years of cigarettes had left him with a legacy of emphysema. But the death of his beloved wife last July had taken the greatest toll of all.

"I'm Celia, Grandpa." She pulled a chair up to the side of his bed.

His lower lip trembled and his gaze slid away. "Guess I was just...dozing."

"I miss Grandma a lot, too." Celia brushed a kiss against his forehead, then settled into the chair. "I came in to see if I could get you anything. A sandwich and milk? Some ice cream? Vicente says you wouldn't eat any supper."

He lifted a hand in a shaky, dismissive wave. "He...tells me you have a new fella."

"A new *ranch hand,* yes."

His faded blue eyes twinkled. "But one that isn't too hard on the eyes, eh? Someone you knew when you were in college?"

Maybe she didn't completely trust Brady, but the one true thing she knew about Brady Coleman was that he was not hard on the eyes.

Under different circumstances, he would have caught her attention across a crowded room, and made her wish she owned pretty dresses and still knew how to flirt. Those foolish days were over, though, and Coleman was off-limits.

A handsome guy wasn't worth heartbreak, or the risk that her daughter might become attached to a new father figure who wouldn't stay. Not even if he was six feet of solid muscle, with warm, sensitive eyes and a deep, testosterone-laden voice that sent shivers dancing over her skin. The fact that he was armed, capable and DEA made him all the more appealing.

There was no chance of any future with him, though. In a few months he'd be gone, and she could never leave.

So how in heaven's name was she going to pretend that Brady and she had once had a "relationship"—or deal with his pretense about being interested in her now?

While he was faking, she'd be trying to ignore her honest attraction to the most intriguing man she'd met in years.

"This guy is just another cowhand to me," Celia lied. She reached over and took one of Jonah's hands in hers. "I'm not looking for a man, either. You know that."

"Vicente tells me that you knew this man long ago. Is that true?"

"Not really. I mean—" Here was another lie, and this time it lodged in her throat. She swallowed hard. "We went out a couple times, but I didn't know him well."

"Maybe he will be the one." Giving her a knowing smile, Jonah rested his other hand on top of hers and squeezed. "That daughter of yours needs a dad and you need someone, too. I'm not going to be around forever."

"I can run this ranch by myself. I'm doing fine."

His chuckle gave way to a spasm of raspy coughing that shook his gaunt frame. "That I know," he agreed after he caught his breath. "From that first pony, you were hell-bent on proving yourself more capable on horseback than anyone else in the county."

"It's more than just the horses. I've got the cattle coming along well—increased our herd by twenty percent and have had a better weight gain on our feeders compared to last year. If the prices come up in the next three months we'll do okay."

None of it had been easy. Gaining acceptance from some of the proud, patriarchal Mexican ranch hands had been a battle, and she'd finally had to let Carlos and Pedro go. And she'd never shared with Jonah any details about the escalating dangers surrounding the drug traffickers in the area.

Jonah levered himself up against the headboard. "This is Remington land...from fathers to sons... and now...to you. But promise me..." His voice trailed off as he coughed weakly.

Worry slid through her, as it always did when he started talking about dying. He'd been her partner, her best friend, ever since she'd left college to help run the ranch after her father died. Life without Jonah's love, advice and companionship was unimaginable. "You're not going anywhere—you'll be stronger in a few months."

He rested against the headboard with his eyes

closed for so long that she thought he'd fallen asleep. But then he rolled his head toward her and gave her a sad smile. "Don't…hang on to memories. If this place goes under, don't look back. Find something else. A new start."

"That won't happen. We're going to come through this fine, and you're going to be around to see it. Understand? You weren't a quitter, and I'm not one either."

The heritage of her grandfather and the generations before were all around her—in the thick adobe walls of this old house. In the fences and old wells and the massive Triple R cross pole suspended over the road leading from the highway to the ranch buildings. All her life she'd felt the fierce pride of belonging to this land, along with the ghosts of her tough, indomitable ancestors.

Only once had she thought of leaving it forever—during those brief, glorious months of first love with Lacey's father—but after recovering from her broken heart, she realized how close she'd come to making a grave mistake.

She'd been born here and she would die here, because this was where she belonged.

MIA TWISTED HER long, black hair up into a knot on top of her head to let the back of her neck cool.

The ancient window air conditioner rattled and hummed, leaving the air inside the old house almost bearable—but only if she sat a few inches away. Walking two dusty blocks up to the air-conditioned cantina for a Coke now and then had been her only respite.

"At least it's cooler at night," she grumbled, pulling her damp shirt away from her skin. "I think you need to move to Alaska."

"Wait until summer," her newfound great-aunt Dominga said in heavily accented English, a smile creasing her broad face. "Then, it is hot. I don't go outside until evening."

"I can't even *imagine* summer here."

Mia had spent the past few years wondering about the relatives she'd never seen, and looking forward to visiting the town where her late mother had been born.

She'd imagined a quaint, folksy place. Perhaps even something artsy, filled with small galleries and pretty little restaurants capitalizing on a south-of-the-border motif. Reality had hit the moment she stepped off the bus. *No wonder my mother left and never looked back.*

"Maybe you'll come to New York to visit me someday?"

Dominga laughed. "El Paso is too big, and that is far as I go. New York would be like going to the moon."

Mia felt a wave of sympathy for her. The old woman seemed oblivious to the oppressive heat, the clutter around her and the dreary scenery just outside her windows. How sad was it to live out a whole life here, so far from everything that mattered?

Except for Dominga, the only interesting thing Mia had seen in three days was the cute guy at the cantina.

After getting off the bus, she'd gone inside to gather her waning courage before trying to find her relatives. She'd been hot and tired and horrified at this dusty little town with its handful of shabby businesses.

She'd barely said a word to the guy, though, and he'd taken off like a scared bunny. How pathetic was that? Not that she had any real interest in flirting with some local who couldn't find the East Coast on a map.

"So, you got all your things together?" Dominga hoisted her bulk out of her tattered recliner and slowly moved through the small house. She stopped by an end table. "Ah—your photo album. You'll want this to show your grandfather Vicente, *si?* I hope he will be pleased to meet you." She lifted it with both hands and clutched it to her bosom, then held it out. "I am so proud of you, Mia." Her eyes shimmered with emotion. "My niece—I know she must have been proud, too."

They looked at each other, both aware that telling Paulina anything about this visit would have been a waste of time, because she'd wanted nothing to do with the father and other relatives who'd once shunned her.

"She died a very bitter woman," Mia said quietly. "My father left her before I was born, and she struggled financially all her life. This past winter, when her cancer spread, I tried to get her to talk about her past. She refused. If I hadn't found some old papers in her desk, I wouldn't have even known where you lived."

Dominga nodded, her eyes sad and distant. At the sound of a truck pulling to a stop outside, she crossed the room and pulled aside a curtain to look out the window. "Gilberto is here to take you to the ranch," she said heavily.

"You're sure he doesn't mind taking me all that way?"

"His ranch is next to the Remingtons', where your grandfather lives." Dominga turned to her and gave her hand a comforting pat. "Don't worry. I cleaned Gilberto's house for many years, and I trust him. He will treat you well."

"I'm more nervous about meeting Vicente," Mia admitted.

"You will be a surprise, but give him time. It just might take a little while for him to realize his good fortune. And please, come to see me again before you go back to New York."

"Of course." Mia hesitated just a moment before stepping into her great-aunt's arms for a quick, fierce hug. "I promise I'll write, from now on."

"Mi muchacha querida." Dominga's voice trembled as she held Mia's arms and searched her face,

as if memorizing each detail. "You're sure you don't want me to call Vicente and say you are coming?"

"Nope. Bad things happened between him and my mom, and he might not want to meet me. I don't want him to disappear before I can get out there."

"Your grandfather is a proud man. A difficult man. Give him a chance, *si?* He has many gifts, but patience isn't one of them."

Mia bent to gather her duffel bag and tried for a confident smile, though now her insides were quaking.

After Mom's death on Christmas Day, she'd decided to take spring term off and go to Texas. She'd only found a number and address for Dominga, but she'd hoped to find a host of relatives who would welcome her into their fold—cousins and aunts and grandparents who would help her find a sense of family and belonging, now that she was alone.

Instead, she'd discovered her only family consisted of one elderly, impoverished great-aunt and a crotchety grandfather.

"I'll be fine," she said breezily. "I'll just stay a few days, and then I'll be on my way."

But already her hands were starting to shake as her mother's last warning echoed through her thoughts. *Don't look for trouble, Mia. Some things are best left alone.*

Chapter Three

"WHEN ARE YOU coming to see me, Uncle Brady?"

Funny, how the child's voice still had the power to shred away yet another piece of his heart.

Brady closed his eyes and saw the five-year-old's pale, tear-streaked face the day of his father's funeral. The glimmer of accusation in the eyes of Chuck's widow, who'd probably wished it had been Brady instead of her husband lying in that casket.

There'd been more than a few times during those early days when the guilt over his friend's death had overwhelmed him—and when he'd almost wished the same thing.

"Soon, Tyler. I'll come to visit you soon. Is your mommy there?"

He held the phone away from his ear at the sound of Tyler dropping the phone at the other end of the line, followed by the patter of running feet, a slamming door, and a high-pitched voice squealing, "Mo-om! Mo-om!"

Adan stood at the open doorway of the barn holding his horse's reins, and glanced at his watch.

"Just a minute, Adan. I won't have good cell phone reception when we're way out in the pastures." Brady held up a hand, urging him to wait. "Melissa?"

Her voice came on the line, cool and distant. "Tyler talks about you all the time, Brady. When will you be back in town?"

Since Chuck's death, Brady had tried to stop by to see the little boy every week and do guy things with him—man to man—though God knew it was hardly enough to replace the daddy he'd lost. "I'm not sure. At least a month. Did you get the check I sent you?"

He heard her suck a breath through her teeth. "Yes, but you don't have to do that every month. We can get by."

But *getting by* wasn't what she deserved. She deserved a husband coming home to her every night. A father for her son. A comfortable life. And because of Brady, she'd lost all of it.

Looking up, he saw Adan watching him with obvious interest, so he turned away and lowered his voice. "I want you to have the money. I know you and Chuck were in the midst of fixing up that place of yours, and with that plus Tyler's after-school day care, it's got to be tough. When I get done here, I'll help finish the basement for you."

"I appreciate your offer…and the money. I truly do. But it's been two years now, and—"

"Chuck was one of my best friends. I'm Tyler's godfather. Please, just let me do these things." *Please, let me make amends.*

She gave in as she always did, with a tremulous sigh, and he knew that they were both thinking about the gentle bear of a man who'd gone out on that last joint operation with the border patrol and the DEA, but never came back.

Two other agents had lost their lives that night as well—dedicated, intelligent, experienced agents who'd also been Brady's close associates.

Ending the connection on his cell phone, he strode down the barn aisle toward Buck's stall. He'd always be there for Tyler and his mother, in every way he could. But he was also going to make sure—absolutely sure—that Chuck's killers were caught and tried.

He allowed himself a grim smile.

Thanks to perseverance and a touch of luck, he was in just the right place to do it.

TRYING TO OBTAIN information from a teenage boy rivaled interrogating a prison lifer who had little to gain by cooperating. After two hours of riding with Adan while checking the herds, Brady had come up with nothing.

The report he'd just received from Luis indicated that Adan had a long juvenile record and a fringe association with some members of the Mafia Mexicana.

Given that, there was a chance that he'd had been planted here by the Garcia drug organization, to help smugglers crossing Triple R land.

He shot a glance at the sullen kid lounging on his horse with one knee hooked over the saddle horn, and decided to try again. "It sure is pretty here."

They'd stopped on a low rise overlooking a broad valley rimmed by rocky outcroppings and, on the far side, a trio of buttes. A mountain range loomed along the horizon, purple now that the sun was riding low in the sky. A herd of cattle—224 head, all bearing the Triple R brand—ranged across the land below them.

Adan gave a noncommittal grunt and shook out some slack in his reins, then reached into his saddlebag and pulled out a plastic-wrapped sandwich. His black gelding lowered its head and started grazing.

"Do you know what those mountains are to the northwest?"

That earned an impatient shoulder jerk. Which meant the boy didn't know, didn't care, or considered conversation a waste of time. Brady tried another tack. "Nice horse you have there. Is he yours?"

Adan shook his head.

"I had a black gelding when I was a kid." Brady gave a self-deprecating laugh. "Named him Spitfire, of all things. I figured he'd win the Kentucky Derby someday and then I would use him to become a world champion roper."

That earned a snicker.

"Problem was, he was just a tad over fourteen hands and had the build of a Shetland on steroids. Poor thing waddled instead of walked, and the only time he moved fast was when we turned for home."

After wolfing down his sandwich, Adan watched his horse graze for a long moment. "You had a ranch?"

"Until we lost it. Drought...cattle prices...you know the drill. How about you—did you come from these parts?"

"No."

"Where, then?"

A vague wave of Adan's hand might have meant El Paso or any number of tiny, dusty towns between here and there, though Brady already knew exactly where he'd come from.

"How long have you worked for Celia?"

The boy shot him an irritated look. "Long enough." He balled up the plastic wrap, stuffed it in his saddlebag, and dropped his foot into the stirrup. "Ready?"

Brady urged his gelding into a brief lope to catch up, then settled him into an easy jog beside Adan's horse. "I just figure we might as well get to know each other, seeing as how we'll be working together. Know of any good places to eat around here?"

"You're kidding, man."

"Isn't there a cantina in town?"

"Food's okay." A dull flush worked its way up the boy's neck. "I guess."

"Sometimes those back-of-beyond places are the best. Not much atmosphere, but they have cheap food that's darn good." Brady scanned the horizon, then reined his horse up another draw. "One of my favorite places in the world is a place called Ruby's in a little Wyoming town in the middle of nowhere. Prime rib you can cut with a fork and the homemade pies—" Brady closed his eyes briefly in blissful appreciation "—unbelievable."

That caught Adan's attention. "You been to *Wyoming?*"

"Most states west of the Mississippi, and a lot of them on the other side."

"And you came back *here?*" If Brady had sprouted wings and flown, the boy couldn't have appeared more incredulous.

"Why not? Good, solid people. Beautiful country. Last place I'd ever want to be is where you spend your life in bumper-to-bumper traffic, and see crowds of people you don't know, every time you step out your front door."

The brief conversation faded to silence as they moved up into the draw, where deeply fragmented rock jutted from the high walls on either side. The horses picked their way through the ruggedly beautiful terrain, past the sharp, swordlike leaves of yuccas and the spines of low-lying cacti.

His thoughts drifted to Celia. She was as strong and tenacious as she was beautiful, although she had a few dangerous qualities herself. Rather like, he thought with an inward sigh, his former fiancée, who'd placed dedication to her law enforcement career above all else.

At least, until she met someone else.

Given Celia's staunch defense of her long-dead druggie boyfriend and her dedication to this ranch, Brady guessed that she wouldn't be nearly as shallow as Jane.

At a sudden loud and angry buzz, Brady's horse balked, then lurched sideways, beyond striking distance of a mottled rock rattler coiled and ready on a sun-drenched rock by the trail.

The gelding stumbled and fell sideways against one of the knee-high boulders littering the base of the draw. Then he staggered to his feet, his sides heaving and nostrils flaring.

The snake, apparently impressed by fifteen hundred pounds of careening horse, slithered away.

"Easy, Buck. Easy now." Brady settled him with a hand on his neck, took a good look at the ground, then swung out of the saddle. Blood dripped from a ragged scrape across the buckskin's right knee and welled up in a smaller laceration along his pastern.

Adan pulled his horse up close. "How bad is it?"

"Superficial, but I'd better take him home." And home was a good two miles to the south. "You can go on if you want—I'll be okay."

"Can't you ride him at a walk?"

"I'll just lead him. I want to take it real slow."

Frowning, Adan rested his crossed wrists on the horn of his saddle. He glanced at the rocky ledges high above them. "You know how to use that rifle on your saddle?"

Brady gave him a wry grin. "I think they're standard issue in these parts, given the two-legged and four-legged varmints a guy might run across."

"But can you *use* it?"

Surprised by the kid's concern, he nodded. He'd scored ninety-eight during his last recertification on the firing range, but to the boy he probably looked old and inept.

"I heard Alvarez—the foreman on the next ranch north—found a mountain lion just after it killed a calf last week. He shot it."

Brady pulled the rifle out of the scabbard on his saddle and loaded it, then gathered his reins and started leading Buck back down the draw, keeping an eye out for snakes on the ground and any suspicious movements on the rocks above. "That's one less mountain lion to worry about, then."

"But its friends will smell the blood on your horse." Adan wheeled Rowdy around and followed. "I'd better come along—Celia won't like it if I let them eat you for lunch."

"Thanks, kid," Brady said dryly.

"If you want, we can ride Rowdy double."

Brady eyed the boy's gelding. Barely fifteen hands, it didn't have the stout, muscular build of a quarter horse, and it wasn't shod, either. "I'll walk, but thanks."

On the way out they'd taken numerous side trips into gullies and draws, searching out cattle to count and assess for general condition. Now, heading straight for home, they topped the last rise above the home place in less than an hour.

Adan jerked his horse to a halt and stared down at the assortment of pole barns, corrals and sheds, and the white adobe house beyond.

A white truck was parked close to the house. A stocky, older man and a young woman with long black hair stood next to it, talking to Celia.

"Damn," Adan muttered under his breath.

Surprised, Brady looked over Buck's neck at him. "Who is it?"

Without a word, Adan pivoted his horse back toward the hills.

BY THE TIME Brady had seen to his horse, Celia and her guests were seated at a wrought-iron table on the patio by the side of the house, under the wide-spreading branches of an ancient live oak. Pitchers of beverages, glasses and a tray of cookies were arranged on a second, smaller table at the edge of the patio.

Vicente stood near the others, but with a dark and troubled expression on his face. Curious at both Adan's abrupt departure and Vicente's obvious discomfort, Brady ambled toward the patio on the pretext of delivering information.

Celia rose and met him halfway. "Come over and join us."

"Don't mean to interrupt," he said, holding his hat at his side. "Just thought you should know about what happened up in the hills."

"Maybe you'd better tell me here. Privately." She lowered her voice. "Did you have problems?"

"A few. My horse ran into some rocks, so I led him home. Adan came back with me, but he took one look at your guests and skedaddled."

"For all his bravado, he's a shy kid around strangers." She gave Brady a quick head-to-toe glance. "Looks like you survived okay. What about the horse?"

"A laceration on his knee, and one on his pastern. I cleaned him up with peroxide and used an antibiotic spray, then wrapped the pastern."

"Does the vet need to come out?"

"Both would be hard to suture, given the constant flexing of those joints. I'd probably keep him in a stall so the wounds can be kept clean, and also get him started on a round of IM antibiotics."

"I'll take a look later on. Anything else?"

"We quit counting the herd up there after Buck

got hurt, but Adan thinks that some of the stock is missing."

Celia's expression sharpened. "We'll all go up there tomorrow at first light. We had a few cattle stolen before you came. A week later, we found a steer that had been shot."

"You reported it to the sheriff?"

"Of course I did. But old Aubrey pointed out that with twenty-thousand acres on this ranch alone, he could hardly patrol our boundaries. I called the new sheriff last week and he drove out to talk to me, but Ramon is facing the same challenge Aubrey did—too much county, too little manpower."

"Any other ranchers in the area having problems?"

She nodded toward the portly, gray-haired man seated next to the young woman. "Gil says he lost three about the same time. Otherwise, no."

"What do you know about him?"

"He is—or was—my uncle, and he's my closest neighbor. He owns the Rocking B."

"Do you two get along well?"

"Our family goes back generations on this land, but he's a newcomer—he married my aunt and bought his place when I was a kid. They divorced a few years later." She gave a rueful laugh. "Since my dad died, he's appointed himself my unofficial guardian, of sorts. Come on over and get something to drink, and I'll introduce you."

He followed her and couldn't help but admire the

view. Dressed in her usual jeans, boots and western belt, she now wore a ruby sleeveless shirt that set off her slender arms and deep tan. Silver concho earrings dangled at her ears, catching the sunlight that filtered through the leaves above.

She was, Brady thought, rather like a jewel hidden away along a mountain path. Why hadn't some rancher snapped her up long ago? If they'd all been threatened by her strength, they'd made a big mistake. One, he realized grimly, that he shouldn't be quite so thankful for.

He was here for an investigation. Period. And anything else would not only be unethical, but could also jeopardize his last chance to see justice done.

At the table, she poured a glass of lemonade and handed it to him. Her eyes flared wide when their fingers brushed, and she took an abrupt step back.

So she feels it, too. Ignoring his own reaction to her touch, he glanced at the others across the patio. "Easy, now. Pull back like that, and they'll think you're afraid of me."

"Not if they have a lick of sense," she retorted.

Grinning, Brady winked at her and sauntered over to the table. "Howdy, I'm Brady Coleman. And you are..."

"Gilberto Banuelos." The older man stood and gave Brady a quick once over. "You're new here."

"Just since yesterday. Always did love this part of Texas."

"Well, if you get tired of working for Celia here, give me a call. I'm always on the lookout for a good man or two."

Celia laughed. "Don't listen to him, Brady. He might seem charming, but he's the meanest old coot this side of the Rio Grande."

"And Celia is the toughest boss you could find," he retorted. "Of course, she's a whole lot nicer to look at than I am."

The young girl at the table watched them with avid interest. Celia caught Vicente's eye and raised a brow, and when he gave her a brief nod, she motioned to the girl.

"This is Mia Holden, Vicente's granddaughter from New York. She's visiting us for a few days, then she'll head back to college."

"Nice to meet you, ma'am."

She awkwardly accepted his handshake. "Thanks."

He hid a smile, remembering Adan's abrupt departure. Given a chance to meet a gal like this one, the kid should have been heading for the house, not in the opposite direction. When she matured, the girl was going to be flat-out gorgeous, with that fall of silky black hair reaching her waist and those exotic dark eyes.

"What's your major?"

She blushed. "Um…music."

"We hadn't even gotten that far," Celia said, glancing at Vicente. "What sort of music?"

"Violin and piano."

"That's wonderful. Maybe you can play for us sometime while you're here. What do you think, Vi—" Celia turned and scanned the patio. "Now where did he go?"

"Inside," Gil said, his voice amused. "He seemed to be in quite a hurry."

Brady touched the brim of his hat. "I'd better go take another look at my horse and start chores. Good to meet you, Gil, Mia."

He'd only gone a few paces when he heard Gil come up behind him. The older man fell in step with him on the way to the barn.

"Lovely little gal, isn't she?"

"Vicente must be proud of her."

Gil laughed. "Maybe someday—at this point he's still in shock. Never met her until today."

"I'm new here. I wouldn't know."

"I gave her a ride from town myself, because she came clear across country on a bus just to meet family she's never seen before. Spunky kid, if you ask me." Gil gave Brady a curious look when they entered the cool, dark aisle of the main barn. "I hear you have a little connection with Celia."

Brady reached for the halter he'd hung on a hook outside Buck's stall. "College days."

"Figured as much. You're not the kind of guy we usually see just dropping in for a job." Gil braced a hand on the frame of the stall door as Brady went inside to halter the gelding. "But why would a college boy end up working on a ranch?"

"I like ranching...and I like to move around a lot, I guess. I needed a job for a few months, then I have another offer up in East Texas." Brady led the horse into the aisle and cross-tied him, then reached along the wall to turn on the lights.

"You from here?"

Brady laughed. For all of his questions, the guy did have a twinkle in his eye, and with that smile he could probably charm women of his generation into falling at his feet. "What is this, an inquisition?"

"Just concerned. Celia's like family to me, and she's a soft touch for anyone with troubles. She hired that wild kid who came from God knows where—" distaste flitted across Gil's face "—and with her grandfather laid up, she needs looking after."

Remembering the fiery gleam of independence in Celia's eyes, Brady knew she'd disagree, but he just nodded. "Sounds like you're a good neighbor."

"People watch out for each other." The hint of warning in his voice was unmistakable.

Brady reached for a plastic tub on the floor containing antibiotic ointment and dressing materials, and pried off the lid. "I'll bear that in mind."

"Consider this as well, *gringo,* because I have reason to worry." The older man moved closer. "Celia has run a lot of *Mexicanos* off her land. She thinks she is seeing *hombres* behind every tree, and goes out into the night with her rifle like some old gunslinger in the movies." Gil spat on the floor near Brady's feet. "If she isn't careful, she's going to get herself killed one of these days. Tell her to stop. Protect herself. It isn't worth trying to fight a war by yourself, and she does not listen to what this old man says."

Brady applied a smear of the salve to Buck's pastern, then rose and met Gil's gaze. "I don't think she'll take any stock in what I say, either."

Gil shook his head slowly. "She's got to listen to someone, or she isn't going to be around much longer. Tell her."

Brady watched the old rancher stride back to the house.

Celia was the kind of independent woman who probably wouldn't change her tactics no matter what anyone told her—whether he was her nosy neighbor or an agent with the DEA.

And that, Brady thought, could prove to be a problem.

Chapter Four

THE MOMENT Mrs. Andrews and Holly dropped her off at the ranch, Lacey raced for the barn.

Vicente sat by the open door, saddle-soaping a bridle. His weathered face split into a broad smile at her approach. "Been too quiet this week, without you chasing off in all directions on your horse. How was camp?"

"Okay." She dumped her duffel bag on the ground and scanned the darkened aisle behind him, then the corrals to either side of the barn. "Where's Mom?"

"Town. Oughta be back in an hour or so."

Her heart sank.

"Maybe sooner," Vicente added, his voice gentle. "I s'pose you want to tell her about all your adventures, and your new friends."

She looked down at the toes of her boots and gave a deep sigh. "Nah. I was just gonna tell her that I'm home. Is Loco up by the barn?"

He jerked a thumb toward one of the corrals. "Waitin' for you."

She'd been homesick from the first day she'd been at camp and had been counting the minutes during the long drive back today. No matter what happened at school or anywhere else, talking to Mom always made it feel right again. But taking Loco out for a good long ride would be the second best thing.

In a few minutes, she had him caught, cross-tied in the aisle of the barn and saddled.

"Where are you heading?" Vicente asked as she led the gelding out of the barn.

"Not far. I'll be back in an hour or so." She tightened the latigo on her saddle, tested the girth, then flipped the stirrup off the saddle horn. Loco bent his head around to nose at her pockets. "Beggar! No treats today, buddy."

She swung up into the saddle and gathered her reins, then turned toward the lane leading out to the west pasture. A feeling of peace settled over her. Camp *sucked.* How could those other girls talk about nail polish and clothes and boys twenty-four hours a day?

Shuddering at the memory, she nudged Loco into an easy jog past the house.

A tall, dark-haired guy stepped out through the open screen door onto the porch, settled his hat into place, then waved at her, his lean, tanned face creased by a smile that flashed even white teeth and crinkled the corners of his eyes.

Stunned, she pulled Loco to a stop and stared at him.

With endless miles of rough road, sagebrush and sand between here and town, strangers never found the place and locals rarely made the trip. The nearest ranch—Uncle Gil's—was a whole five miles away, even if you took the shortcut cross-country instead of going out on the highway.

"You must be Lacey." The guy took the steps two at a time and sauntered over, rested a hand on Loco's neck, and studied the horse with an approving eye. "Nice horse. Is he yours?"

She gave him a wary nod. "Does my mom know you were in our house?"

"She does. There's someone else here who you'll want to meet—Vicente's granddaughter."

Granddaughter?

Just then, a drop-dead gorgeous Hispanic girl stepped out onto the porch. Slender and graceful with beautiful dark eyes, she was as pretty as any actress on the cover of *People* magazine. Her waist-length black hair gleamed as it lifted on the breeze.

She was exactly the type of girl Lacey had just endured by the dozen at camp for the past five days. Next to them, with her own kinky red-blond hair, freckles and total inability to giggle with them about stupid girl stuff, Lacey had felt like an ugly stepsister. From their snide little comments and superior glances, she knew they thought the same thing about her.

"Vicente doesn't have a granddaughter," Lacey snapped. "Who are you?"

She sounded rude, but she flat out didn't care. During that endless week at camp she'd longed to be on her horse, on her own, with only the high desert breezes for company. And after her ride, she wanted time with Mom. Strangers here to buy or sell livestock would just take up Mom's time when Lacey *really* needed her.

"That's Mia," the guy said. "I'm Brady Coleman. Your mom hired me on Saturday."

A guy who looked like he oughta be in the movies? Lacey's mouth fell open, then she snapped it shut.

He must have read the surprise on her face, because he laughed. A nice, deep, gentle laugh, not the catty kind that she'd heard all week at camp. "I knew your mom long ago," he added. "I called her because I needed a job for a few months. She said she needed help, so this works out for both of us."

Grandpa Jonah's words came back to her...words meant only for her mother's ears. *Those young bucks from town keep sniffin' around, but they're after this ranch, m'girl. You be mighty careful.*

Was this one of those guys? Seemed likely, because he sure didn't look like the sort of dirt-poor cowboy who usually turned up at the Triple R looking for work.

The thought of some jerk trying to slither his way into her mom's life made Lacey's teeth clench. "When Mom gets home, tell her I've gone up to the mesa," she said. "I'll be back before supper."

Beneath the brim of his hat, she could see him frown.

"Hey—wait a minute—"

With a light touch of her boot at Loco's shoulder, she spun the gelding into a neat one-eighty and loped off in the opposite direction, leaving Mr. Hollywood in the dust.

Once she passed the barns and corrals and willows clustered by the creek running through the home place, she slowed to a walk and kicked her feet out of the stirrups. "Yeah, right—like I'm gonna wait a minute for you, you creep," she muttered, glancing over her shoulder toward home.

The last guy who'd started hanging around her mom had thought he could play "daddy" and had started bossing her around. He'd even tried to tell Vicente what to do, too, but at least Mom had caught on and put an end to *that*.

Maybe this time Mom wouldn't catch on. One of these times—Lacey shuddered—Mom might even think she was falling in love with someone and want him to stick around.

But everything was perfect just the way it was, and no one was going to move in on them and take over if Lacey had anything to do about it. Not this man, and not the pretty girl on the steps.

No one.

"WE NEED TO TALK," Brady said.

Celia looked up from her pile of bills and receipts and glanced at the old Big Ben clock on her desk, then surveyed the man silhouetted in the doorway.

Yesterday she'd been gone all day hauling cattle to auction in El Paso, determined to be home this afternoon when Lacey arrived. Then, because she'd had to run to town after a tetanus vaccine for an injured calf, she'd missed her daughter's return.

Interruptions now would mean less time with her daughter after supper. "I'm busy," she said.

"It's important," Brady added. He walked into the room, shut the door tossed his hat on an empty chair, and settled into a hide-covered chair across the desk from her. "First of all, your daughter is out alone on that horse of hers, and it isn't safe."

"She doesn't go far." Celia swiveled her desk chair toward the window and tugged on the miniblind cord. Outside, a light breeze kicked up a cloud of dust in front of the barn, and late afternoon sunshine pierced the willows, throwing black lace shadows across the empty yard.

"That doesn't matter. She needs to stay close to home, at least until this investigation is over."

The veiled criticism in his voice grated against Celia's nerves—all the more because Lacey knew better than to stray very far, but sometimes she did it anyway. "We aren't in the big city, Mr. Coleman. There are few of us on this ranch and there aren't any neighbors for miles. It's broad daylight."

Brady leaned back in his chair and crossed a booted foot across his opposite knee. "Even during the day, I don't want to take chances."

The reminder hit Celia like a bucket of ice water down her back. "Neither do I."

"Have you said anything to her about me?"

"Nothing. She was at camp, and I haven't seen her since she got back."

He lifted a brow. "Well, when I told her I'd be working here for a while, I got the feeling that she'd like to drop me into the nearest rattlesnake-filled ravine."

Not a good start, then, and knowing Lacey, she was already planning to make life difficult for him. "I haven't dated much over the years, and she hasn't taken well to the idea when I have. Maybe she thinks you're potential trouble."

"Then she's a potential problem." Brady uncrossed his ankle and leaned forward to brace his hands on the rim of her desk. "No one but you should know why I'm here. Not even her. Can you deal with her, without giving her any detailed explanations?"

Celia let her voice drop a good ten degrees. "I'm not sure what you mean."

"She's upset about me being here. If she gets

suspicious, or says the wrong thing to someone in town, she could jeopardize this operation." He shook his head. "And when I asked her to stop, she just took off on her horse. What if there's real trouble brewing and she refuses to listen?"

"I'll talk to her." Celia leveled a stern look at him. "But I can't guarantee that she won't be asking you some tough questions. She's going to wonder why I've never mentioned you before."

"You couldn't have told her about everyone you ever met when you went off to college." He gazed at her thoughtfully. "Platonic or otherwise."

"I'm trying to avoid lying to my family and neighbors, Coleman, and I'm still uncomfortable regarding what to say when you leave."

"That I was interested, and you weren't, I guess." He flashed a wicked grin. "That would be believable, wouldn't it?"

"Hardly," she muttered. "Why would a guy like you be swept off his feet by a woman who practically lives on a horse and doesn't even own a dress?"

He laughed at that, and reached across the desk to take her hand. "You have no idea how beautiful you are."

She knew he was only being kind, but the contact of his hand on hers instantly quickened her heartbeat and sent ripples of sensation across her skin.

Their eyes met, and something indefinable sizzled between them, reminding her of just how dangerous this ruse was.

To him, it was simply a cover so he could do his job.

But to her, after just a few days, it was getting harder to remember the line between fiction and reality. It was all too easy to become entranced by those warm, compelling eyes and to imagine things that would never be.

Brady abruptly released her hand, leaned back in his chair and cleared his throat. "Uh...on to other things. There'll be times I need to go to town— like tomorrow—so try to think up errands for me. At least the first time, I'd like you to come along."

"An eighty-mile round trip to town isn't something I do often," she said dryly as she scanned the calendar on her desk. "I could try to move my appointment with our banker. What else?"

"I'll also be doing surveillance most nights—you can assign me to watch your herd, given the cattle you've lost in the past, but sometimes I'll need to be in other places as well."

"And what about me?"

"Just stay absolutely clear of any action that happens here. That goes for your family and hired hands as well." His voice lowered as he caught her gaze with the intensity of his own. "The less everyone knows, the better."

"I protect my land and family, Mr. Coleman. I've run off a lot of interlopers."

"So your neighbor tells me."

"Gil?" She couldn't quell her derisive snort. "He fusses at me like an old hen, telling me to just shut my eyes and ignore anything that happens around here."

She sensed Brady's sudden interest in that, though he didn't betray it with so much as a twitch.

"Tell me more about him," he said, adjusting the cuff of his shirt.

"You don't have all of those details in your report?" Lifting a brow at him, she tapped a stack of paper into a neat pile and then folded her hands on top of them. "Someone didn't do their job?"

He sighed. "Look, Celia. We're on the same side, here. I understand that you resent any intrusion into your privacy, but it's policy for us to know all we can about a situation and the people we're dealing with. Too many good men have died in this job, and we don't take needless risks."

Something flickered in his eyes—was that a flash of deep regret? Sorrow over a good friend who'd been killed in the line of duty?

And that's what this man does for a living, too—he puts his life on the line. Anyone who loved him would deal with anxiety and uncertainty every single day, wondering if he would come home. It was a sobering thought, because she could well imagine the fear of listening for the phone to ring when he was away.

Chastened, Celia bit her lower lip. "There was

once some bad blood between him and my dad, but by the time Dad died, Gil was here most every Sunday for dinner."

"And now?"

"I don't see him that much, but he still keeps in touch. With Jonah ill, I think Gil feels obligated to offer...advice."

"I'm guessing that you don't need it." Brady studied her for a moment, then cracked a smile. "Or want it, particularly."

"He's conservative, and he wasn't born here." She pushed away from the desk and stood. "I've worked this ranch since I could sit a horse. I've run it for thirteen years now, with Jonah's help."

"Do you trust Gil? His men?"

"Trust? Out here, we all depend on each other come time to move herds or brand or when disaster strikes. We work together, or this country will eat us alive."

"Not exactly what I meant."

For just a heartbeat, she imagined trusting this man. The joy of facing life together, no matter what happened. The image was as appealing as it was improbable, for it was a luxury she would never enjoy.

"I believe in myself, Coleman." She leveled a look at him, then glanced at the steel gun safe along the wall near the door. "I don't trust anyone to make decisions that will affect the future of this ranch or the safety of the people who live here. If anything goes south with this operation of yours, I'll do whatever it takes to keep my family safe."

BORED, MIA WANDERED around the living room, studying family photographs on the fireplace, an old upright piano and absorbing the definite South-western flavor of the sprawling adobe house.

Everywhere she looked, there was native pottery decorated in rich peach-and-turquoise geometric designs. Navajo blankets or animal hides draped over the backs of furniture. Old West cowboy prints hung on walls, along with pictures of Lacey from birth until now. Celia on beautiful horses at shows, holding trophies and ribbons. Some were of a much older man on horseback—probably Celia's father or grandfather, though with the lowered brims of their hats, it was hard to tell.

Trying to find a way to start up a conversation with Vicente, who seemed to prepare most of the meals, she'd hung around the kitchen for a while before lunch. He'd mostly grunted in response to her questions and acted as if his cooking was the most important thing in the world. How often did he have a granddaughter come to see him? As far as she knew, she was the only one he had.

She'd finally given up on trying to talk to him and offered to deliver Jonah's lunch.

The old guy in that back bedroom sure didn't look much like the big, burly guy in these photos.

Now he was pale and gaunt, and his hands shook. But like Vicente, he didn't have much to say, either.

And Lacey—Mia blew out a long sigh. Celia's daughter had glared at her with serious dislike before taking off on her horse. Dislike, for heaven's sake, and they hadn't even met each other yet!

Nothing on this trip was turning out like she'd hoped.

She picked up a horse-shaped trophy from an end table and ran her fingertips over the polished surface, then put it back down. It was clear, she finally decided in disgust, that her gifts and talents had not come from her *mother's* side of the family.

What kind of guy worked as a common laborer on a ranch and never cared about owning property of his own? She'd imagined so much more, choosing to believe her mother had lied about Vicente.

Now, frustration tied her stomach in a knot. *All this way—I came all this way!*

Her frustration heated to anger, then cooled to resolve. Running her fingers through her long hair, she marched back to the kitchen where she heard the clang of a pot lid and the sound of the dishwasher running. Vicente would be starting supper now, so he couldn't stalk off to his cabin or disappear into the barn.

He spared a brief glance at her, then turned away and opened a cupboard door.

"Hi, Grampa, what's up?"

His shoulders stiffened.

She crossed the room and propped a hip against the counter. "What's for supper?"

When he just kept rummaging around in the stupid cupboard, she moved a few inches closer. The back of his neck was deep brown, like heavily creased leather. His salt-and-pepper hair was still full and shaggy, but beneath his heavy red flannel shirt his chest appeared sunken, and bony where the top button gaped open. Not much taller than her own five-foot-five, he probably didn't weigh much more than she did, either. Maybe he'd been much stockier and straighter in his younger days, but it was hard to imagine that now.

Now, he looked old and bent, and she knew this trip would probably be the one and only time she'd see him.

She followed him over to the stove, where a stock pot of something spicy was simmering and a frying pan filled with crumbled ground beef sizzled and spat. "Secret recipe?"

"No."

Surprised and a little encouraged, she moved close enough to almost brush his shoulder and watched him shake a dash of cumin into the stockpot. "My mom loved to cook, too, but she didn't make good Mexican food." Mia inhaled the aroma of spices. "She just did the usual American stuff."

"Go. I'm busy here," Vicente growled.

He didn't so much as *look* at her. Hurt, Mia felt her mouth tremble and sudden tears burn behind her eyelids. Just her third day at the ranch, and she already knew that coming here had been a mistake.

Vicente hated her. Lacey ignored her. And wouldn't you know, that cute cowboy from the cantina worked here—and *he* avoided her like the plague. Yesterday, she'd gone out to the barn to apologize to him, but he hadn't even nodded or met her eye. He'd just finished saddling his stupid horse, then mounted and rode off without a word.

The only friendly person here was Celia, but she never seemed to stop working and was rarely in the house.

Mia sighed. Two more days. Two more long, boring days, and then on Saturday she could get on the Greyhound and head back to New York, where she would kiss the ground the minute she arrived.

She turned toward the kitchen door and nearly ran into Celia, who stood with a hand on the door frame and a frown creasing her brow.

"Sorry. I—I didn't see you," Mia mumbled. She brushed past Celia and headed for her bedroom, pretending she didn't hear Celia call her name.

Why had she ever thought this trip was a good idea? Trying to piece together a family to love just wasn't going to work. Her late mother would have scoffed at Mia's desire to come out here, and for once, she would have been right.

THE MAIN STREET of Saguaro Springs was all of two blocks long, flanked by dusty side streets and a few dozen homes. Most of the buildings were of adobe, battered tin or faded clapboard that must have been around since the 1800s. If the town had ever boasted the existence of a spring, it probably couldn't do so now. Thick dust blanketed the sidewalks and the asphalt of Main, and even at the southeast end, where a cluster of fine old brick homes stood, the front yards were dry and desolate.

"Aren't you glad you made this trip?" Celia asked, tipping her sunglasses down with a forefinger to glance across the front seat of the crew cab pickup at Brady. "I'm not sure what you were hoping to find, but it probably isn't here."

"Oh, it is. Banking..." He shifted his gaze from the Saguaro First National Bank across the street to Juan's Cantina, down at the corner, and past that to a metal framed building belonging to Coriolos Hardware. "Maybe a cold beer and some conversation, and a pair of work gloves. Mostly, a chance to check out the town and be seen as your employee. Thanks for the check, by the way."

"Any time." She slanted an amused look in his direction. "I like paying you, because you plan to give it right back."

"Don't get too used to it." Angling toward her, he dropped his arm along the top of the seat and brushed her shoulder with his fingertips, then gave in to temptation and caught a silky strand of her hair and tucked it gently behind her ear. "Your next cowboy might not be so agreeable."

Her smile faded as her gaze lowered from his eyes to his mouth, then jerked up again. "Right."

He was tempted to curve his hand behind her and try drawing her closer, to see if he was reading her hesitant invitation correctly—or if it was just a trick of the light, coupled with a lack of sleep.

The moment was lost when a young cowboy strolled by the hood of the truck, gave it a thump, then whistled and gave them a double thumbs-up.

"The Baxter kid." Celia straightened up behind the wheel, suddenly all business. "I'd better get going."

"Sure…whatever you say." Opening the door, he stepped outside, slammed it and braced his forearms on the open window. "Meet here at noon?"

"Probably. After I pick up the salt at the feed elevator, I need to sign some papers at the bank. I'll stop in to say hello to Vicente's sister and see if she needs anything, then pick up some groceries." She gave the deserted street a wry glance. "It won't be too hard to find you if I get done early, and I want to be back at the ranch before Lacey gets home."

He watched her shift the truck into Drive and head toward the grain elevator on the west edge of town.

With her denim ball cap, faded plaid western shirt and jeans worn white at the knees, she might have looked like any other hardworking West Texas ranchwoman he'd seen when he'd first passed through town on his way out to her place.

But there the similarity ended. More than once, Brady had found himself captivated by that straight blond hair caught in a simple ponytail and pulled through the back of her cap. The healthy, tanned glow of her skin. The occasional, unexpected glimmer of amusement lurking beneath that no-nonsense exterior.

And just a moment ago, he'd been damned close to kissing her.

Pretending that he was an old flame shouldn't have been difficult, but it was, because he wanted it to be *real*. That wasn't the sort of thing he ought to be thinking about. Not now, when he had a job to do, because nothing could interfere with his need to see justice done. *Nothing*.

He had only to recall Tyler's tear-streaked face and the grief of the boy's widowed mother to remind him of that fact.

Brady turned away and stepped into the cool interior of the tan adobe bank. Inside, a single teller leaned on her counter, inspecting her manicure. She straightened when he approached her window and slid a check from the Triple R beneath the old-fashioned, ornate metal grill barrier.

Easily in her midforties, with wispy, mouse-brown hair rimming her round face, the woman's eyes widened behind her thick glasses as she read the front of the check. "You're that new guy out to the Remington place," she marveled, looking up at him with even greater interest. She patted down the springy curls at her temples. "Heard tell they finally found someone."

"Yeah, well…I'm glad to find the job."

The clerk's mouth pursed. "So what do you think of Celia?"

"She seems like a good boss, so far."

"Boss, eh?" A corner of her mouth quirked up, as if she were sharing a private joke with him. "That girl ain't had an easy life, out there trying to make ends met. Met her grandpa?"

"Just briefly." The old guy had given him a piercing look and managed a credible handshake, but he was obviously ill and stayed in his room whenever Brady was in the house for dinner. Apparently, he spent most of his time in his bed or at his window in a recliner, dozing the day away.

"Strong stock, that family. Real hard workers and honest as they come. You planning to stay long?"

Brady glanced at the clock on the wall over the massive door leading back into the safe. In a town this size, there probably weren't many customers walking in on any given day, and this woman was obviously lonely and wanting to talk. "Nice town."

Confusion flashed across the woman's face at the abrupt change of topic, but she rallied fast. "Yessir. 'Bout big enough to stuff down a gopher hole, but the people here's real friendly."

"Quiet place?"

Her cheerful expression faded a little. "If Joe Henson's dog crosses the street, it's something to talk about. 'Course, being three-legged and a mite old, he don't find it an easy trip."

Brady grinned. "I don't suppose you see many strangers coming through."

"Not unless they're lost or selling something," she snorted. "Except for rodeo weekends up in Montrose, but those only run every third Saturday, June through September. Why—you lookin' for someone?"

Behind her, a half-closed door led into a small room where the edge of a desk and a computer were mostly hidden from view. Someone inside cleared his throat, and the teller stiffened. "Oops," she whispered, tipping her head toward that door. "I'd best get to work."

Brady watched as she counted out six twenties, three tens and a five. "Thanks, ma'am."

Her full cheeks pinkened. "I gave you smaller bills—easier to use around here."

Touching the brim of his hat, he folded the bills, stuffed them in his back pocket, and headed out the door toward the hardware store, where he bought a pair of work gloves and shot the breeze for a few minutes with Angelo. A lean, elderly Hispanic man with a broad smile and sharp, dark eyes, Angelo gave Brady a serious once-over the moment he stepped into the store, then grilled him for a good five minutes on where he'd been and why he'd come to Saguaro Springs.

A man who asked so many questions would

likely share his findings with his cronies, establishing Brady's "identity" even further.

Two down, one to go. And with his last stop, he'd be done.

At Juan's Cantina, he stepped into the dark interior and hesitated for a second as his eyes adjusted to the light.

A woman who had to weigh a good three hundred pounds braced her arms on the bar and cocked her head at his approach. Her handsome brown face creased into a friendly smile when he dropped a five in front of her. "Corona in the bottle, with lime," he said. "Keep the change."

She expertly squeezed a lime wedge over the mouth of the bottle, then skated a cardboard coaster across the bar and pinned it with the bottle, dead center in front of him. "You must be that new hand at the Triple R," she said, standing in front of him and watching as he savored a long swallow. "First time in town?"

"Since I hired on."

She extended her hand. "Trinidad Fuentes. My husband Juan is out back somewhere."

"Brady Coleman." He raised a brow. "Sure must not be much action around here—one look and everyone figures they know who I am. I'd think you'd have a regular parade of strangers crossing the river and heading through here on their way north."

She tipped back her head and laughed. "Not so easy nowadays. With the old sheriff, there was a lot. Now—Ramon keeps pretty good tabs on what's happening. After just three months, I think the word is spreading. The illegals and the drug runners, they give this town a wider berth."

The hinges of the front door squealed. Sunlight and a blast of hot, dry air poured inside, silhouetting a stocky man in a Western hat.

Trinidad stiffened, and a sixth sense told Brady that this guy was no ordinary, Saturday night rowdy. He turned his back to the door and lowered his voice. "Who is that?"

Trinidad sucked in a low breath. "Trouble."

"Got a name?"

She hesitated, then grabbed a bar cloth and began scrubbing at the gleaming bar. "He isn't around here much, and Efrain is all I know. With some guys, it's better not to ask. Comprende?"

Brady nodded. "Last thing I want is trouble."

The man called out the name of a beer, and Brady heard him settle into a creaky chair at a table in the far corner of the room.

"Then watch out for this one—big scar on his jaw, mean look in his eye." She bustled down to the beer taps and drew a tall glass, took it to the newcomer, then disappeared into the kitchen.

Brady nursed his Corona and waited until long after the man left, then strolled to the men's room and flipped open his cell phone.

Efrain. A common enough name, but one that

might turn up in a records search, or trigger someone's memory at the El Paso DEA office.

Any lead, however small, was worth a try.

Chapter Five

MIA CAREFULLY sidestepped something disgusting on the ground and halted beneath the shade of a willow. Mojo ambled over to her side and flopped at her feet, looking up at her with soulful eyes before heaving a sigh and resting a golden muzzle on outstretched legs.

On the other side of the corral fence, Vicente patiently flipped a Navajo blanket over a young horse's back, legs and neck, as he crooned softly to the wild-eyed creature.

Talking, Mia noted with irritation, a lot more to the horse than he'd ever talked to *her*. The first night, he'd disappeared soon after the neighboring rancher brought her out. The following days, he'd worked from dawn until long after dark cooking, training horses in this corral, or doing something with the cows somewhere out in the vast reaches of the ranch.

His own granddaughter obviously ranked low on

his list of priorities. "His loss," Mia muttered under her breath, batting away a persistent fly.

And it wasn't even like he was anyone special or important. He was just some farmhand, wasting his life on a godforsaken ranch in the middle of nowhere. And Lacey, like Vicente, had totally ignored her for the past two days.

Annoyed, she adjusted her broad-brimmed straw hat and glared at the action going on in the corral. Lacey was perched on the fence along the opposite side, watching Adan hold the colt's lead rope as it tried to dance away from the waving blanket.

He methodically rubbed its neck and head to steady it, and Mia found herself mesmerized by the constant, almost gentle movement of his long fingers.

Tall and muscular, with an indolent sort of grace, Adan was so different, so...*dangerous* looking, compared to the soft city boys she knew back home. She found herself watching him all the time—drawn to the air of mystery about him.

A little shiver slid down her spine when he briefly lifted his dark, mocking gaze to hers, then turned away, his sensual mouth curled in a sneer.

Vicente barely noticed her and had little to say, but *this* cowboy was almost like a phantom. Right now he was trapped in the corral, working with that horse. But whenever she ran into him in a barn or up at the house, he disappeared into the shadows faster than she could say hello.

Sweat prickled beneath her pale-yellow crop-top and matching shorts, and her heavy hair felt hot against her back, but she stayed, watching the two men gentle the young horse, and felt oddly melancholy. After four days here she still felt inept, out of place.

It wouldn't be hard to leave this dusty wasteland behind tomorrow and get home to the real world, where she had a cool summer job at a little boutique, and a scholarship starting with her summer term of college.

She and three of her all-time best friends had leased a sweet little apartment near school, too, and they'd all be moving in next week.

"Mia—telephone!" Celia waved to her from the door of the barn. "Long distance. You can take it in here."

Adan glanced up and scowled at her, and Mia savored the moment. Maybe he thought he was too special to be friendly, but *he* probably didn't get phone calls from New York. And tomorrow, she would leave this place behind.

Affecting a bored, nonchalant smile, she waved her fingertips and turned.

Stumbled.

Her feet sliding sideways out of her sandals as they connected with the sleeping dog, she waved her arms trying to regain her balance.

Mojo yelped, struggled to her feet and bumbled into Mia's knees.

With a startled cry she went down, pain lancing up her leg when she fell against scattered rocks and a low-lying cactus.

Adan chuckled. Lacey laughed out loud.

"Mia!" Vicente called out. "You okay?"

She sat up and contemplated the small, bloody scrape and dirt on her knee. Almost invisible cactus spines burned her shin and the palm of her hand. Tears of embarrassment welled in her eyes. Apparently it took an *injury* for the old coot to even notice she was alive.

A warm, wet tongue slurped up one side of her face, and she found herself nearly eye to eye with Mojo, who stood over her with her head cocked.

The dog wagged its tail, then playfully crouched low and snatched the brim of Mia's forty-nine-dollar straw hat. In an instant she slipped under the corral fence and romped away, tossing the hat in the air and catching it like a favorite toy.

"No, Mojo!" she begged. "No—come here!"

The colt snorted and shied. Reared high. Then again, higher yet, striking out with its forelegs before dropping down to earth and dodging backward as the pup raced in circles at it's feet.

Through the veil of her tousled hair, Mia saw Celia come running for the corral, and Lacey take off after the dog. Adan and Vicente struggled to calm the frightened horse. Mojo gaily dodged Lacey's efforts to grab her as she raced in circles through the billowing dust with the floppy yellow prize still clenched in her teeth.

Cursing, Adan released his hold on the colt's lead rope and tackled the dog, gently bringing it to a quivering halt.

"Easy, boy…easy, now." Celia moved into the center of the corral and snagged the rope. "It's okay, buddy."

Mia scrambled to her feet. "I'm sorry…."

But no one turned to look at her, except Lacey, who threw her a disgusted glance.

Adan, one hand on the dog's collar, tossed the offending hat into the dirt outside the corral. Celia led the colt through the far gate and unsnapped the rope to let him trot into another pen. Then she came back and hunkered down in the dirt beside Adan.

Mia stared, horror washing through her.

Vicente was lying on the ground, and he wasn't moving.

ADAN HAD SPENT two years in juvie, locked up with guys tougher, stronger and with even less to lose. He'd watched his back, tried to stay out of trouble and counted the minutes until freedom.

Before that, he'd had too many run-ins with the law to even remember. As much as he'd missed his sisters, he'd needed a new start, away from his old gang and the sheriff who knocked on his door whenever anything happened around town.

The Triple R had felt like home from the day

Adan showed up here asking for a job. Whatever his reasons for coming here, these people were his family now, whether they realized it or not. And Adan Calaveras took care of his own.

Now, up at the main house, he glared at Mia across Vicente's bed, wondering why he'd ever thought she was cute that first day he'd seen her at the cantina. Arrogant, stubborn and rude, she'd given him enough disdainful glances to last a lifetime. And yesterday, her carelessness had hurt Vicente bad.

"I'm so sorry," she whispered. She raised her tear-filled gaze to Adan's, then looked down at Vicente's grizzled face. "I knew the long-distance call had to be my best friend in New York, and I hurried. It was an accident."

"Yeah. Some accident." She could act as sorry as she wanted, but her suitcases were stacked at the front door and she was leaving in an hour. She'd go off on her merry way and leave a lot of trouble in her wake. How would they manage with Vicente laid up with an injured back and only that greenhorn *gringo* in his place?

At the sound of footsteps coming down the hall, he grabbed his Stetson and turned to go.

Celia appeared in the doorway with a pitcher of water, a glass, and two prescription bottles on a tray. She was worried, too—he could see it in her eyes.

She set the tray on the bedside table and rested

a gentle hand on Vicente's forehead. "Has he been awake at all?"

"No." Mia's voice trembled. "Not since you gave him those pills a couple hours ago."

"Yesterday, the doc said his pain medication would make him drowsy, and that sleep would be the best medicine right now." Celia gave her a reassuring smile, then turned to Adan. "Would you mind taking Mia into town? I'd like to stay here in case he needs something, and I still need to make breakfast for Jonah."

"Sure." Celia now had *two* old guys to take care of and a ranch to run, and she still managed to be nice to the person who'd just made things worse. Adan didn't feel nearly so generous. "Sooner the better."

Mia went pale.

At Celia's warning frown, he added lamely, "Uh…so I can get back to work." He stalked out the door. "I'll put her stuff in the truck and wait outside."

He had to wait a good fifteen minutes before she finally showed up and crawled up into the truck. The engine roared to life when he turned the key. "Got everything?"

She looked over her shoulder at the suitcases he'd thrown into the bed of the pickup. "I guess so."

He reached over and turned the radio on, cranking up the volume so he wouldn't have to think up anything to say on the long trip into town. From the corner of his eye he saw her bow her head and fold her hands in her lap. Her dark hair swung forward, obscuring her face.

She didn't say a word until he pulled to a stop in front of Grover's Drug, where the Greyhound stopped on its way through town.

"Thanks," she said in a small voice as she unbuckled her seat belt. "You don't have to wait."

She'd acted like a princess since she'd arrived and he'd purposely avoided her—the way she'd treated him in the cantina that first day still embarrassed him. But now she was almost making him feel guilty, and that was even worse.

He stepped out of the truck and hauled her suitcases up to the bench in front of the store.

She followed, and sat on the bench. Her short white skirt hiked higher when she crossed her long, slim legs, and that snug red top hugged her slender figure. She looked like someone in a magazine, not someone who would be sitting in Saguaro Springs waiting for a bus.

A couple of cowboys passing in a dusty white Chevy pickup apparently thought the same thing, because one of them whistled at her. The truck slammed to a halt and backed up.

The driver was hidden in the shadow of the cab, but the passenger took a deep drag from his cigarette, then reached through the window and beckoned. "Hey, sugar," he called out. "Need a ride?"

Mia shuddered and stared at him with horrified

fascination. "He *must* be joking. Oh, God—he's getting out!"

Adan had intended to drop her off and head straight back to the ranch. Now, duty made him stay. "When does your bus come?"

"Half an hour." She cast a nervous glance toward the front door of the store. "Maybe I should go inside."

Adan considered the elderly woman who ran the store along with her young grandson, and the time it usually took for a county deputy to arrive. When Celia found some cattle stolen, it had taken over a day for one to show up. "Go ahead, but I think I'd better stay anyway."

The cowboy was swaggering up the sidewalk, now, with the cigarette dangling from a corner of his mouth and an ain't-I-cool jut to his chin. The ragged scar on his jaw suggested he'd seen trouble before.

Adan surveyed the guy's stocky frame and age—he had to be almost forty—and flexed his fists. "She's not interested."

"And what would you know, punk?" The cowboy spat on the ground and smirked, his eyes pinned on Mia, who now stood frozen, one hand on the front door. "Hey, honey, I haven't seen you around here before."

"She isn't interested," Adan repeated. "Leave her alone."

"Son, don't mess with me." His eyes glittered with challenge. "I could have you for breakfast."

Maybe the guy was a bar room brawler, but *he* hadn't spent time at Millville Detention Center, where fights were common and never fair.

Adan caught him in midstride with a right cross to his jaw, then plowed a fist into the guy's gut. The cowboy doubled over, gasping, and then Adan caught his chin with his knee, sending him backward to the ground.

"Adan, stop!" Mia's voice rose to a frightened wail. "You could kill him!"

Glaring down at the jerk on the ground, Adan ignored her. "You get the hell out of here. And you tell your buddy that I'd look forward to dealing with him, too. You hear?"

The cowboy winced, scrambled backward, then staggered to his feet and stumbled toward the pickup. Once inside with the door closed, he glared at Adan. "You ain't seen the last of me," he snarled. "You can bet on it."

From behind the wheel, the driver leaned forward and gave Adan a long look, then the truck roared off, kicking up a spray of gravel that pinged against the handful of dusty ranch pickups parked beside the road.

An uneasy feeling settled in the pit of Adan's stomach. The driver's face had been hidden by sunglasses and the brim of his hat, but there had been something eerily familiar about the guy. Threatening.

Across the road, a woman in front of Saint Mary's turned to watch, and he could see an old guy scowling outside the grocery store, with a hand shading his eyes as he stared down the street. Did they sense it, too?

Mia tugged on Adan's arm, her mouth open and eyes round. "My God," she whispered. "What would he have done?"

Adan rubbed the tender knuckle of his right hand. "Nothing you'd like." He gave her a cursory glance. "Maybe those clothes of yours made him think you were in business."

That brought her old fire back. "A skirt? Top? Are you insane?"

"Take a good look. See any other women in this town dressed like you?" Actually, a lot of the teens wore even less, but they didn't look nearly as good. "No wonder those guys thought you were hot."

She flounced away from the door and sat on the bench next to her suitcases. Adan leaned against a light post a good ten feet away, where he fully intended to ignore her until the bus came.

After a few minutes of silence, she cleared her throat. "Thanks for staying with me. And…thanks for dealing with that creep."

Adan hitched a shoulder.

"Look, I know you don't like me much. But it really wasn't my fault yesterday."

He didn't even bother to respond.

"I tripped on the dog. That's all. Mojo was part of that ruckus, too."

The petulant tone of her voice set him off. "Not your fault, maybe, but you've upset an old man, and now he's hurt, and you're taking off without a care in the world. What's gonna happen now?"

"It's not like he broke anything," she retorted. "He just has to rest and he'll be better."

"No, he's got badly strained muscles in his shoulder, and he's in awful pain. He can't use that arm for *weeks,* and the Doc says he might even need physical therapy." Adan's voice lowered to a growl. "You know what trouble this is? We need him, and he can't help with Jonah or meals or pitch in when we need him outside."

"I can't change that. It was Mojo—"

"Yeah, yeah. With *your* stupid hat. Who the hell wears a hat like that out here?" It was unfair to rant at her, really, but he'd been frustrated and angry since the day she showed up, and he just couldn't stop. "Vicente's seventy. He helps some with the horse and cattle, but mostly he helps take care of Jonah. He cooks. He keeps the home place going so Celia can concentrate on the ranch. Now she has *two* old guys to care for, plus everything else."

"But Brady—"

Adan snorted.

"And you."

"I don't know ranching like she does. And I sure

as hell don't know how to take care of two old guys and cook."

"My Great-Aunt Dominga said she'd heard Celia has a cousin coming for the summer. A woman. Maybe she can help."

"Celia says she isn't coming."

Mia braced her hands on her thighs and studied the tips of her flimsy little red sandals. "I'm sorry. I never would have come here if I'd known how badly everything would turn out. I only—" her voice caught, and she swallowed hard. "I just wanted to see what my family was like. There's so much I don't know. My mom never…"

Her voice trailed off at the sound of air brakes, then the rumble of a large vehicle coming down Main.

Guilt lanced through Adan over what he'd said to her. Vicente's accident had been his fault, too. If he'd held that colt better—protected the old guy— maybe nothing would have happened beyond a couple of bruises.

A second later, the bus pulled to a stop at the side of the road in a billowing cloud of dust. The door whooshed opened, and the driver descended the stairs. Motioning to them, he opened the side luggage compartment.

Adan grabbed her two suitcases and stalked over to the driver, who tossed the luggage inside. He touched the brim of his hat in farewell and stepped back, waiting for her to climb aboard.

"Thanks, Adan. That awful cowboy…" She gave a delicate shudder as she handed her ticket to the driver. "Tell Vicente I'm sorry."

She followed the driver up into the bus and Adan turned toward the Triple R pickup parked a few yards away. He'd already gotten in and started the motor when he realized the bus hadn't taken off.

Seconds later, Mia emerged and gave him a determined wave. "Wait!"

He glanced at the floor of the cab and the truck bed. "Forget something?"

The bus driver appeared, too, and hurried to the luggage compartment, where he flung open the door and pulled out her two cases. "You're sure, ma'am?"

She nodded decisively and accepted her ticket from him. "I have to stay, just a while longer."

The driver shifted his gaze toward Adan, then grinned down at her. "Guess I can see why."

Adan stared at her as she marched toward the pickup with one suitcase in each hand.

She was snobby. Arrogant. She'd embarrassed him, made him angry, and during the last few minutes she'd made him feel guilty. And now she was apparently delaying her plans to help at the ranch—something surprisingly thoughtful—which made him feel small.

If only he'd kept his mouth shut, maybe she would have gone away and left everyone in peace.

Chapter Six

BRADY RETURNED from El Paso after supper, and knocked on the back door. "Do you have a minute?"

After dealing with both Jonah and Vicente—who were both even grumpier than they'd been this morning—just the sight of someone young and healthy filled Celia with relief.

But then Brady's gaze traveled over her, warm and appreciative. And given his six feet of solid, sculpted muscle, glossy black hair and rugged features, it was almost impossible to rein in her errant thoughts.

He tipped his head toward the kitchen and grinned. "I'll even help you with the dishes."

It took a second for his words to register. "Um… Lacey is doing them, I hope."

He followed her into the kitchen, where Lacey was loading the last of the dishes into the dishwasher. Celia gave her a quick hug. "Thanks, honey. Do you want to come out to the barn with me in a few minutes?"

"I can't. I've got a test on Monday, and a paper due." Lacey hesitated. "Um…maybe I should make supper tomorrow."

Celia chuckled. "What, you didn't like my hamburgers?" Charred on the outside, a tad too pink on the inside, they'd been a far cry from the fare Vicente usually served, but she'd tried to make them too fast in a skillet on the stove. "If I can get in here earlier tomorrow, I'll do a little better. Otherwise, I may just take you up on your offer."

"'Kay." Lacey shut the dishwasher door. Without so much as a glance in Brady's direction, she bounded out of the room.

Leaning one hip against the kitchen counter, Brady waited until she was gone, then turned back to Celia. "You look exhausted."

"Long day. Vicente was restless last night. Even his pain pills didn't help much, and he had them at midnight and four. A mare needed help foaling, and a few head of cattle got out."

"Mia?"

"She and Adan headed for town around three o'clock so she could catch her bus at five. I'm surprised he isn't back yet."

Brady checked his watch. "Maybe he stopped to eat at the cantina." He glanced at the kitchen door, then lowered his voice. "I didn't plan to be in El Paso overnight, but things took a little longer than I thought."

A girlfriend, maybe. Celia imagined a sophisticated blonde or a leggy, intelligent brunette, and was surprised at her own flash of irritation. She grabbed the dishcloth hanging over the edge of the sink and started scrubbing the counters. "Whatever. Beyond your cover as a ranch hand, you don't owe me any explanations."

"I've received word about—"

Footsteps came across the porch. The kitchen screen door squealed open, and Adan walked in carrying two suitcases, his expression grim.

Mia came in right behind him.

Celia looked at her in surprise. "What happened, did you miss the bus?"

With a nervous glance between Celia and Brady, Mia stepped forward. "I got to the bus stop and started thinking...it's my fault Vicente got hurt. I...um...know you probably don't want me here, now, but I thought maybe I should offer to stay a while longer and help out." She took a deep breath. "I'm not a great cook or anything, but at least you wouldn't have to try to do everything yourself. If you need me, I can stay until April 25. If not, I'll catch the bus on Monday."

For someone who'd come so far to meet her family, the girl had certainly arrived this week with a chip on her shoulder, Celia thought. The friction between Mia and Adan had been palpable, and Vicente had avoided her like the plague. But whatever issues they all had, maybe now there'd be enough time to settle them.

"Of course. We'd love to have you stay longer. But I won't let you just volunteer." Celia gave her a quick hug. "I'd be happy to pay you for the hours you work. And if you can make supper without burning it, you're a better cook than me."

At an indrawn breath over by the living room door, Celia turned to find Lacey standing there, her face sullen.

"Look, honey—Mia's back. Won't this be nice?"

Lacey's frown deepened. And then she turned and walked away.

AFTER MIA SETTLED back into her old room and Adan left for his cabin, Brady tipped his head toward the back porch. A few minutes later, Celia finished brewing a pot of coffee, brought out two steaming mugs and handed him one.

"You were saying…?"

"I hear there's a big shipment coming through this weekend." He took a long, slow swallow of coffee. "When we were in town a couple days ago, I saw a guy named Efrain. Stocky, midforties, maybe. Scar on his left jaw. Last name could be Fernandez, from the information I got back from the DEA office. Do you know who he is?"

Celia nodded. "A guy with a scar like that did stop here, just a couple of weeks before you came. He said something about trouble in the area…and that people who got in the way were likely to be hurt. He meant it as a threat, I'm sure of it. I figured he was another one of Garcia's men."

"Possibly. He could also be an independent contractor, of sorts. With the arrests of some major drug cartel leaders, there's been a proliferation of smaller, fragmented gangs. Alliances shift—sometimes guys will help with large shipments and then take a cut. A man like Efrain would be very useful."

"So he *is* bad news."

"Front page. He was an enforcer for the Mafia Mexicana while he was incarcerated."

"Will he recognize you again?" She suppressed a shudder, imagining a man like that following Brady back to her ranch, seeking vengeance for that arrest and conviction.

"No. I turned away in time, and he just downed a fast beer and left." Brady pushed away from the railing. "Let Adan and Vicente know that you want me to watch over the herd tonight—tell them you're concerned about cattle thieves."

"Not a problem. I'm sure they'll just both be glad that it's not them out there." She rinsed the dishcloth under the faucet and then attacked the stovetop. "Are you going to try to make some arrests tonight?"

"No. These guys are just the runners."

She turned to face him and sighed, waiting for him to elaborate.

"I want you to stay home tonight. Promise?"

"I'll try, but I can't promise." Armed with her

Ruger, she was more than enough match for anyone daring to cross her land, whether Brady thought so or not. "I can't afford to stay home and risk losing my cattle. Adan found a section of fence cut yesterday. Not just down, but *cut*. My problems aren't over."

He pinned her with a searching gaze for a moment, then set his coffee mug on the porch railing and rested his hands on her shoulders. "This is important."

His words registered, even if she didn't intend to obey. But unfortunately the warmth of his hands registered, as well—all the way to her bones. Just that simple touch stirred up emotions and desires she'd ignored for a long, long time. She swallowed, her mouth suddenly dry.

Maybe he felt that same sensation, because his eyes turned dark and smoky, and his gaze burned into hers with an intensity that nearly took her breath away.

He blinked and stepped back. "I…" he faltered, then found his voice. "I mean it, Celia. I've got to stake out a spot a few miles from here, and there'll be other agents positioned out on the highway to take up pursuit if our tip was correct. You and the others need to stay here, where you'll be safe and out of the way."

She gave a vague nod.

"Why," he muttered with obvious exasperation, "are you so stubborn?"

"Why," she challenged, "is a woman with a mind of her own called *stubborn,* while the same sort of man is called *assertive?*"

A long silence stretched between them as their eyes locked once more, and she knew that if she didn't move, he was going to kiss her. It was as inevitable as the scorching Texas heat of summer or the rise of the moon at night. And heaven help her, she wanted him to.

She tipped her chin up and held her breath as his mouth hovered just above hers and his gaze seared her.

Instinctively, she knew that he would be more sensual, more powerful, than anyone she'd ever known, and the anticipation sent tiny shivers zipping through her that sensitized nerve endings in places that had been dormant for years.

The first brush of his mouth against hers was a promise.

The second was a dare.

Wrapping a gentle hand behind her head, he fitted his mouth to hers, at once tender and possessive and demanding in a way that made her knees go weak and her heart go wild. She slid her hand behind his neck and pulled him closer, wanting more—more of his mouth, more of him against her—as everything inside her seemed to melt.

It had been so long since anyone had kissed her. Years since anyone had made her feel so desirable.

And she'd never, ever wanted anyone with such blinding need.

Brady pulled away. "We can't do this."

Breathing hard, Celia stared at him, feeling unfocused, dizzy and completely embarrassed. One little kiss, and she'd practically undressed in the middle of her porch.

"I...don't know what happened there," she began, searching for the portion of her vocabulary that seemed to have gone missing. "I don't usually—I mean—"

Brady's sensual mouth curved into a smile and then he brushed a swift kiss against her brow. "Me, too."

"What I'm saying," she continued, trying to ignore the warmth in her cheeks, "is that I agree. I'm not interested in complicating my life, and you're just here as part of your job. Nothing more than that."

"Right. Nothing more." He fell silent for moment. "So, how's everything going?"

His question, so ordinary after the most extraordinary kiss she'd ever had, caught her by surprise. If he could slip back into the mundane so quickly, he hadn't been nearly as affected as she.

It took her a second to gather her thoughts. "I... have to haul a load of cattle to auction tomorrow afternoon. Jonah's not feeling well, and Vicente probably won't be able to do anything for four to six weeks. I'm not too happy with him right now, to tell you the truth."

"He's not a good patient?"

"He totally blew off his granddaughter's arrival and won't listen to a thing I say. The poor girl came clear across this entire country by bus only to be completely ignored. Why on earth would Vicente treat her that way?"

"WE'VE GOT FOUR new foals, Jonah," Celia said as she helped him swing his legs down to the floor. Hooking his arms over her shoulders, she grabbed the belt at the small of his back and helped him move slowly to the window.

He grunted in response as she helped him turn and ease into his chair.

His hands were shaking more today, despite the medication, and he'd had more trouble than usual with his supper. He wouldn't let anyone help him, and with half of his dinner in his lap, he hadn't gotten nearly enough to eat before shoving the bedside table away and refusing the rest.

That pride had led to the loss of a good thirty pounds over the past six months, and he didn't have much more to lose.

"We've got twenty foals on the ground, now," she continued as she tucked a lap blanket over his bony legs. "The new ones are out of our good cutting mares. Two bay fillies and a big, rangy buckskin colt. Want to go out to see them? I can get your chair—"

He gave a single, sharp jerk of his head at that. He had a wheelchair now, but despised it and the weakness it represented. She'd seen the anger and frustration simmering in his eyes whenever they had to go to town for a doctor's appointment.

"Please, Gramps—wouldn't it feel good to be outside? It's seventy degrees out, and the sun is still shining."

He didn't so much as look at her.

With a sigh, she reached for the bell kept at his bedside, and placed it on the table by his chair. "I've got to clean up the kitchen. I'll check on you in about twenty minutes. Okay?"

Knowing he wouldn't answer, she turned to go, and came almost face-to-chest with Brady, who stood at the open door. Her pulse stumbled, then picked up a faster beat. "I didn't realize you were here."

"Sorry. Just wanted you to know that I'll be riding out soon." His voice was all business, but something else flickered in his eyes—something dark and compelling—that had nothing at all to do with the investigation, and everything to do with the kiss they'd just shared. "I might not be back until morning. If you have any trouble, use Luis Mendoza's personal cell phone number. He'll get someone out here right away."

BRADY SADDLED HIS horse at dusk and headed out over the hill above the ranch, thankful for the clouds in the sky and the sliver of moon behind them.

Last Monday night, a high-flying helicopter with FLIR video technology had tracked the ghost-white heat images of human movement across eight miles of the Triple R—from the Rio Grande to the rocky, rugged northeast section of the ranch. At that point, the travelers had swung wide, then headed toward Saguaro Springs.

The nearly impassable terrain in that area accounted for the route of those warm bodies through the night. But even the relatively gentle, rolling grassland through the center of her property didn't make any of those eight miles easy. Wiry sagebrush, cacti, and rocky outcroppings still made the going treacherous.

Tonight, a couple of special agents and several border patrol officers were posted along the river and ready to radio ahead with any sightings, though the rough terrain and darkness could easily mask the movement of experienced drug runners. The Rio Grande was shallow through here—easily fordable on foot—and a few makeshift carriers made of old inner tubes would keep packages dry while blending nicely into the black-on-black tones of night.

Two other special agents were posted along the highway, with their car well out of sight but ready to follow any suspicious vehicle if given a signal. All Brady needed to do was watch and wait, and try to get some decent film of the suspects, then radio the other agents.

Only that, he thought wryly. With a 300-millimeter telescopic lens and superfast ASA film that might be too grainy to read. And in terrain that offered little cover for him.

He shook some slack into the reins and alternately loped Buck for a half mile, then jogged, swinging wide to the south from the expected route of the suspects.

The solitude gave him entirely too much time to think about his mistake back at the house—a kiss that shouldn't have happened. Not with someone involved in this operation—and especially not with her, because just that brief kiss had stunned him more than if he'd taken a hit by a Taser.

Even now, he could smell the lemony scent of her shampoo, and feel the sensual, inviting warmth of her lips beneath his own. How the hell was he going to keep his professional distance and objectivity now? Growling in frustration, he forced his thoughts back to the plan for tonight.

With perseverance and a touch of luck, this operation would ultimately bring down the man responsible for the deaths of Chuck and the other two agents. And that was what was at stake, here. He couldn't let anything—or anyone—jeopardize the chance to see justice done.

Not even a woman who could fill his thoughts and shatter his control with just a touch.

AN HOUR LATER, he stopped at the top of a low rise, where he could make out the faint, dark line of the highway a mile or so ahead.

He settled Buck into a walk as he turned to the east, and let the horse cool down. At the bottom of a ravine, he dismounted and tied the horse to a scrubby pinion pine. "I'll be back, buddy," he said, giving Buck a pat on the neck. "Don't leave without me."

The rest of the way he moved on foot, traveling low to the ground where thorny mesquite, scrub live oak and dark mounds of sagebrush camouflaged his progress, walking tall where profuse stands of giant yuccas towered above him.

This stage of the operation sent memories from two years ago flooding into his thoughts as he made his way to his vantage point.

The tip they'd received about a multimillion-dollar shipment of cocaine by the Garcia gang.

The stress of quickly pulling together a top-notch team.

The waiting…and waiting…and waiting at a predetermined spot.

The ambush that he'd failed to predict—and the hail of bullets that had cut down three good agents. Three good friends.

If he'd only arrived sooner, he might have been

able to stop Agent Vickers from insisting that she and the other two proceed before backup arrived—and those agents would still be alive. His failure was never far from his thoughts.

Since then, he'd lost endless nights of sleep, reliving every moment of that night. Putting on his badge for this current operation had sharpened his pain and guilt and remorse, because this one might finally give him a sense of resolution.

Once he made sure Garcia's organization was destroyed and those vicious killers were in custody, he would end his career.

Finding the rocky outcropping he'd discovered earlier, he settled in and got his camera ready, welcoming the cold and rocky ground as just one more act of penance.

And he waited.

AT A GENTLE TOUCH on her shoulder, Celia sat bolt upright and swung around, her heart in her throat.

Adan stood by her chair, clearly just as startled as she was. "I'm sorry. I didn't realize you were asleep."

She reached over to switch on the table lamp and blinked at the burst of light in the dark living room. "What's wrong?"

Guilt flooded his face. "I turned in—then I suddenly remembered that I forgot to tell you about the paint broodmare—out in the north pasture. I…

guess I was in a hurry to get cleaned up to take Mia into town…then I didn't get back until late…."

"What mare? What's wrong with her?"

"The bay-and-white overo. She looked really close…she looked sort of soft and sunken in around her tailhead, and her teats were waxed. I think one was dripping, but she was so cranky that I couldn't get real close on my gelding."

"Sounds like Santana, but she isn't due for another couple of weeks. I was planning to bring her up to the barn on Monday, because she had problems foaling last year. Maybe Mother Nature beat us to it."

Celia quickly considered and discarded Brady's warning about staying home. She had no intention of prowling the remote areas of the ranch—she only had to reach the mare. Santana was worth a good five grand in any sales ring right now, and the stud fee for that foal had been fifteen hundred. But beyond that was concern for the life of a good mare.

She threw aside her afghan and stood up. "I'd better get out there and check on her."

"I'm sorry. I should've let you known. Earlier."

"That's all right—we've all been distracted lately, and it's my fault for not going after her sooner. Stay here at the house and keep the doors locked, okay? I'll go tell Mia I'm leaving, in case Lacey or one of the guys needs something."

Within thirty minutes, Celia had her saddlebag

loaded with vet supplies, had her horse saddled, and was well on her way into the north pasture.

From the long slope behind her came the sound of hoofbeats. She turned and found Adan coming at a lope, his black horse nearly invisible in the deep shadows. He slowed Rowdy to a walk beside her.

"I thought I told you to stay at the house and keep the doors locked."

Adan's smile died. "I made sure all the doors were locked, and woke up Mia so she'd know what's going on. I figured I should come out here with you, in case anything happened."

Chastened by his concern, she softened. "That's nice of you, Adan. Thanks."

His horse Rowdy suddenly dodged a cactus, nearly unseating him. "You brought flashlights, right?"

"I've got to save the batteries in case we need light to help that mare." Celia buttoned up her jacket against the cold night air so typical of this high desert area. "With luck, she's got a good healthy foal at her side right now. But you just never know."

They'd traveled a little over a mile when the thin crescent moon slipped from behind the clouds, casting weak light over the desolate, almost lunar terrain.

"Look—is that her?" Adan stood in his stirrups and leaned forward, pointing toward a dark shape moving behind a stand of yucca.

Celia reached for the binoculars she'd slung over

her saddle horn and lifted them. Night, with its landscape in shades of black on black, made it difficult to see what Adan pointed at. "There...no, wait a minute...."

It wasn't a horse.

In one swift motion she reached for the scabbard on her saddle and pulled out her rifle. "I want you to quietly turn your horse around, and get the heck out of here. *Now*."

"But—"

"I can't tell who's out there, but we've had cattle stolen and one steer shot in the past few months. This could also be runners packing a load of drugs on up to the highway."

He sidestepped his horse next to hers. "If you fire," he whispered, "they're gonna shoot back."

"I don't intend to fire. Not yet."

"Let's go home and call the sheriff."

"And wait for him to show up next week? I have to protect my ranch, Adan. I'm going to see how many guys there are and find out what they're up to...and I just might give them a warning once I know the odds."

"*Please*. Let's—"

A semiautomatic rapid-fired, the noise echoing through the landscape. Not three feet away from Celia, a cactus shattered and a bullet ricocheted off a rock with an eerie whine. "Go, Adan—*go!*"

Swearing, Adan spurred his horse around and urged him into a dead run toward the safety of a rocky outcropping. Celia followed and pulled to a stop next to him. She lifted her binoculars again.

From this angle she could see the intruders better—three figures on foot, dressed in black. So they weren't cattle thieves on horses...and at least two of them were armed. *So where are you when I need you, Brady?*

She raised her rifle. Aimed for the sky, and fired.

Wheeling her horse around, she loped to a different position just as another round of semiautomatic gunfire resounded in the darkness. This time, from farther to the west.

"*Celia!* Where are you?" Adan called out. "Are you okay?"

Through her binoculars she watched the figures fleeing through the brush along the Rio Grande. Anger burned through her, setting her nerve endings on fire. How dare they? *Again*.

She turned her horse toward the sound of Adan's voice. "I'm here...and they're leaving. Let's go find that mare."

The kitchen lights of the main house were on when Brady reined in his horse, dismounted, and led him into the barn.

He found Celia's mare and Adan's gelding in their stalls and cooled down, but there were still saddle marks on their long, winter coats, and in the tack room, two saddle blankets were damp.

Growling with frustration—yet relieved that the

two had arrived home—he spun on his heel and strode to the house, his teeth clenched. He'd told her. He'd *told* her not to go out there. Yet apparently, she'd gone and taken that kid with her, and put both of their lives in jeopardy.

He took the porch steps two at a time and rapped on the door, then bent to one side and peered through the window next to the door.

Celia stood at the sink, still dressed in jeans and a shirt, her hands braced on the edge and her head bowed. Lines of exhaustion marked her face.

She lifted her head wearily when he knocked a second time, so he considered that an invitation and let himself in. He headed straight toward her. The temptation to take her shoulders in his hands and shake her was so strong that he jammed his hands in his back pockets. *What if she'd gotten herself killed?*

"*Why* did you go out there tonight? Are you crazy?"

She stared silently at her hands.

"I can't force you to stay home, but you were dammed reckless if you took that boy out with you tonight. I heard the gunfire, Celia, yet I was too far away to get there in time. Do you have any idea what you're dealing with here?"

She looked over her shoulder at him, her eyes dull and her face blank.

"The worst thing would be to have you or the boy hurt. But by going out there you scared those guys off, and also screwed up a careful operation involving nearly a dozen agents and officers. We could have traced tonight's shipment and laid the groundwork for nailing the major drug distributors later on."

"I—I'm sorry. I didn't think past trying to help that mare. You're right."

She stood like stone for so long that he finally took her shoulders and gently turned her to face him. And then he saw the bloodstains on her shirt. He froze. "What happened, Celia? Are you okay? What about Adan?"

"I was worried about one of my pregnant mares, so I went out to check on her." Her voice sounded flat, hollow. "Ran into some trouble, though—probably the guys you were after. They fired—so I fired once in the air to scare them. They fired a few more rounds, then took off like jackrabbits. Adan wasn't supposed to be out there. I told him to stay home, but he followed me anyway."

Remembering his suspicions about Adan, given his troubled past, Brady frowned. "Why?"

"He said he didn't want me out there alone." Celia's voice broke. "Later, we found the mare, and she did need help delivering that foal. We also found three of my cattle shot. Nice young heifers, and those bastards hit them. Not even clean kills—I had to put two of them down myself so they wouldn't suffer. When I heard those last few shots—I thought they were shooting at *me*."

"Awww, Celia." Brady pulled her into his arms and tucked her head beneath his chin to hold her close, remorse settling deep in his gut for the way he'd attacked her with his words. What else could he expect, from a woman who'd single-handedly defended her land and family for so long? "I'm sorry."

"No, I put the safety of livestock above you and the others, and that was a stupid thing to do. I'm the one who needs to apologize, not you."

She stiffened, then gradually melted against him as he stroked her back. It felt so good to hold her that he might have stood there all night.

But then she pulled away and braced her hands on his chest. And he discovered that her eyes were filled with grief and anger rather than tears.

"I didn't realize that Mojo might have followed us—I never heard her bark. But Adan said he saw her. She never came home. My God—what if they shot that sweet puppy, too?"

Chapter Seven

UNABLE TO SLEEP, Celia had paced through the house long after Brady went to his cabin. And now, standing on her porch in the early morning light, her thoughts kept returning to the gunshots. The dark figures moving through the shadows.

As a rancher, she'd felt compelled to go check on that mare last night, but she couldn't ignore the truth. Brady had been right. She never should have gone, and she should have sent Adan back home the moment he showed up.

Her heartbeat hitched at the thought of the dead cattle and Mojo's disappearance.

Men who would kill defenseless animals were lower than scum. Even now, she found herself watching for the pup to gambol about in the barnyard, or to be lying in her favorite spot under the porch. The loss of her dog filled her with sadness, but what if something had happened to Adan?

Over the years, she'd run off a lot of trespassers—though the actual number of illegals who hauled drug shipments across the most remote areas of the ranch was anybody's guess. If she happened to see them, a few shots fired in the air, or aimed nearby, usually made them turn tail and head back to the river.

But last night had been different. These guys had carried powerful weapons and hadn't hesitated to use them. Just the thought, given her young daughter and the two defenseless old men who lived with her in the main house, made her blood chill.

She'd been a good shot since childhood, but she couldn't be everywhere on the ranch twenty-four hours a day. She couldn't stand against a whole organization bent on making huge amounts of money through drug shipments. But she *could* be more cooperative and make Brady's job easier.

Heaving a sigh, she stepped off her porch and headed for the farthest cabin under the willows. She knocked a few times, then turned to survey the barns and corrals for any sign of him. Maybe he was gone again—having a big powwow about the botched operation last night. Maybe he was out searching for shell casings or other evidence.

Either way, he was probably dealing with the aftermath of her interference.

"Celia!" Adan called out. "Look!"

She turned, and saw Adan and Brady riding into view. Adan swung his hat wide in the air and let out a bloodcurdling victory yell that made both horses dance and toss their heads.

When Brady's horse started an anxious sidestep, Celia saw the limp, furry bundle draped across his lap. "Oh, my Lord," she whispered, her feet frozen in place and her heart in her throat.

"She'll be okay," Adan said, punching a fist in the air. "She's hurt, but not bad."

"She has a bullet wound in her shoulder." Brady cradled the dog in one arm as he stepped off his horse. "It isn't bleeding now, but I don't know how deep it is. She's pretty tuckered out from trying to crawl home."

Celia ran to meet them. She crooned to the pup as she stroked its soft fur. "So they *did* shoot her, the bastards."

"As a warning, probably. They're letting you know that you need to back off, or else. You've got to do that, Celia—leave this situation alone."

An apology lodged in her throat when Mojo whined and feebly licked her hand. "How can I *not* take a stand?"

Brady handed Buck's reins to Adan and watched the boy disappear into the barn with the two horses. "We'll get these guys, I promise you."

"And then what? A little jail time, a fast probation and they're out on the street." Trembling with anger, she crossed her arms across her chest. "Back to terrorizing innocent people, creating threats?"

"When this current operation goes down, we're planning to snare some big players in the net." His expression turned grim. "Until then, we need to give you and Lacey better protection. I'll call Luis and ask for at least one more agent."

"I don't think…" Her breath caught at the image of her daughter, riding her horse or getting off the school bus, or even just playing out in the barn. Anyone could be out there, waiting. Anytime. The thought chilled Celia's blood. "You're right, of course. Thanks."

Adan appeared in the barn door with two bridles slung over his shoulder and a saddle propped against his hip. His gaze narrowed as he looked at them. "What next, boss?" he called out.

"Feed the mares out in the corrals, then start cleaning stalls. Later this afternoon you can help me move some cattle."

Brady waited until he left, then lowered his voice. "Make sure your daughter stays inside or within sight of these barns, unless she's at school or with you." The exhausted dog stirred in his arms and whined. "Do you want me to take Mojo to the vet?"

"Thanks, but I will. If there's any surgery decision to make, then I'll be there myself to make it." She held out her arms for Mojo, but Brady shook his head and carried the dog over to the truck, where he laid her on a pile of horse blankets on the back seat.

Celia rounded the truck and climbed behind the wheel, then slammed the door and rested her elbow in the open window. "I'll be home in two hours or less—then I need to round up a load of cattle. Be ready to ride."

"Hold on, pardner," Brady drawled. He handed her his cell phone. "Call the vet. He might be out on farm calls, so ask if he'll meet us there."

"I can go alone, but thanks."

"Actually, I'd rather come along, and Lacey should, too."

"But—"

"The risks are escalating, and I'd rather not have you two alone. Like it or not, you've just found yourself a sidekick. Me."

THE TRIP TO the vet went well. The vet extracted the bullet and started Mojo on antibiotics, with no long-term complications expected, to Celia's heartfelt relief.

The pup was now sleeping off her anesthetic in a box stall in the barn, with Lacey at her side. Brady nodded to Celia and walked to the end of the aisle, on the pretext of checking one of the mares in a box stall.

"I'll talk to Luis at the DEA office and see about getting more backup into the area." He paused for a moment, clearly weighing the options. "From now on, I need to be closer to the main house at night. In fact, I should be inside. I could use that small bedroom off the kitchen, or just crash on the couch in the living room."

An expected—and inappropriate—flash of

awareness shot through her at the thought of him staying in her house, night after night after night.

Safer for Lacey, certainly...but not for my heart. "Sure. Of course."

"It doesn't matter where—I probably won't get much sleep anyway."

She studied him under her lashes for any hint that he was implying—or expecting—something more, but he was all business, one hundred percent professional control. "You're welcome to the bedroom off the kitchen."

"I'll need to have access to your phone line for faxes and the Internet. Is there a phone jack in that room?"

Celia thought for a minute, then nodded. "You could also use my office."

Brady paused. "However you want to deal with my presence in the house is okay with me, but it might be hard to explain to everyone here. You could hint that we've resumed our 'affair' from years ago."

"Oh," she said faintly. That idea conjured up images that made her blood heat and her pulse pick up its pace—but the reality was that her daughter and grandfather lived in the house, too. Hints given to anyone would soon spread throughout the ranch and beyond. Maybe today's kids were more blasé about these things, but Lacey was still young and impressionable. "I think I'd better pass."

"I would stay in the spare room," he assured her,

but the devilish twinkle in his eyes told her that he
hadn't really expected her to say yes. "Or, I can
figure out another excuse so I'd have to move into
your house for a while. Maybe something could
happen to my cabin's wiring or plumbing, so the
place is uninhabitable for a while. The other cabins have no room for an extra person and Vicente
will soon be back in his."

"Isn't that awfully extreme?"

Alarm must have shown on her face because he
grinned down at her, curved an arm around her
shoulders and gave her a quick, reassuring hug.

"I promise to fix whatever I break. Honest. And
otherwise, how will you explain me moving into
the house, when I have a perfectly good cabin?
You know Adan and Vicente will think we've got
something going, and if you don't want this to look
fishy, we need an excuse."

Relief mingled with a flash of disappointment at
so prosaic an alternative. With the warmth of his
hard muscled arm around her shoulders, the affair
idea sounded so much more…intriguing.

And when he gave her a little squeeze and then
lifted his arm away, she felt almost bereft. How
long had it been since anyone besides Lacey had
hugged her?

A very, very long time.

"Tell me," she said finally, "what you're going
to do to my cabin."

"I could have a small fire in the electrical breaker panel—as long as Vicente and Adan aren't good at electrical work. Or the pipes running into the cabin could suffer an unexpected break. I think the fire would be best—the nights are cold here, so not having heat from the electric baseboards would be chilly, and there could be a little smoke damage, too, which would take a while to air out."

Celia thought about the clean but tattered old quilts on the bed. The swaybacked couch and burnt orange upholstered chair. "There's probably nothing in there that couldn't be thrown out. But this sounds like arson—or vandalism. And that's illegal."

"Only if we reported it, and made a claim to your insurance company. I'll fix or replace anything that's damaged at no charge, and promise it will look better than before. Consider it," he added with a smile, "a little overhaul."

"How much time do you need?"

"I already checked the Saguaro Springs phone directory, and there don't seem to be any electricians in the area. Given the distances out here and how busy those guys are, we could figure on a few weeks, easy. We could always delay making the call, too."

She fixed him with her sternest look. "You'll take care of any damage?"

He held up his right hand in a scout salute. "Honest."

THE SEARCH FOR the cattle wasn't going well at all.

"Too bad you don't have a helicopter," Adan observed, taking off his hat to wipe his brow. "Lots of the bigger ranches have them."

"I'll add that to my Christmas list. In the meantime, let's fan out over this next ridge. Brady—you head south, toward the ranch road. Adan—keep going east. I'll go west. Fire a shot in the air if you find a dozen or less, two if you find a big herd."

The land was vast, but it took a hundred acres of sparse grama grass and greasewood to support a single cow here. The animals tended to range through great distances, often breaking off into smaller herds, but the one limiting factor out here was water. They always needed to be within traveling distance of one of the old-fashioned windmills that still whirred with the breezes and drew water into sixteen-foot galvanized steel watering tanks.

Over two hundred head of stocker cattle were supposed to be in this pasture—young cattle she'd intended to bring up to around seven hundred pounds and then sell at auction to feedlot buyers. There'd been recent, muddied tracks by one of the water tanks, but so far, she'd seen just a handful of animals—and had only spotted those through her binoculars. Where the heck were the rest?

Celia rode on through gullies and over ridges, scanning the horizon, her frustration mounting as one hour passed, then another.

The distant crack of a rifle—followed by two

more, in quick succession—filled her with relief. Pivoting Duster to the south, she urged the mare into a lope toward the sounds.

Once enough cattle were rounded up and herded into the pen by the loading chute, she could go home to get the aging semi parked behind the barn.

And there'd still be time to make it to El Paso this afternoon.

The ride back—a straight shot, this time, rather than one sweeping north and south hunting for signs of the herd—took almost an hour. At the top of Eagle Butte, she found Adan and Brady waiting for her, where they could be easily seen from a distance. The corral and loading chute were just on the other side, filled—she hoped—with cattle close to the right weight.

At her approach, Brady and Adan rode down the steep flank of the butte and loped over to meet her.

"I didn't find any," she said. "How many do you have?"

Adan and Brady exchanged glances.

"Adan found ten of them," Brady said on a long sigh. "I found just three."

"We'll keep looking—most of them have to be out here somewhere," Adan added. "It'll just take time."

A sudden uneasiness made the back of her neck prickle. "Then why did you fire all those shots?"

"Take a look."

Brady reined his gelding toward the holding corral and took off at a lope, with Adan and Celia behind him.

At the corral, he stopped and waved a hand toward the loading chute.

Her uneasiness had changed to dread. And now, as she surveyed the scene, her dread turned to outrage.

Fresh truck tire tracks led toward the ranch road.

The sand in the corral had been stirred by milling hoofprints. A lot of them. There was fresh manure in there, too.

Someone had been here. With a potbellied semi, they could have taken a good thirty-five head or more in just one trip.

The chute was miles from the home place and well out of sight. A good team of cowboys could have rounded up a nearby herd, loaded them and hit the road in an hour or so, and disappeared without ever being seen. Perhaps have even returned for a second load.

Brady sidestepped his horse next to hers. "These were all branded?"

It took a second for her to speak past the knot of anger in her throat. "Of course they were. They couldn't be taken straight to a sale. Not when the sheriff could be notified and a bulletin faxed to every auction barn in this part of the country."

"Then someone has to rebrand them, and let the brands heal."

Celia drew a deep breath and forced her clenched

fists to relax. "The Triple R brand isn't easy to alter, and our ear notches are unusually long and hard to mask. With that combination, thieves could sure find other herds much easier to deal with."

"I'm sorry, Celia. You don't deserve this."

Adan rode up on her other flank, his face a mask of worry.

"What about that sale?"

"I've got several hundred young steers in the southwest pasture, but none of them have gained anything even close to market weight." She worried her lower lip with her teeth. "I'll go after my semi, and call the sheriff while I'm at home. With luck, maybe someone saw something or will have some leads. Ranches out here are so few and far between that most people notice if a strange truck comes through. I want you two to go after the cattle you found already, then round up anything else you can find. I've *got* to ship a load today."

Adan frowned. "But we've been looking for hours, already."

"And the market isn't that good right now," Brady added.

"I know," she retorted grimly. "I'm going to lose money, but I need that cash by tomorrow for a loan payment, and waiting isn't an option."

ON MONDAY, MIA studied the two lunch trays she'd prepared, then adjusted the angle of the folded napkins. Maybe she wasn't exactly the best cook on the planet, but no one could say that she didn't understand presentation.

She'd found breaded chicken patties in the freezer and nuked them. The canned green beans she'd lined up like perfect little soldiers. A fan of apple wedges completed the plate, adding a dash of red and some nice crunch to the textures. And the pièce de résistance, the brownies she'd made from a box up in the cupboard, had just the right dusting of snowy powdered sugar. Who could resist?

Satisfied, she grabbed a tray with each hand and headed through the living room, down a long hallway, and then to the right, where two of the five bedrooms were occupied by two old guys who were going to enjoy the prettiest meal they'd ever seen.

She grinned to herself, wishing Lacey was around to see *this*. With spring break over, the girl had started back to school this morning. She'd left without a word, though she'd grudgingly accepted the waffle Mia made, and had almost cracked a grin at the bulging eyes and wrinkled smile Mia had created on it with two hard-poached eggs and a strip of bacon.

Sliding one tray onto a table in the hall, she knocked on Vicente's door and nudged it open to peek inside. "Lunchtime," she called out. When he didn't answer, she bumped the door open wider with her hip and stepped inside with a flourish. "Here you go!"

The bed was empty.

Startled, she walked around the bed and checked the floor. The walk-in closet. The bathroom. His boots were gone too, no surprise…and he'd left the sling for his arm tossed at the foot of the bed.

As grumpy as he was, he probably much preferred his own company and had headed for the solitude of his own cabin.

Heaving a sigh, she headed to the next room and knocked, then entered with a tray in her hands. This guy was in bed, as always, poor thing. She hadn't even spoken to him yet, because he always seemed to be asleep.

"Hi, there. I brought you lunch!"

He rolled his head against the pillow to look at her, then turned away and closed his eyes.

Glancing down at the food she'd prepared, she curbed her impatience and marched to the other side of the bed. "Let me crank up the head of the bed for you," she said breezily. "I made you a *nice* lunch."

"No."

He didn't even open his eyes, which was certainly rude, and from what she'd heard, Jonah didn't eat enough to keep a bird alive. Maybe Vicente was on the loose again, but this was one guy who could use her help. "You don't think it's a nice lunch?" she demanded. "Look!"

His eyes opened just a crack. "Go away."

"Nope." She pulled up a chair to the side of his

bed. "If you don't want to eat, I can at least tell you stories."

When he didn't answer, she tapped a forefinger against her lips and affected her most outrageous Southern accent imitation. "You know, you just wouldn't believe it, but my friend Marcy Burton— you know, of the Burton's grocery store chain out in Pennsylvania? Well, you just wouldn't believe what she did this last spring. I saw the cutest little red skirt in a display at Bloomingdale's—exactly the right color for my kicky new sandals—so I put it on layaway. Ten percent down, the rest in six months. And I found just the right sweater, too— midriff long. Cute little heart buttons. Well, I told her about how *thrilled* I was. And she went right out and bought the *very same thing.* Only she paid for it right then, because she gets to use her mother's credit card, and she *wore* it to school. Three times! And everyone said how *cute* it was, so they would all remember it—and if I wore my outfit they'd think I was trying to copy her. Can you believe that? I mean, *really.*"

Jonah swore under his breath and opened his eyes just enough to glare at her.

Encouraged, she rolled her eyes toward the ceiling as if deep in thought. "Of course, now we're going off to different schools, so I guess it doesn't matter. But I just *know* that someday I'm going to be wearing that outfit somewhere in town, and

Marcy will be there in hers, and she'll say, 'Well, Mia—how cute that you decided to get an outfit *just like mine.*' Now my friend Hollis—she's a girl, even with a name like that—would never think of embarrassing her friends like that. She's got class, you know? Why, one day we were shopping together, and I didn't have enough cash, and when I saw a pretty little purse with all sorts of beads dangling from the bottom, and the sweetest smiley face design on the front, she loaned me the money. Of course, I gave her the money that same week, but she never went back and got one like it, even though she—"

"Enough!" Jonah roared. "Get out!"

"But I brought you lunch."

"You're *fired!*"

"Can't be," she said primly. "I volunteered."

"Why in God's name did you do that?" he growled.

She grinned at him. "Because you're such a charming guy. Ready for lunch?"

He sat partway up, then fell back against the pillow. "No!"

"It's so sad," she murmured. "We had a neighbor once—a nice old guy. But there was something wrong with him. Not like it would kill him or anything, but he just totally gave up. Can you believe it? He sat around and moped, and wouldn't go out, and he didn't eat…and one day the landlady let herself into the apartment to check on him, because he hadn't paid rent for like two whole months, and she found him dead. He was sort of shriveled up and dry. The weird thing was that he wouldn't have died from the disease he had—he died because he just gave up. What a waste."

"Well, there's the difference, because I *will* die. So take that tray and get out of here."

She found her most imperious tone. "I *arranged* your green beans!"

"What?"

"Look." She held up the tray, and after a good minute, he finally did.

She had lined them up like pencils in a box, with a twist of pimento across the top.

"What the hell did you do that for?"

"Presentation. Style. Appeal. All considered and executed," she added darkly, "to make you feel guilty enough to eat."

"And why in the Sam Hill would I feel guilty?"

"Because someone cared enough to make you something really, *really* special."

He eyed the canned green beans. The woefully flat brownie—which made Mia wonder just how many years that box of mix had been on the shelf. The soggy chicken patty, which probably should have been baked instead of microwaved, but who knew?

A chess set sat on the bureau in the corner, its pieces well-worn and a few of them chipped.

"You eat, and I'll play you a game of chess. Either that, or I'll bring in my violin. I've had it in my luggage this whole trip and haven't even practiced once. Isn't that terrible?"

"Bluegrass?"

She pursed her lips. "Never, but I could sure try to learn—let me go get my case."

His mouth twitched as his gaze lifted from the plate to her face. "You aren't really a nitwit, are you," he said flatly.

His bitter expression had changed to irritation, then defeat, but now his features softened into something close to a faint smile. Mia thought wistfully of Vicente, wishing that just once she could have gotten through to him, as well.

"Give me the danged tray to eat in peace, then I'll beat you at chess."

Mia nodded and left, and waited outside Jonah's door for a moment until she heard the clank of silverware against the stoneware plate. Then she grabbed Vicente's tray and headed out the door and down the long path to his cabin. "I'm on a roll," she muttered to herself, "so it won't hurt to try."

At the door, she knocked twice, then tried the handle. The door swung wide, revealing a Spartan, immaculate sitting area with a table and two chairs on one side, a tiny galley kitchen, and a door at the far end that likely led to the bedroom and bath.

There wasn't so much as a sock or a magazine

out of place, and the effect was almost sterile despite the homey glow of the deep-golden pine paneling and the soft, crimson-and-black woven rugs on the oak planked floor. The only picture in the entire place was a gold-framed photograph of an elderly Hispanic woman placed dead center on top of an old-fashioned TV.

"Hellooo," she called out. "Anyone here?"

Taking another step inside, she found Vicente in a recliner just behind the narrow room divider that held the row of kitchen cabinets that faced the door.

He appeared pale and drawn, and probably a bit woozy as he stared at her from beneath several multicolored afghans.

"I brought you lunch." She walked in and scanned the sitting room, spied a TV tray set, and unfolded one next to his chair. "Here you go…are you hungry?"

"No."

She put the food tray down and smiled, ready for battle, and he must have seen a gleam in her eye because he gave an indifferent wave.

"Leave it here," he said wearily. "I'll get to it."

"How come you came down here?"

His eyes drifted shut. "This is where I belong."

"Can I get you anything? Are you due for medicine, or anything? What about the sling and the ice?"

When he didn't answer, she continued. "I…um… want to tell you how sorry I am about what happened." He didn't answer, so she plowed ahead. "I didn't mean to trip over the dog, and then she grabbed my hat, and I couldn't get it back before she got under the fence."

Celia had said that he'd been sleeping most of the time because of the pain medication, and now his breathing deepened, slowed. He'd probably just drifted off again.

"I'll just put this tray in your refrigerator," she whispered. "You can have it later."

She stood for a few moments, though, tray in hand, and studied his craggy features. "I'm sorry you didn't really want a granddaughter," she said softly. "But meeting you sure meant a lot to me."

VICENTE WAITED UNTIL the door of the cabin opened and closed, and his granddaughter's footsteps faded away. Then he opened his eyes and gazed at the photograph of his Consuelo.

He talked to her still, even though she'd been gone over twenty years now, and sometimes he could almost feel her smiling back at him, her beloved face full of love and forgiveness.

"I just can't do it, *mi querida,*" he whispered, though he knew that she could read his thoughts. "I can't let her into my life. You understand…I know you do."

But as he drifted off to sleep, he imagined Consuelo's troubled eyes watching over him and her soft voice begging him to forget the past and move on…before it was too late.

The same words she spoke on the day she died.

Chapter Eight

CELIA CLIMBED out of the semi, pocketed the keys, and headed for the house, feeling her daily dose of parental guilt.

Lacey would have gotten on the school bus hours ago, thanks to Mia. And when Celia left last night for El Paso with the load of steers, the poor kid had gone to bed without the usual good-night routine they always shared. Given Lacey's inexplicable dislike for Mia, the morning had probably been as chilly inside the house as it was outside.

Trying to estimate the number of missing steers and finding enough of the others had taken far longer than she had expected, and by that time Celia had needed to load and go. Paying off the loan due today had been crucial, yet Lacey needed time, too, and there just wasn't enough time in the day.

Now, after the three-hour drive home from El Paso—one that had included stopping at the local bank to make the loan payment—she had a morning appointment with the sheriff. *If* he showed up as planned.

"Which isn't likely," she muttered as she wearily shucked off her boots at the back door.

The house was quiet when she walked into the kitchen, with the pleasant aromas of cookies cooling on the kitchen counter and fresh-brewed coffee, but no one in sight. Curious, she walked through the living room. Checked her office, and the flagstone patio behind the house.

Walking down the hall to the bedrooms, though, she heard a deep male voice that could only belong to her grandfather, laughter that could only belong to Mia. If Mia had him talking, she was worth her weight in gold.

Celia stopped at his open door and watched Jonah studying a chessboard set up by the side of his bed. Sitting on the table on the other side of the bed was a lunch tray, and from the looks of the plate, he'd done pretty well.

"Gotcha," he announced, laboriously moving a chess piece with a trembling hand.

Mia looked up at Celia and winked. "Your grandpa is *waaay* too good a player for me."

"He's darn good, all right." Or he had been, before his sight had started to fade and his mild confusion began.

Moving to the side of the bed, Celia leaned over to study the board. Her estimation of the girl kicked up another notch, because there were at least three moves she could have used to avoid being beaten.

"He doesn't like to play with just anyone," Celia added, giving his shoulder an affectionate squeeze.

"He had to. I threatened him with my violin."

"She threatened to teach herself bluegrass," he corrected. "Right here in my room. The thought made my teeth ache."

Thank you, Celia mouthed to Mia.

The girl nodded. "By the way—Vicente moved back to his cabin. He said he couldn't sleep right up here, so I took him some lunch. Brady went to town on an errand he said you needed him to do. He'll be home around three. Oh, and Lacey left a note on the counter—says she needs some props for a play at school. She wants to go through the storeroom in the barn, if that's okay."

"Tell her she's welcome to anything of mine she needs, but she has to stay out of Jonah's things unless she asks him first. Did she say what she was after?"

"I'm not sure. She has a list that the teacher gave all the kids, and whoever comes up with the most gets extra points, or something. It's on the counter, too." Mia frowned at Jonah. "I should let you sleep a while. You look tired, pops. But if you want, I can offer you a choice of Chopin or world-class chess before supper."

Jonah hadn't looked that perky in months, Celia thought as she headed down the hall. He'd never be strong and healthy again—fifteen years of advancing Parkinson's was inexorably dragging him into a downward spiral—but he'd been understandably depressed these past months as well.

She glanced out the windows facing the ranch road, then took a quick shower and changed.

The sheriff's patrol car was just pulling in by the time she got to the kitchen. Gathering her damp hair into a ponytail, she went outside to meet him.

"Hey, Ramon. Good to see you." She offered her hand and gave his a firm shake.

After Aubrey Booker, Ramon was a welcome change—not more than thirty and physically fit, he had the energy and the obvious desire to see things done right.

"I lost at least thirty head either Saturday night or Sunday morning, best as I can tell."

Pulling out his metal-backed notebook, he started filling out a report form. "Branded?"

"With the Triple R brand, and you've seen how tricky it would be to alter it. Our ear notches are the same way."

"Not easy to change, either. Someone would have to hold on to those steers for a while so the changes wouldn't look fresh."

"That's what we figure. Your office said they've already faxed bulletins out to the sales barns throughout Texas, and did that e-mail report thing as well."

"You have insurance?"

"Not enough—and this is the second time in the past six months. My agent is getting a little testy. If these guys got one of my bulls…" The thought made Celia's stomach twist into a knot.

Ramon frowned. "Any evidence?"

"Truck tire tracks, mostly. Some cigarette butts, but I don't imagine you're going to look at DNA for a cattle thief." She fished into her back pocket. "Out about fifty yards from the chute Adan found this key chain, though I guess we don't know if it's been there two days or two years."

Taking it from her, he turned it over in his hand. "First Avenue Ford, Dallas. But no keys?"

"Nope."

"Did y'all hear anything? See anyone suspicious hanging around?"

She gave a frustrated wave of her hand. "Those pens and the chute are a few miles up the ranch road, and well out of sight. I did see some illegals or drug runners crossing my land from the river Saturday night. I fired a warning shot and they fired back. But they were on foot, so they weren't after any cattle."

He lifted his gaze from his notepad. "Anyone hurt?"

"I don't shoot to hit, Ramon. You know that. But I sure as heck want those people to steer clear of my property."

He shook his head. "You be mighty careful with that gun of yours, ma'am. One of these days you might get a tad too close and all hell will break loose out here. You understand what I'm saying?"

"So when," she asked evenly, "are you going to do something about it?"

She'd promised Brady she wouldn't relate any details about his reason for being out here, or about his part in the events of that night. Apparently, the operatives with the DEA and border patrol had chosen to work without the knowledge of the sheriff's department on this case.

But one day Brady would be gone, and she would be facing the same old problem, with the same lack of action on the part of the local police force. It wouldn't hurt to keep Ramon apprised of her situation.

"We've got a task force. All we need is about triple the funding and quadruple the staff, and we'll be able to make a good dent in the drug trafficking that goes on through here." He studied the form in his hands and wrote a few more notes. "Back to the cattle...the weigh stations out on the highways have been notified also. There haven't been any reports of illegally transported cattle, but we'll keep looking. I'll let you know if anything turns up."

"Have you talked to any of the other ranchers in the area?"

"Our dispatcher did, last night. No other reports." He slipped off his sunglasses and rubbed the bridge of his nose. "If this is a cattle ring, we'll be hearing about other thefts nearby. If it's an isolated case, it's gonna be much harder to solve…unless a brand inspector or sales barn owner gets suspicious about falsified documentation."

She sighed. She hadn't expected a miracle. But she'd hoped for something—*anything*—that might be a solid lead right away. A few years ago, there'd been some organized cattle thieves who jumped from one county to another, changing the license plate and the color of their semi and tractor as they went.

They'd been apprehended not more than fifty miles from Saguaro Springs, based on a tip from someone who'd seen the vehicle parked at a quickie car paint shop in West Dallas.

It was unlikely that she could ever be so lucky.

"Thanks, anyway." She offered her hand again, then watched as he drove away, taking with him all her hope of ever seeing her cattle in time for the next loan payment due.

LACEY CLIMBED DOWN the steps of the school bus and trudged up to the house.

Mom's truck was gone. *Again.* But then, when was she ever home? The cattle and the horses and all the stuff it took to run the ranch took up every last minute of her time.

Lacey scowled, remembering the kids at scout camp. Sure, they were mostly airheads, and thought the wrong nail polish was a complete fashion disaster, but they got to do a lot of things Lacey couldn't even imagine, like going to Dallas for school clothes.

Dumping her backpack on the porch, she headed for the barn and looked in on Mojo. The dog had a bare, shaved square on her shoulder and wiry-looking stitches, but she thumped her tail and whined when she saw Lacey at the door.

Lacey went inside and shut the door behind her, then sat down on the thick bed of straw. Mojo crawled into her lap—way too long to be a lap puppy, but still imagining that she fit—and tipped her head back when Lacey rubbed under her collar.

At the sound of footsteps, Lacey looked up and saw Brady at the door.

"Hey, how're you doing?" He had a nice smile, but he used that same one on Mom, too. He probably thought he was Mr. Personality or something. As far as Lacey could tell, he wasn't a very good worker around the ranch because he was gone an awful lot, and he didn't seem to have the kind of respect that most of the hands had shown her mom.

He talked to Mom like she was a friend, instead of his boss, and Lacey had overheard him actually *lecturing* her about something, which was way out of line. The fact that Mom hadn't put him in his place had Lacey worried, big time.

"How's the pup doing today?" Brady came into the stall and hunkered down next to Lacey, then reached over to stroke Mojo's head. "She's one lucky dog, you know. A few inches over, and the bullet would have hurt her pretty bad."

When Lacey didn't answer, he got back to his feet. "It's a beautiful day for riding, isn't it? I suppose it gets too hot to enjoy it, come July."

If he didn't know, he was gonna be in for a big surprise. She smiled at that, figuring he wouldn't stick around long once the temp hit a hundred.

"How's school going?"

"Fine," she mumbled, clambering to her feet and dusting the straw off her jeans. "I gotta go."

She brushed past him and headed down the aisle for the ladder at the far end, wishing he wouldn't try so hard to be friendly. He'd never done or said anything wrong, except that's what her mom's old boyfriend had done—he'd tried to be nice to Lacey just to win points with Mom, and that was just so *shallow.*

Greg, thankfully, hadn't lasted very long, and Mom hadn't dated anyone since then. But this guy... Lacey gave a little shudder. He was cute and tall and she'd overheard Adan telling Vicente that the night he brought Mia back, he'd actually caught a glimpse through the open kitchen window of the guy *kissing* Mom. *Eeeuw!*

She glanced over her shoulder to make sure Brady hadn't followed her. Then she climbed up the ladder nailed to the wall, hoisted herself through the trap door and fumbled for the light switch on the wall.

A half-dozen bulbs high overhead bathed the hayloft in light. A discordant choir of half-grown kittens mewed and blinked and stretched on top of the hay bales stacked along the opposite wall.

Most days, Lacey came up here to play with them, and they were already starting to scramble down the bales when she reached the storeroom built across the far end of the barn.

"Not today, guys," she called out.

They were all winding around her ankles and batting at her shoelaces by the time she wrestled the heavy brass snap out of the hasp-and-loop closure on the door.

Scooping up a handful of wiggly kittens, she nestled them to her chest and opened the door wide—glad to have some company, even if kittens wouldn't be much defense against the spooky shadows inside.

She jerked a string to turn on the single lightbulb in the room and frowned at the piles of boxes, old furniture, rusty bicycles and old toys tumbled haphazardly into every available space.

She needed those extra points for the class scavenger hunt project. She really, truly did, after that last unexpected quiz and that paper on the History of Pioneer Women in Texas, which had been a page too short and just a *little* shy on facts.

Edging into the room slowly, holding the kittens tight and keeping a wary eye on the floor for any unexpected critters, she surveyed the trunks closest to the door. The only ones, she decided with a shudder, that she dared check out.

Blowing at the thick dust on top, she slipped open the two hasps on a tall trunk with a bowed top and crumbling leather hinges. The kittens mewed anxiously and stapled themselves to her T-shirt with razor-sharp claws as she leaned over to peer inside.

In awe, she stared at the contents of what must surely be a trunk belonging to Vicente. "Perfect!" she breathed. "This is so totally cool!"

A small voice in her head whispered a warning, but she ignored it. Surely he wouldn't mind if she borrowed a few things, just for a little while. After all, what could it matter?

Back on the main floor of the barn, her arms full, she grinned to herself as she headed down the aisle. The moment she saw Mia walk in the door, though, her excitement faded.

"Hi, Lacey. I saw you come out here—need any help?"

Mia's golden skin glowed. Her black hair hung loose, gleaming under the aisle lights, and her tight black jeans and cherry-red sweater were perfect, as always.

First Mia had won over Mom, then Grandpa Jonah…and now Adan seemed to watch the princess whenever she wasn't looking. Sparing a glance at her own baggy Texas A and M sweatshirt and threadbare jeans, Lacey scowled and just kept walking. *It isn't fair.*

Mia touched her arm as she passed. "I'm sorry we can't be friends, Lacey. It would be so nice to have another girl here to talk to. Maybe we could write each other, after I leave."

She was *lonely?*

"You're lucky, you know that?" Mia's voice sounded wistful.

Lacey hesitated at the door. The thought that anyone so beautiful could ever consider someone *else* lucky was beyond belief. Shifting the weight in her arms, Lacy turned and narrowed her eyes. "Why?"

"You've got such a nice family." Maybe it was just the light, but Mia's eyes looked bright. "I'll be gone in a few weeks, and I probably won't come back. My grandfather sure wasn't all that thrilled about meeting me."

Lacey had been prepared for an arrogant putdown, or a backhanded compliment delivered with a smirk. Now, guilt slithered through her midsection and made her feel small.

Memories flashed through her thoughts—the times Vicente had helped her learn to rope calves, and use an awl to repair leather equipment. The times he'd hitched up a team to take her for sleigh rides when they'd had a rare snowfall. He'd been like a second grandpa, yet Mia had had none. "Maybe he'll get used to you."

Mia shook her head. "I wish you could tell me what to say to him. My mom said he was cruel to her, but I didn't want to believe her. Now I do."

Cruel? *Vicente?* Lacey's mouth dropped open, then she snapped it shut. "Maybe he'll like you better by the time you go home."

Mia's laugh was the saddest Lacey had ever heard. "Don't count on it. There's a better chance he'd dye his hair pink and do somersaults across the barnyard."

Chapter Nine

On Thursday, Celia announced that she had to pick up some hay at the Rocking B, and needed both Adan's and Brady's help.

On the way there, Adan drove with one wrist draped over the top of the steering wheel and a cigarette dangling from the corner of his mouth.

Unlit, Brady noticed with amusement, because Celia gave the kid a dark glance the moment he reached for the cigarette lighter in his front pocket.

Resting an elbow on the back of the front seat, she looked over her shoulder. "This won't take long—maybe twenty minutes to load, and another twenty to get away. Gil's quite a talker. If we're lucky, he won't be home."

Brady nodded.

With an empty hay wagon bouncing over the rough road behind the crew cab truck and the roar of the engine—glass pack mufflers, probably—there wasn't much possibility of conversation.

Given Celia's preoccupation and the kid's body language, there wouldn't have been much anyway.

The buildings at the Rocking B were similar to those at the Triple R. The typical, sprawling adobe ranch house. Pole buildings. Corrals. Cattle bawling in the lots nearest the buildings.

But where the Triple R was utilitarian—clearly a working operation with its roots spreading back to the 1800s—this place had the quiet aura of success.

Professional landscaping set off the large home, and pristine white pipe fencing enclosed the arena and corrals. A couple of white pickups—with Rocking B emblazoned in gilt on the sides of one, and dealer's stickers still in the side window of the other—were parked at the barn. From somewhere up by the house came the fierce barking of what sounded like a large dog.

Adan honked the horn as he drove past the barn, then he turned up a lane on the far side of the last pole building. He pulled to a stop with the empty trailer next to a towering stack of hay bales that ran along one side of a feedlot.

"We're buying a hundred," Celia said as she stepped out of the truck and pulled on a pair of old leather gloves. "Just enough to get by until my next semi load arrives. I'll throw 'em down, and you boys can stack."

Brady watched her swing easily up onto the empty hay wagon, then step off onto the hay stack and climb to the top, each foothold a narrow space between the tightly packed bales.

It was a particularly nice view from where he stood, given her slender curves and tight jeans. There was nothing quite like a cowgirl—especially this one.

Strong, lean and tanned, with a no-nonsense attitude and obvious belief that she could handle anything that came her way, she stood at the top of the stack and looked down, a sixty-pound bale already hoisted and ready. With long, slender legs and a trim waist like hers, most women couldn't have lifted it.

"Heads up!"

The bale sailed into space and landed with a thud on the trailer, in perfect alignment for Adan and Brady to grab it and put it into position. Another ninety-nine arrived as fast as Adan and Brady could stack them.

Dust and prickly hay chaff covered his shirt. Sweat trickled down his back as the load on the trailer grew higher and harder to build. Even with gloves, the twine strings around the bales bit deep across his palms. But the hard work, crisp air and brilliant sunshine were exhilarating—a step into his own past.

If the bank hadn't foreclosed on his dad's ranch, he'd probably be working there right now—with a rich and satisfying life spent on a good horse, with the wide open-spaces and the rugged beauty of nature as his constant companions.

A life, he thought wryly as he shoved the last bale into place, where he wouldn't be facing the regret and guilt that still kept him up at night.

Brady sauntered over to a freestanding hydrant along the fence, tossed his hat on the ground and lifted the handle. He held his cupped hands under the stream of water, splashing his face and neck. "Want me to go find one of the boys so we can pay up?"

"No one came when we honked. They must be gone." Celia walked over and held her own hands under the water and followed suit. "Gil knows what I came after and how much I needed, though. I'll just put a check on his kitchen counter."

Adan plunged his hands under the water. "Want me to run the check up to the house?"

Celia gave a dry laugh. "It's a thought, kid. Might be faster that way. Especially if Gil's home."

With Brady at the wheel, they pulled the hay wagon up in front of the barns and Adan stepped out. He hadn't gone more than a few yards when Gil appeared on the shady patio outside the front door of his house, with his hand on the collar of a white German shepherd.

"Come on in," he called out. "Coffee's hot."

Brady looked down into Celia's expression of stoic acceptance. "You can refuse. Tell him you're in a hurry."

"I'll tell him we need to get going, but we can't just drive off," she sighed, already reaching for the door handle. "He'll think something is wrong and then he'll drop by, and those visits last even longer. Come in with us."

Brady detoured toward the pickup with the dealer sticker in the window. "Nice truck," he called out. "Is the mileage as good as the sticker claims?"

"Never is." Gil chuckled. "But it makes me feel good thinking it's even possible."

He ushered them through a broad, Spanish-tiled entryway lit by a chandelier hung from a two-story vault above, past the dining room, and into a far more casual family dining area just off the kitchen.

Here, towering plants in terra cotta pots bloomed prettily in the corners of the room, and a large, Mission-style oak table was set with bright Mexican placemats.

"Rosita—coffee, please," Gil called out, waving everyone to a place at the table. He gave Celia a benign smile as she handed him a check. "Sorry I didn't have anyone out there helping load. A couple of the guys are moving cattle and one is helping the vet treat some calves. I've got a new man who'll be up here in a minute, though."

Adan held back as everyone took a chair, then grudgingly went to the far end of the table and slouched into his seat, his eyes downcast. Knowing the boy's history, Brady sympathized with him—he'd surely never had this sort of luxury in his life.

After Rosita bustled in with a tray of fresh, hot *sopapillas* and poured coffee, she nodded and hurried to the kitchen.

"You've got a beautiful place, here," Brady said with a lift of his coffee cup toward Gil. "You must be quite a rancher."

"One would think. Actually, my investments have paid off better than the ranch has." Gil chuckled. "It's hard to get rich on land with nine inches of rain per year, so I dabble in the stock market."

"But you do run cattle, don't you?"

"Around five hundred head of mother cows. A few dozen broodmares. There were those," he said with a faint edge to his voice, "who said I'd never last out here. But I proved them wrong."

Brady felt Celia tense in her chair next to his. Under the table, he reached over and found her clenched hand, then he enveloped it with his own until she relaxed. He interlaced his fingers with hers.

Sparks of warmth radiated through him at that contact—and from the faint pink in her cheeks, he suspected she felt the same thing.

"You certainly have, Gil," she said evenly, without so much as a glance in Brady's direction. "You have a showplace, now."

At the far end of the table, Adan eyed the plate of soft, pillowy pastries covered with cinnamon sugar. Brady nabbed one and slid the plate in his direction.

"Have you had any more trouble at night, Celia?" Gil darted a look between Brady and Celia. "I understand you had cattle stolen."

"We were out yesterday checking the herds. I figure I lost thirty, including a young bull."

He shook his head in sympathy. "Bad luck, there."

"That Brangus bull was new stock. With his bloodlines, I was planning on heavier weaning weights, and it took a bank loan to buy him."

"A shame. It's a hard life out here—dealing with drought and predators, not to mention cattle thieves preying on unprotected livestock. One of these days maybe you'll decide to just throw in the towel and sell out."

Celia rolled her eyes. "Not in this lifetime, as you well know."

"But a young woman like you—" he sputtered to a halt and threw his hands up in obvious frustration.

"I'm posting night watch, now. At this point, I think I'll shoot first and ask questions later, and you can tell that to anyone you meet." Celia took a long swallow of coffee. "It won't be easy to market my stolen stock, though—our registered brand and ear notch are tough to alter."

"Everything still okay over here, Gil?" Brady asked.

"Yes—knock on wood." He rapped his knuckles on the table for luck, then shifted his attention to

Celia. "I've just got to tell you again, it isn't a good idea for you to go traipsing out in the—"

"I appreciate your concern, but I can handle things myself, Gil." With a quick glance at her watch, Celia pushed away from the table. "I didn't realize how late it was. I need to get home and get some things done before Lacey gets home from school. Thanks, Rosita," she called out toward the door leading into the kitchen. "Come over sometime and show Vicente how to make good sopapillas, will you?"

The housekeeper appeared in the doorway with a smile on her face, wiping her hands on her apron. "*Sí, señora.* If he will listen."

"I guess that would be a first." Celia laughed. "Good luck."

Gil walked out with them to the truck, hovering like a doting uncle, and opened the driver's side door for her. "I do care about you," he said. "Please don't ever believe otherwise, when I get a little too pushy. With your dad gone, and all—well…" At the sound of an approaching vehicle, he lifted his gaze to the driveway and frowned. "This world just isn't a safe place anymore."

His expression cleared as a Rocking B pickup barreled into view and pulled to a stop in a cloud of dust in front of the barn.

"Here's my new man, Jose Nieto—he and Alvarez are in command, around here." Gil smiled apologetically. "My arthritis and the back of a horse just don't do so well together anymore. It's hell to get old."

Celia hesitated, then rested a hand briefly on his shoulder. "You've got a lot of good years left, Gil."

Brady watched the driver get out and slam the door.

The wiry cowboy touched the brim of his hat in greeting and turned toward the barn. Then he pivoted and froze, staring at Adan. His teeth bared in an eerie semblance of a smile before he wheeled around again and disappeared into the barn.

Adan drew a sharp breath.

"Is he a friend of yours?" Brady asked him in a low voice. "He sure seems to know you."

"Nope." Adan gave a jerk of his shoulder and climbed into the back seat of Celia's truck.

A sixth sense told Brady that Nieto was no stranger to trouble, and that he'd clearly recognized Adan.

The kid was lying. But why?

CELIA KNEW BRADY was planning to do something to engineer his move into the main house; she just didn't know when, where or what. So when Adan thundered up the porch steps on Saturday morning, flung open the door with a crash and skidded into the kitchen, she did her best to feign surprise.

"Fire extinguisher! Where is it?" Adan spun around, searching the kitchen walls. *"Hurry!"*

Lacey bolted out of her chair at the kitchen table

and raced to the end of the kitchen counter next to the stove. Flipping open the plastic holder, she pulled the extinguisher from the wall.

"What is it? *Where?*" she cried as Adan grabbed it from her and took off like a rocket out the door. She whirled back to Celia, her face white. "Should we call 911?"

Not if Brady handled this right. "Let's go check this out first, okay?"

Lacey darted after Adan. Celia followed, close enough to make sure that it was indeed Brady's cabin and not something much worse.

Sure enough, she could see Adan racing for the last cabin along the creek, where Vicente stood outside, motioning wildly for him to hurry. Celia ran to the cabin and schooled her features into an appropriate amount of anxiety.

Which, if Brady wasn't as good at this as he'd indicated, might just be warranted. What if he inadvertently did burn the place to the ground? Could she really expect him to rebuild before he was on his merry way to some other assignment?

"What's going on?" she said as she pulled to a breathless halt next to Vicente and Lacey.

Adan was already inside.

"Fire—electrical panel," Vicente wheezed, gripping Lacey's shoulders with both hands to hold her back. "We came running when we heard the smoke detector go off. Brady shut off the electricity quick, but the fire started to spread."

Mia came at a run as well, her black hair flying behind her. "Is everyone okay? What happened?"

"You all stay here," Celia ordered. "I'm going in. Lacey, you wait here. *Promise.*"

"But Mom!" Lacey's voice rose to a wail. "Don't go in there—please!"

Celia dropped a swift kiss on the top of her head. "I'll be right out."

A faint haze of smoke met her as she stepped inside. Moving cautiously, she walked through the kitchen, the living area and back to the single bedroom, where the electrical panel was set in the wall.

Adan and Brady had already opened the windows wide to air the place out, but an acrid odor of burned wiring and melted plastic hung in the air.

"Fire's out," Brady said. "Let's leave—these fumes are toxic."

Celia held a hand to her mouth as she backed away. "The damage?"

Adan raised his hands about two feet apart. "The wood paneling burned—this much. The electrical panel is *toast.* There's no fixing it, that's for sure."

Brady shooed them both out, then joined everyone out in front.

Lacey rushed forward and hugged Celia. "I was so scared—what if the place *exploded,* Mom? You shouldn't have gone in there!"

Celia wrapped her arms around her. "I was really careful, honey. Don't you ever go into a dangerous situation like that." She looked up at Brady. "So how bad is it?"

"No structural damage. Mostly just the electrical panel, which will need to be replaced, along with some wiring. The place will need to air for a few days, but there won't be any electricity in there for lights or the baseboard heaters. Know any good electricians?"

Vicente rocked back on his heels and frowned, one hand cupping his chin as if he were thinking hard to remember a familiar name that was just on the tip of his tongue.

"There's one I can call up in El Paso," she said. *That part is true, anyway.* "He's definitely the one I want. He's done work in the house before, and he's…a second cousin, so he'll give me a decent quote."

Brady studied the cabin for a few minutes. "Got any flashlights? I could sleep on the couch in there, still…if it airs out enough by tonight."

Mia shuddered and wrapped her arms around herself. "Do you know how cold it gets at night? Last night it was thirty-six degrees! You'll freeze in there."

"And that swaybacked old couch would be awful," Adan added.

"Maybe you could use one of the spare bedrooms up at the house," Celia said. "You certainly can't stay out here without lights or heat."

"I couldn't do that, ma'am. It isn't right to put

you to that much trouble. I could camp on Adan's floor…or Vicente's. Or even out in the barn someplace."

He spoke with such sincerity that she almost believed he meant it, despite their previous plans.

"Both guys are used to their privacy and the barn's too drafty." She rested her hands on Lacey's shoulders. "Honey, come on up to the house and help me get a room ready. He can have the room Vicente was in for a while. It's down a hall by itself, where he'll have some peace and quiet away from the rest of us."

Over her daughter's head, she met Brady's eyes. "If that's okay with you?"

"Thanks. I'll grab what I can from my cabin— if my things aren't too smoky—and bring them up in a few minutes."

She nodded to Adan and Vicente. "I'll be out in the barn in a half hour, if you want to start saddling some colts."

The two men moved toward the barn, and she turned toward the house. Brady had pulled off his little plan without a hitch. He'd now be up at the house at night, watching over everyone there. His presence would be reassuring, considering her concern for Lacey's safety. But one disturbing thought kept resurfacing as she walked.

Brady Coleman had been totally believable from beginning to end—as believable as any Oscar winner on the silver screen. She'd need to keep that in mind.

He'd been affectionate, he'd kissed her and held her close. He'd given her comfort and reassurance. But he also had a clear agenda that involved fitting into life at this ranch and appearing close to her.

And nothing that he'd said or done was real.

Chapter Ten

SINCE BRADY HAD moved in today, Celia expected to see him at the house after supper. Expected awkward moments that hinged on the crazy sense of awareness that she felt whenever he was near. But after he moved some of his clothes into the spare room, he went out to the barn and didn't even come in for supper.

More surveillance, she suspected, though he rarely told her when he was coming or going at night and never, ever shared what he saw.

During the day, he was just another hand fixing fences and doing other chores. At night, he was a phantom who disappeared into the darkness. Didn't the man ever sleep?

Now, at 3:00 a.m., she heard the faintest creak of the back door hinges and the scrabbling of Mojo's toenails across the kitchen floor. Given the dog's sweet nature, that could mean that either a best friend or a serial killer had just come inside.

In her robe and already reaching for the rifle

in her closet, Celia caught the sound of Brady's low voice calming the dog—who'd surely retrieved some item to carry in her mouth as a welcome offering.

Shelving the rifle, Celia wrapped her robe around herself and cinched the belt tight, then went to the kitchen. Only the light over the stove was on, and in the dim yellow glow Brady looked unshaven and more than a little dangerous, given his size.

Until he held up his hand. "This yours? Mojo seems to think I should have it."

Celia blinked and focused on the limp object dangling from his crooked forefinger. "My *underwear?*"

The dog sat at his feet wagging her plume of a tail, clearly pleased with herself.

Brady tipped his head toward the laundry alcove at the far end of the kitchen. "I think she got this out of one of the baskets of clean laundry over there."

Celia groaned. "She's border collie and part retriever—so she's either trying to herd the barn cats or bring us anything she can lift in her mouth. Once she got mixed up and tried fetching a cat—got one whale of scratch on her nose."

"Guess this was safer," he observed, tossing Celia the...

Oh, no—black lace panties.

Embarrassed, Celia stuffed them into her robe pocket, wishing Mojo had found something else. Maybe she lived in jeans, boots and flannel shirts, but what she wore underneath satisfied her girlie side—the side she never revealed as a hardworking, no-nonsense rancher, because in her world she needed to be taken seriously.

"Well…um…you missed supper. There's leftover chili in the fridge, and a pan of corn bread on the stove."

"Thanks, but I'm not hungry."

"Then I'll go get you some fresh towels. We made up your bed earlier, but I forgot the towels for your bathroom. I bet you're ready to turn in."

"I'm not really tired, Celia."

She slid a glance at the clock over the stove. "You must be. You were up at dawn to help do chores. It's past three in the morning, now."

"I'm not going to take advantage of this situation." He toed off his boots and lined them up with all the others by the door. Slid off his jacket and hung it on a peg. His eyes locked on hers as he sauntered across the kitchen toward her until he was just a few inches away. "It wouldn't be right."

Beneath her heavy terry cloth robe Celia felt her heart pick up a faster beat.

"But," he said in a voice so low that she felt it vibrate through her, "I just want to check one thing."

Lifting her chin, she gave him a cool look. "And that is…?"

"I've been wondering if kissing you was as phenomenal as I remember—or if I only imagined it." He gave an apologetic motion with his hand, but there was no apology in the devilish gleam in his eyes, or in the sensual undertone of his voice.

She softened as she remembered that kiss, understanding exactly what he meant. No one had ever kissed her like that. Even now, just the thought of it made her nerve endings tingle and hunger sing through her veins. How could she have known him for two short weeks and feel such a powerful reaction? Maybe fantasies, coupled with long hard days and too much stress, had clouded her judgment.

Everyone else in the house had been asleep for hours.

The house was dark, quiet, and expectant—as if time stood still in hushed anticipation of an event that would change everything. Irrevocably.

"I believe in pursuing dreams," she murmured. "But also in making sure I know the difference between dreams and reality."

She closed the space between them and reached up to pull him down into a sweet, soft kiss that spoke of tentative exploration and fledgling emotions.

That plan lasted a heartbeat and then he took over—his hands framing her face as he eased her back against the cupboard, his mouth on hers... seeking, demanding.

A hot, restless ache grew inside her, and she curved her arms around his neck and drew him closer, deeper into the kiss, wanting more—

And then he pulled away. His hands slid down her arms and captured hers.

Disoriented, she swayed forward, but he stopped her with a gentle, apologetic smile, and if it hadn't been for his darkened eyes or rapid breathing, she might have thought he'd never started to lose control.

"Guess I was right. It was phenomenal," he murmured, his thumbs sketching lazy circles against her hands. "I'm sorry...I shouldn't have done that."

She stared up at him, her brain still reeling and her pulse still pounding.

He probably had beautiful, sophisticated women back home. Women who were urban and classy, with upswept hair and little black dresses, and who knew how to flirt. They didn't haul hay or clean stalls or spend fifteen-hour days on a horse checking cattle, or spend hours on difficult calvings and come home covered with mud and blood and amniotic fluids, and need to hose themselves off in the yard before even coming into the house.

And they certainly wouldn't have callused hands and a .30-06 rifle in their closets. Black lace underwear or not, she was probably the least feminine and enticing woman he'd ever met.

Brady frowned, searching her face. "I'm here on assignment, Celia. I couldn't start something now, no matter what I wanted. And," he added, his voice hoarse, "I'm just not a good bet. For you or anyone else."

"But—"

"No. You need someone you can count on. Someone worth staying with, no matter what happens. And that guy just isn't me."

His eyes filled with such deep sadness that she wanted to know more, and wished she could ease his pain.

But he just shook his head and released her hands. "Good night, Celia."

And then he turned and walked away.

BALANCING THE CARDBOARD box on her knee with one hand, Lacey fumbled with the slippery doorknob as rain pelted the back of her neck.

Rain was rare. It was precious. But right now, it was seeping through the loosely closed flaps of the box and maybe getting the contents wet, and that was not a good thing.

Suddenly the door swung open wide and she stumbled inside, and found herself face-to-face with Mia.

"I thought I heard something down here," she said. "Here—can I take that for you?"

Lacey handed over the box and went outside to retrieve the guitar case she'd leaned against the door, then braced a hand against the wall to kick off her Western boots. "It wasn't easy, getting that home on the school bus. On Fridays the kids are all hyper, and everyone kept wanting to see what

I was carrying. Kip Thompson even tried to grab the box. He is *such* a creep."

"What's in there?" Mia lifted a corner of one flap to peek inside.

"Stuff for the treasure hunt. Vicente isn't around, is he? I…um…need to get some of it put away, quick."

Mia glanced at the clock on the wall. "He's feeling a little better, and said he was tired of just sitting around. He went to town for some groceries after lunch, so he should be home pretty soon. What do you have there?"

"We were supposed to bring examples of our heritage to school, because we had this big unit on pioneers."

"Cool. So what did you find?"

"Mom found some photo albums, and there were some really old draft horse bits hanging out in the barn, so I used those." Lacey opened the top of the box and reached inside. "I went out to the storeroom and found some other old stuff, too. Look at this—isn't it awesome?"

She lifted out a bundle of water-stained silk and brittle lace, and unfolded it on the kitchen table.

"Oh," Mia breathed. She ran a hand over the hundreds of tiny pearl buttons sewn from the top of the dress to the bottom hem. Almost invisible hand stitching caught the bodice into intricate tucks. "It's pretty. I think it must have been a wedding dress, don't you?"

"That's what Miss Ventura said. But even better—" Lacey reached for the battered guitar case and set it on the table "—look at this!"

She lifted the rusted hasps and opened the lid, revealing an old classical guitar—its gleaming, deep russet surface a rich contrast to the dusty black velvet lining of the case.

Mia sucked in a sharp breath. "Wow. That was out in the *barn?*" She reached out with reverent fingers and stroked the glass-smooth surface. "I don't know much about old guitars, but I bet this one is special!"

"My teacher said you can't play old strings like that—it needs new ones to sound good. She tightened them up, though, so we could hear what it sounded like. She played some easy songs, too."

Leaning over, Mia searched for a label. "It's…" She squinted at the faded words. "A Paulino Bernabe, I think. Is that good?"

Lacey shrugged. "It was out in the storage room in the barn. If it's worth a lot, why would Vicente leave it out there?"

"Oooh." Mia frowned at her. "Does he know you have it?"

Fidgeting, Lacey plucked a guitar string. A sweet, bell-like note rang out. "I was in a hurry, and I just looked through the trunks closest to the door. I'm going to put it right back."

She leaned over to shut the case.

Footsteps thudded up the steps outside. The door

opened and Vicente stepped inside with two bags of groceries in his arms. He nodded a welcome at Lacey. His gaze skidded past Mia, and landed on the table.

He froze almost completely, his jaw working. "What have you done?" he roared, slamming the grocery sacks on the kitchen counter. One tipped, spewing cans and paper goods onto the floor. A jar rolled to the edge of the counter. Teetered. Crashed on the floor at his feet.

But his furious gaze never left the guitar case and the dress laid out on the table. "Who did this?" He glared at Mia, his hands clenched at his side, and the veins in his neck distended and throbbing. "You? You dared this—this *violation?*"

Lacey wanted to run. Disappear. But at Mia's quiet sob, she swallowed hard and gripped the back of a kitchen chair. "I-it was me. I—I had a school project. I just needed some things and—"

"No!" He slammed a fist on the counter. "You had no right. I've done so much for you—and this is how you repay me?"

"B-but I only borrowed—"

"You have no idea what you have done!" He took a step forward, then stopped and bowed his head. "Please…just leave me alone."

Guilt flooded through her as she stared him. He was angry, but there was something else in his voice, too—something so deep and sad that she felt like crying. "I'm s-sorry. I didn't think—"

"Go!"

She turned and fled through the house to her own room, where she locked the door and threw herself on the bed. And wished she'd never, ever opened that trunk in the storeroom.

AT THE FIRST LIGHT of dawn on Monday morning, Brady rose from his surveillance point up in the bluffs, his bones stiff and muscles aching from hours on the cold, damp ground. At thirty-four he felt like seventy when he did things like this—old injuries came back to haunt him, hinting at worse things to come if he didn't slow down.

Not that he could ever face a desk job, he thought as he shook out his bedroll, rolled it up and tied it behind the cantle of his saddle, but with this operation he would finally see his friends' killers brought to justice. And afterward, he was definitely looking into a new career.

He gathered his binoculars and camera, and stowed them in the saddlebag. With a last look around, he swung up into the saddle. *Another wasted night.*

He'd watched for the past seven hours. There'd been nothing—no furtive movement through the sagebrush and rocks below. No sudden beam of a flashlight or glint of metal in the moonlight.

"Well, old boy—time to go home." He gathered up the reins and swung into the saddle. Buck tossed his head and sidestepped in the direction of home, obviously looking forward to his warm stall and feed. "Easy, buddy."

He dropped some slack into the reins and gave the horse his head, and Buck took off at an easy jog, straight for Celia's place. Brady chuckled, feeling just as relieved to be heading for home. "You could be a homing pigeon, you know that?"

The trail was familiar, though Brady varied between several options each night, and kept well out of sight of the route most of the drug runners followed along the flat valley floor. This time he swung farther south, though Buck tossed his head and lashed his tail, clearly wanting to take the most direct route.

"Safer, pal," Brady murmured. "Predictability is a big mistake."

A niggling worry about Adan surfaced as Brady rode on. Something wasn't quite right there. Nieto, the new ranch hand at the Rocking B, had clearly recognized the kid when they'd gone over there for hay, yet Adan had denied ever meeting him—even when Brady casually mentioned it the next day.

Maybe they knew each other from Adan's wilder days, when the boy had been in a lot of gang-related trouble in his hometown. That alone could account for Adan's reaction, now that he was apparently trying for a fresh start.

Or was he?

Brady's thoughts drifted to Celia as he rode on, scanning the terrain for any unexpected movement.

He hadn't intended to kiss her last Saturday night. Lord knew, the first time had been a mistake, because she'd stirred up emotions he'd thought were long dead. But seeing her in that soft light, her long hair tumbling over her shoulders and her eyes heavy with sleep, he'd thought about what it would be like to follow her to her room and make wild, passionate love until the sun rose and they were both too exhausted to speak.

Because if there was anything he sensed about her, it was that she was a strong, passionate woman who didn't waver in her loyalties or her goals, and who went after what she wanted with focus and determination.

It would be incredible to make love to her... though there was so much more that he wanted that had nothing to do with a set of sheets and everything to do with who she was inside, deep in her soul.

The glint of silver sparked so unexpectedly off to the right that he barely had time to reach for his rifle scabbard before a shot rang out—

And another.

Pain seared his shoulder as Buck shied violently to one side, then reared high.

The rocky ground spun in dizzying circles. Closer and closer...then even greater pain exploded through him, and everything went black.

Chapter Eleven

CELIA GLANCED out the kitchen window, then finished braiding Lacey's hair and gave her a kiss on the cheek. "Brady's usually here for breakfast by now. Have you seen him this morning?"

"Nope."

"Your bus will be here any minute. Are you ready?"

Lacey nodded and pushed her chair away from the kitchen table, her face glum.

Concerned, Celia rested her hands on the child's shoulders. "You've been quiet all weekend. What's wrong?"

"Nothing."

"Vicente seemed grumpy this weekend, too. Did you two have an argument?"

Lacey's silence was a pretty good clue. "Let me go talk to him," Celia said.

"No! Please, no…it's all right."

"But honey, just stewing over things doesn't make them better. If you two talk this over—"

"I was wrong, all right? I found some old stuff in a trunk and took it to school, and I didn't ask him first. Just leave me alone." Lacey jerked away, grabbed her backpack and jacket, and rushed out the door.

Through the window, Celia saw the school bus pull to a stop. Lacey climbed aboard without a backward glance. With a sigh, Celia turned to the stove and finished serving up a plate of scrambled eggs, sausage patties and toast for Jonah.

Vicente had done some grocery shopping and had made a few lighter meals, though he hadn't been up at the house as much as usual. Probably avoiding Mia, Celia guessed as she carried the tray down the hall. She'd tried to talk to him about his granddaughter several times, but he'd refused to even listen.

She rapped on Jonah's door, then stepped inside. "How are you doing, Gramps?"

He lifted a shaky hand in greeting. He appeared weaker, now, and she'd seen signs of more problems when he swallowed. Without saying anything to him she'd begun serving him softer foods that might be easier for him—casseroles, and meats that simmered in a slow cooker all day.

She tried not to think about what was ahead. If he had to move into a nursing home, the move alone would probably kill the proud old rancher who'd been able to weather every other storm in his life with sheer determination.

This time, he wouldn't win.

"Do you want me to crank your bed up higher, or do you want to sit in the chair by the window?"

He rolled his head against the pillow. "Just leave the tray here by the bed. I'll…get to it."

"But it's nice and hot right now," she wheedled. "The coffee's strong, hot and black, just the way you like it."

His eyes drifted shut. "I will…in a while."

I'm going to miss you so much. She set the tray on his bedside table and brushed back the wispy white hair that always tipped over his forehead at a rakish angle. "Don't wait too long to eat, okay?"

At a light rap on the door Celia turned. Mia stood there, urgently beckoning to her.

Celia followed her to the kitchen and found Adan pacing by the door, his face ashen and his mouth a grim line.

"It's Buck," he said. "He came home alone. When I walked in to the barn he was standing in the aisle, still saddled, with his reins dragging on the ground. I checked everywhere—Brady isn't here."

"Was he still hot? Sweaty?" Celia searched her memory for any clues about where Brady usually went. A man down, with 20,000 acres to search, could be almost impossible to find.

"He was cool but wet—hadn't dried off yet. I figure he got back sometime in the last hour or so."

Celia went after her rifle, then jerked on her boots and a jacket. "I remember Brady once saying that his ride meant two hours of solitude. That probably puts his location somewhere past our number 5 windmill in the east section. Mia, watch after Jonah, will you? If he starts eating breakfast someone needs to be close by."

Mia nodded. "I'll be praying for Brady's safety."

"There's one other thing—" Adan's voice caught. "There was blood. On the saddle, and on the edge of the saddle blanket."

Icy fingers crawled down Celia's spine. She hesitated just a second, then spun toward the phone and found the business card she'd tucked between the pages of the government listings in the phone book.

"Saddle two horses, Adan. We're heading out right away—but first I'm calling for help."

MIA SIGHED AS she stared at the clock.

The day wore on, minute by minute. Jonah barely ate and wasn't up to his usual game of chess. Supper—like most of the meals Celia requested these days—was in the slow cooker, this time a nice six-pound pork roast sprinkled liberally with mesquite seasonings and pepper, that would be moist and fork-tender by evening.

Two guys wearing black clothes and dark sunglasses had driven up in an all-terrain vehicle a few hours ago, but Celia must have already given them directions because they took off into the vast pasture without coming up to the house.

There hadn't been a word all day.

Mia glanced at the kitchen clock then went to stand at the window. Vicente, still unable to ride or handle much of anything with his shoulder injury, sat out on the patio.

Stubborn and silent, he'd spent most of his time out there since the explosion over his stupid guitar and the wedding dress.

Mia thought about poor Lacey, who'd moped all weekend.

She thought about the distance she'd traveled to see this angry, asocial man who pretended she didn't exist.

And she thought about far greater reasons for a person to be upset—Brady, for instance, who could be dead or dying this very moment, or suffering terribly with no one able to find him.

Her anger rising, she stalked out the kitchen door and strode to the patio, where she pulled up a chair directly in front of Vicente. "We need to talk."

He grunted and shifted his gaze toward the barn.

"This is childish," she snapped. "You're old enough to communicate when something's wrong— not just sit here like an angry boy."

"You know *nothing,*" he snapped, his voice filled with loathing. "What right have you to say these things?"

She recoiled from the venom in his voice, but gathered her courage and continued. "Then maybe you can tell me, huh? You've treated me like dirt since the day I arrived. Now you're giving Lacey the same treatment. She's only a kid—she made a *mistake*."

He jerked himself to his feet. "Leave me be."

"Well, you know what? I think you are a hateful old man.

"You wallow in whatever it is—self-pity or spite—and you make people around you miserable. You drove my mother away, and I finally see how." Mia choked back a sob. "Because you're doing the same thing to me. Don't worry—when I leave, I'll never come here again. But for God's sake, please be nice to Lacey!"

He glared at her. "You know nothing—nothing at all," he repeated. "It's better that you go."

Then he lumbered to his feet and walked away, muttering incomprehensible Spanish phrases that were probably better left unknown.

CELIA FOUND BRADY at noon, walking slowly back to the ranch with a good four miles left to go and with blood seeping through the crimson-stained sleeve of his shirt.

Her heart lodged in her throat at seeing his handsome face so pale. With a little less luck, he might have been fatally wounded and never have been found.

He'd never really been hers, but the thought of him not being somewhere in this world filled her with a deep, unexpected sense of loss.

Firing a signal shot in the air, she dismounted,

then grabbed a first-aid kit out of her saddlebag and rushed over to him. "Good heavens—what happened? Are you okay?"

He tipped his head toward his arm. "Damn bullet wound—then Buck didn't much like the noise. He shied hard to the left and dumped me on a pile of rocks."

Horror washed through her, turning her blood to ice. "Did you see the shooter?"

"Nope—" He managed a lopsided grin. "It was too dark out. But I'd guess they weren't particularly friendly."

"You think?" Shaking her head, she gestured toward a boulder. "Take a seat and let me look at this."

She knelt at his side and gently slipped her fingers into the hole in his shirt, then slowly ripped the fabric open.

He winced and turned a lighter shade of pale.

"You aren't going to faint on me, are you?" she asked with false briskness. "This isn't more than a scratch."

But it was. The entrance wound was small and round, but the flesh around it was inflamed and swollen, and there wasn't an exit wound on the other side. The bullet was still in there, and from the looks of things, he'd soon be chilled and running a fever from infection.

"The sooner you see a doctor, the better," she

murmured. "I signaled the others, but we can start home if you think you can get on my horse."

"Others?"

"Your horse came back alone with blood on his saddle. Adan and I had no idea where you were or how badly you were hurt, so I called Luis and gave him general directions on where I thought you might be. He sent two agents to help us search." She cocked her head. "I think I hear their vehicle now."

"I wish you hadn't done that." Brady leaned his head against the boulder and closed his eyes. "It wasn't necessary."

"And how would we know that? Adan and I can cover just so much ground alone, Coleman. I couldn't let you bleed to death out here and not do everything I could to help."

"You...told Adan about me?"

"Of course not. I was vague. Luis told me to say these guys were search-and-rescue volunteers for the border patrol. Tell me—do you think the shooter was waiting for you, or did you just happen across drug runners on their way to the highway?"

"I—I'm not sure. Since no one followed me to finish the job, I'm guessing it was a surprise to all of us. They fired and took off without looking back."

"From the looks of this blood, they did a good job."

"Damn. I don't want to risk being taken off this case, Celia."

"You're worried about *medical leave?*" Celia opened the first aid kit and tore open a moistened towelette, then dabbed away the dirt at the edges of the wound. "I'd be more worried about my health, if I were you. What did you do—fall on this arm?"

He gave a brief nod.

"Ouch. No wonder you look a little bleary." She tore open another package and pressed a stack of four-by-four gauze squares against the wound, then found a roll of adhesive tape and taped the gauze in place. Beneath the other supplies she found a large gauze sheet that she folded into a triangle and fashioned into a sling.

"This will hold your arm still—so it won't hurt as much," she said as she tied it in place.

He tipped his head to study the bandage. "Thanks."

"I'm not going to tamper with the wound itself, or put anything on it. This will hold you together until we can get you to the clinic in town—it's run by a physician's assistant, but I think the doctor is there on Mondays and Wednesdays."

"I can't go to any local doctors."

She inspected her handiwork, then collected the remaining supplies and put them in the box. "Why not? They've been patching up people in Gelman County for years."

"Reports." He opened his eyes to look at her. "They'd have to write reports on a gunshot wound. That would involve the sheriff, and it would end up in the newspaper. That can't happen, or I'm done here and so is everything I've tried to do."

Celia frowned. "So what, then?"

Across the endless, rolling land came the sound of galloping hooves, and much farther away, the growl of a vehicle slowly making its way over the rugged terrain.

He gave a weary sigh. "I guess my buddies will need to take me to El Paso." He reached out to lace his fingers with hers. "But I promise I'll return as soon as I can. Stay out of trouble, hear?"

FROM THE LENGTHENING shadow of the barn, Adan studied the somber expression on Mia's face. She'd been sitting on the patio since supper, her arms folded across her chest and her eyes pinned on some distant point.

Vicente hadn't come up to the house to eat. Lacey had sat silently, picking at her food. Celia had just looked plain worried. And Brady...

Those two search-and-rescue guys had whisked Brady off for medical care. They'd barely said a word to Celia, and from the serious expressions on their faces, Adan guessed that Brady's wound didn't look good. *Just a fall off his horse,* they'd said.

But then why had they taken his duffel bag out of his room, if he was gonna be right back?

Nothing had seemed right, this last couple weeks.

Adan had felt restless and wary, unable to settle down. He found himself watching the shadows.

Wanting to talk to someone—not necessarily *Mia*—he finally gritted his teeth and sauntered across the broad parking area in front of the barn. "Hey," he called out, when he reached the patio. "What's up?"

"What?" She looked up at him, her face cool and indifferent…as always. Her bored tone rubbed like sandpaper across his nerves.

The day had been long. Hard. Searching for Brady had been a tense situation, knowing that if he was hurt bad, every second counted. Celia's worry at supper had added to Adan's edgy mood.

And always lurking among his thoughts was that chance encounter with Nieto over at Gil's ranch when they'd gone after hay.

The guy was bad news, and there wasn't a thing Adan could do about it.

He thought about the threats that had sent him to Celia's, and about his two younger sisters, who were living with their aunt and uncle in a tiny border town three hundred miles southeast of here. They were safe, unless he screwed up.

And then, for the first time in years, he silently prayed to the God he'd forsaken, hoping that trouble hadn't followed him to Saguaro Springs.

"Excuse me?" Mia said, tapping an impatient forefinger on her opposite arm.

"Must be great being so important, Miss College Girl," he snapped. "I guess I was asking why you're sitting out here, looking like you're mad at the world."

Her chin lifted. "If I was, it wouldn't have anything to do with you."

He snorted. "What do you have to mad about? Now Brady, he's got reason to be mad."

Her gaze slid toward the cabins along the creek. "You're right, I suppose."

Adan followed her gaze. "Guess Vicente wasn't too happy to see you."

"He told to me to stay away!" She tipped down her sunglasses. "I'm not all that happy I came to see him, either, now that I'm here. I still can't believe it. Who does he think he is? What makes him think he's so special? He hasn't even *tried* to be nice."

Adan smirked. "I guess he figures it's safer to keep his distance."

"It wasn't all *my* fault that he got hurt. You were there—it was the dog, not me who ran into that corral. If anything, *you* could have caught that dog faster."

Adan jammed his thumbs in his back pockets. It was a shame that Mia was such a knockout, because with that mouth of hers, she sure wasn't the kind of person a guy wanted to hang around for very long.

"I'll see you around, princess." He turned toward the barn. "Unless I'm lucky."

He was halfway there when he heard her chair screech against the flagstones.

"Wait—Adan."

He kept going…and then stopped, considering.

"Please," she called out.

He turned and found her walking toward him, that glorious black hair swinging against her hips.

"Look—I'm sorry. I shouldn't take things out on you," she said. "I've been rude, and I'm sorry."

It was easier being mad, because then he didn't have to come up with something cool to say. "Uh…that's okay."

She looked up at him with eyes prettier than a newborn calf's and gave him a tentative smile. "It's crazy arguing all the time. Maybe we could be friends?"

He scowled at her, remembering all the times she'd put him down. And he thought about all the times he'd wished he had someone here close to his age.

There'd never been anyone in his life like Mia—beautiful and smart and planning to go places—and God knew he hadn't had any close friends at the detention center.

Maybe it was time.

Chapter Twelve

CELIA WEARILY closed out of the accounting program on her computer and flipped off the desk lamp, then swung her chair toward the windows.

The deep shadows of twilight reflected her image on the glass, but the haggard woman staring back at her had to be a stranger. *At this rate, I'll look eighty by the time I hit thirty-five.*

There was a sense of deep satisfaction that came from being a part of this land. Preserving her family's heritage. Seeing her daughter grow up where her family had ranched for generations. But none of it was easy.

Not with loans still due, Jonah's failing health, and so many people depending on her...

And her constant thoughts about Brady.

He'd been gone two days now, but there hadn't been a word from him. Had he developed an infection? Needed surgery? Maybe he wouldn't come back, and she'd never know why or what happened.

She'd simply been a part of his cover for an investigation, after all. Nothing more than that.

Except for the night he moved into the house.

Remembering that heated, hungry kiss they'd shared, her skin warmed. Nerve endings tingled. They'd both shied away from the moment, realizing that any further relationship could have no future. Since then, they'd been oh-so-careful to avoid each other—though she still felt restless, her senses heightened, whenever he walked into a room or said her name.

But that was sheer foolishness, and she knew it all too well. She only had to remember just how believable he'd been over the "accidental" fire in his cabin to realize that the kiss had probably been just a part of his cover—the careful establishment of their so-called history together. He'd planned it, she supposed, so she wouldn't appear alarmed if he took her hand or even brushed a kiss against her cheek to reinforce their "past" in front of someone else.

At the sound of soft footsteps in the hall, Celia turned and found Mia standing just outside the door.

"You got a minute?" Mia bit her lower lip, clearly debating coming in. "I need to talk to you."

"Of course." Celia rounded her desk and settled into one of the upholstered chairs in the corner, waving Mia toward the other. "What's up?"

"I…well…" Mia took the other chair and curled

her feet beneath her, her expression troubled. "I'm worried about Jonah. He just doesn't seem the same. He coughs more when he eats, and he's breathing harder. He also has a lot more trouble feeding himself. I try to help, but he gets mad, and…"

"I know. We're doing the best we can, but at his doctor's appointment yesterday, the doc told him that it was time to think about a higher level of care. Jonah, as you can imagine, wasn't too happy to hear it."

"He tells me he'll never leave here unless it's feet first."

Celia gave a wry laugh. "He said the same to Doc Garmon, but then he was just a tad more blunt. I selfishly want Jonah to have the best possible care so he can live longer. So far, he has refused to think about going into a nursing facility, refused home health workers, and even refuses his medicine, half the time. When the time comes, I just hope he will agree to hospice care."

"He says…he has his pride. He wants to 'go out like a man, not some invalid.'"

"I've heard that a time or two, believe me. I want to thank you, by the way, for all you've done here. You've been a godsend, and I plan to pay you before you leave."

Mia gave a firm shake of her head. "Absolutely not. I stayed on because what happened to Vicente was mostly my fault, and I hoped for a chance to get to know him a little better. My big plan didn't work out very well, but I enjoyed being with the rest of you."

"And we've enjoyed you." Celia winked at her. "It even looks like Adan has come around."

"Since Brady left, I think he's been...I don't know...lonely, or something. He even asked me to go riding yesterday, but I had to say no."

"How come?"

The girl blushed prettily. "Gosh—I've never even been on a horse before. He would think I was a complete dork."

Celia hid a smile. "Maybe I could help you."

"I couldn't let you do that. You work such long hours...." Mia picked at a fray in the hem of her jeans. "I wouldn't feel right."

"Lacey, then. Wouldn't you like to go back East and be able to tell your friends about learning to ride?"

"Do you think she would? I mean, I'm probably the biggest chicken you've ever seen. The closest I ever got to a horse was a carriage ride through Central Park. That horse was *huge!*"

"But gentle, I bet. We've still got Lacey's first horse, Frosty. He's thirty years old and absolutely bomb-proof."

Mia beamed. "Gosh—I've got just a couple weeks left. Is that enough time?"

"I'll talk to Lacey when she gets home from school this afternoon." Celia hesitated. "Now, about Vicente..."

Mia's face fell. "You can't help, there. Luck of the draw, you know? I have a grandfather who won't give me the time of day, and obviously wishes I'd never been born."

"I've tried talking to him, honey. There are things in the past...." Celia hesitated, her wish to help Mia weighing against Vicente's right to privacy. "It's not you," she said finally.

"Yeah, right." Mia's voice turned bitter. "It's been embarrassing, you know? Except for my mom and Dominga, he's the only relative I ever met. *Most* kids have happy memories about grandparents. I've got one who thinks he's too special to even bother talking to me."

"That isn't it, Mia. He's had a hard life. Some very sad things. He..." Celia's voice trailed off as she tried to find a way to explain. "He's a wonderful man with many talents—a man who loved deeply, with all his heart, and who lost a great deal. Give him time."

"I know you're trying to be nice, but you don't need to cover for him." Mia uncurled her legs and stood. "I really don't care anymore. He's a hateful old man who obviously never did anything with his life, and I mean nothing to him. Well, he's not worth my time, either. My mother would have been sooo glad to say 'I told you so!'"

At a sound behind her, Celia glanced over her shoulder.

Vicente stood in the doorway with a bundle of

mail in his hand. An expression of raw pain flashed in his eyes, but his scowl didn't waver as he tossed the mail onto a table by the door and disappeared down the hall.

A SHIVERY TREMOR of anticipation sped through her as Celia watched the bus pull to a stop in Saguaro Springs at dusk on Thursday.

When Brady stepped out and shouldered his duffel bag—his uninjured shoulder, she noticed—she hurried forward.

Did he look pale? Was he in pain? He'd been gone three days, now, and she'd imagined everything from major surgery to him taking R&R with some woman. He'd never been far from her thoughts.

"Let me take that," she urged, reaching for the strap.

"Thanks, but that might look a little strange to the good folks of Saguaro Springs, don't you think?" He grinned down at her. "Then again, with me being your old boyfriend and all, they might just think you were really eager to have me back."

She glanced around, suddenly aware of the woman in front of the grocery store. The ranchers shooting the breeze in front of the cantina down the street.

In a town where people looked up at a tumbleweed rolling down the main street, the bus was sure cause for interest…and every pair of eyes was on them both.

"I've been worried about you, darn it." She turned on her heel and headed for the pickup she'd parked a few yards away. "How come you never let us know how you were?"

"It wasn't a big deal—just a minor scratch is all." His tone was level, all business—a subtle reminder that he was here because of his job and nothing more.

"So what took so long?"

"Business."

He strolled along as if he hadn't left here with a bullet in his arm that could have killed him, had the trajectory been just a little different. Oblivious to the fact that she'd worried about him night and day.

She shot a dark look at him over her shoulder. If he wanted to play Mr. Mysterious Tough Guy, so be it.

He caught up with her at the door of her truck. "Look—I had to follow up on some leads, or I would have come back sooner."

His grin faded when she met his gaze, and she saw that where his words had been casual, there were other, deeper emotions lurking in his soul. *So you aren't so nonchalant as you'd like to seem.*

"I'm sorry," he added quietly.

Well, *there* were a couple of words she hadn't heard a man say in a good long while. She waited until they were both in the truck and on the highway before cutting a quick glance in his direction. "What about your injury?"

"Nothing much to tell. I went to the ER in El Paso, and had the bullet removed. I'll be on antibiotics for another ten days."

"So it didn't hit the bone or major vessels or nerves, then?"

"Nope. Lucky this time around. Luis tells me he has been checking in with you every day. No further activity?"

"Nothing within sight of the house," she said dryly. "But then, not many of the drug runners stop at the back door to say hello."

"Anything new on your cattle?"

"No word on the stolen cattle, but Adan and I dismantled the chutes in the more distant pastures." She flexed her hands against the steering wheel, working at the stiffness and blisters. Her frustration was much harder to deal with. "Those two chutes and pens were a good fifty years old and built like Fort Knox—railroad tie posts and two-inch oak—but there's no sense in making life easy for thieves. Now it'll be a little harder for them to load up my cattle."

Brady shifted into the corner of the bench seat so he could face her. "You figure out how many are gone?"

"Adan and I scoured the brush in every ravine we could find. We found seventy-two head of steers out there. I figure they got thirty. Five shy of a full load—which makes me wonder if they got scared off after seeing someone out on the ranch road."

"That could have been around the time that Adan took Mia to the bus in town, and then came home with her later in the evening."

"That's what I figured, but they say they didn't see anything. Of course, they might have been arguing too much to notice. Adan wasn't all that happy about her staying longer."

The sun had long since slipped beneath the horizon. Celia glanced in the rearview mirror. Behind them, maybe a mile back, she could see the dim form of another vehicle keeping pace with hers.

"That's odd," she said after glancing in the mirror again. "Most everyone here drives like a bat out of hell on this highway—eighty to eighty-five, easy. I'm just going seventy."

"He's been following us since we left town." Brady frowned as he looked at the side mirror on the truck. "Did you see anyone there who lives out this way?"

Celia mentally reviewed the people standing along the street in town and the scattering of familiar pickups parked near the cantina. "Not that I can think of…after my ranch, it's another sixty miles to Brush Flats Ranch and then over a hundred to Coronado—the next town with any sort of trade. Not many people use this highway."

"Slow down."

"You're kidding." She shook her head. "If this is

someone I don't want to meet, I don't want to make it *easier* for him."

"Take a left."

"A what?"

"Next intersection, take a left. I believe it's a country road that winds back to town."

Celia glanced nervously at the rear view mirror again. The other vehicle was gaining, but slowly. "It forks about a mile down—to the left, it heads to town. To the right, there's about fifty slow miles of gravel to Gresham," she said.

Brady reached over and rubbed her shoulder. "Don't worry. I just want to check this out. Cut your lights. Don't signal…and once you get on the gravel, keep going but go slow so we don't kick up a lot of dust. We'll just see what he does."

Her hands shaking, Celia did what he asked. In the dark, with just faint moonlight filtering through the clouds, the road was a study of monochromatic blacks upon blacks, vague shadows barely marking the edge at either side.

At the Gresham fork, she turned left toward Saguaro Springs, then Brady squeezed her shoulder. "Pull over and take a look, Celia."

Leaving the truck idling, she looked over her shoulder and held her breath. Out on the highway, the other vehicle slowed down just past the turnoff. Stopped. Backed up.

After what seemed like an eternity, it jerked into

a three-point turn and sped back toward Saguaro Springs.

"Oh, my God—he *was* after me...or you." A knot of dread settled in her stomach as she considered the implications.

"Maybe."

"Related to your investigation."

"Probably."

"*Talk* to me, darn it."

"I would guess," he said slowly, "that it wasn't someone who knew you, or where you live—or they would have kept going. It was someone hanging around town who wanted to follow and see where I was headed. If he'd wanted a confrontation he would have been right on your bumper—maybe would have tried to run you off the road." He nodded toward the Ruger rifle suspended in the rack along the back of the cab. "I wouldn't have let that happen."

He reached over and tucked a strand of her long hair behind her ear, his fingertips brushing against the sensitive skin below it, and she shivered as much from his potent touch as from the dangers lurking in the darkness.

"Before...I had illegals coming across the river either to disappear into the United States, or to haul drugs," she murmured. "It made me angry, and there was risk. But this—this is far worse."

"While I've been at the Triple R, other members of my team have been tracking the activities of the Garcia gang, both here and in Mexico. These are the people we're after, Celia, and we're getting close."

In the faint illumination from the dashboard, she could see the resolute set of his jaw and the determination in his eyes. This was *personal*…and someone was going down. She said a silent prayer, hoping it wasn't going to be him.

"Why does this matter so much to you?" she asked. "I'd bet that you weren't really supposed to come back here until you healed better. Don't you guys have to take medical leave after an injury, until you're fully capable?"

A muscle ticked on the side of his jaw. "I have to be here. No one else can step into the setup at your ranch and blend in. Not now—there isn't time."

"That isn't all. Tell me." Sitting so close together, in the dimly lit intimacy of the pickup, she felt as if they were alone in the cosmos. Even without touching him, she could imagine feeling the beat of his heart. The warmth of his skin. Remembered kisses heated her blood and lowered her voice to a husky range. "I think I deserve to know."

He closed his eyes and leaned against the headrest, and was silent for so long that she doubted he would ever tell her.

"Two years ago," he said finally, his voice raw. "We had an operation set up on the other side of El Paso—everything going like clockwork, every move planned, reevaluated. Five agents. Six different state and local agencies as peripheral backup. I was instrumental in the planning process, and I was responsible for assigning the agents."

"And something went wrong."

"That implies something vague—an accident. I *failed,* Celia—Felipe Garcia didn't rise to where he is today because he's stupid. Before we even finished moving our people into position, a dozen of his men appeared out of nowhere with AK-47s and flak jackets—hit men who showed no mercy and disappeared without a trace. I blew it, and three good agents died."

Pain etched his lean features, and she knew he was reliving those terrible moments. "You were there?"

"Oh, yes," he said bitterly. "I was there—and I should have been the one to die. I fired every round of ammunition I had and still couldn't save any of them. They were caught away from any cover."

Celia drew in a shaky breath. "How horrible."

"Oh, that isn't all," he said. His voice went cold. "My best friend Chuck took a bullet in the head. He died in my arms—but not before he whispered, 'Don't blame yourself, buddy.' He was dying, and he was worried about me."

"Oh, Brady. I'm so sorry." Celia unlatched her seat belt and scooted next to him, needing to be closer. Wanting to give him comfort.

When she leaned her head against his chest and

wrapped her arms around him, he rested his chin on her head and drew in a shuddering breath.

"The man who ordered that hit is the man behind the shipments coming across your property, Celia. And I'm going to get him if it's the last thing I ever do."

Chapter Thirteen

THEY DROVE BACK to the ranch in silence. Celia constantly scanned the road ahead and behind, her hands clenched on the steering wheel and a sick feeling roiling in her stomach.

An enemy in daylight was terrible enough. One hiding in the darkness was far, far worse. Sure, that vehicle had headed toward town—but what if there were more?

And what if the driver somehow traced her truck to the Triple R? A casual description given to anyone in town might lead a stranger to her door.

The eight miles of rough ranch road had never seemed so long, but all appeared quiet when they arrived. Mojo, asleep on the front porch of the house, raised her head briefly and dropped it to her paws. Many of the cattle in the holding pens near the barns were lying down, chewing their cud.

And the doors of the house, Celia noted with relief, were securely locked.

Brady followed her into the kitchen and leaned

against the counter, his arms folded over his chest, while she made a pot of strong coffee.

"Decaf," she said, pulling two cups from the cupboard. "Want some?"

"No, thanks."

He watched her pour her own cup, his eyes touched with haunting sadness, and the temptation to simply hold him warred with the anxiety and fear that had set her nerves on razor's edge.

She took two long swallows of coffee, welcoming the bitterness and the scalding heat against her tongue, before finally finding her voice. "I need you to let me know about what's going on in your investigation. I have to know."

"I can't do that."

"It's my ranch, damn it. My family and my employees are at risk."

"I can say this much—so far we've seen just nickel-and-dime transport through your property, but the word is out on a major deal—within a couple of weeks. This is what we've been waiting for."

"Weeks?"

"Maybe it's time for you to consider packing up for a while. You've got relatives, don't you? Some place you and Lacey could go?"

"I'm not leaving this ranch."

"Use your head, Celia. Things are escalating here. It's no longer safe."

"My great-grandfather defended this ranch against the Indians and marauders coming across the border from Mexico. My grandfather and father stood their ground. I'm not slinking away and letting these people drive me off my land."

"And what can you do? You've got two old men and a daughter here. A girl who ought to hightail it back to New York, if she's got any sense—and Adan, who has a checkered past of his own. How are you going to defend this place and keep them safe? They won't be any help, believe me."

Frustration and anger welled in Celia's throat. "I thought you were supposed to be our big protector," she snapped. "When you came out here, you said this was all going to end and we would be safe."

"I'm involved in the operation—I can't be at every door and window here as a bodyguard, twenty-four hours a day. When it's over, you'll be safer here. But not now."

She glared at him. "I'm not leaving. We all have our reasons for what we do, and I have mine. If I have to fire at someone threatening my family and property, so be it."

"Celia—"

Her coffee sloshed over the rim of her cup, burning her hand, but she barely noticed. "By Texas law, I have a right to defend what's mine."

He moved across the room and took the cup from her hand, set in on the counter, and gently rested his hands on her upper arms. "This isn't the Old West. It isn't some movie, where the good guys never miss and the bad guys always do. This is real, and it's *dangerous*."

She ignored the disapproval in his eyes. "I'm well aware of that. I also know what I've lost to people like this and I've had *enough*."

Suddenly weary of it all, she leaned into him and rested her forehead against his hard chest, wishing that there was an easy way to make everything right…and safe, once again.

He curved his arms around her and drew her closer, tucking her head beneath his chin. "The important thing is for you to think about protecting the people here. And starting a gun battle isn't the way to do that."

Beneath her ear she could hear the steady, powerful beat of his heart. Feel the reassuring warmth of him, and smell the clean, masculine scents of soap, and aftershave, and laundry starch in his black oxford shirt.

He was a safe harbor, for these few and precious moments, but she'd had to stand on her own two feet and take charge for too many years now, and she knew that soon he would be gone. The only person she could ever truly depend on was herself.

Pulling away, she looked up at him, memorizing the angles and planes of his face. The warm golden flecks in his dark eyes. The dark sweep of eyelashes longer than any guy had a right to own.

"I understand what you're saying," she said slowly. "But you've got to understand this—I lost my first love to drugs. Lacey lost a father she never even got to meet. And I'd stake my soul on the belief that my dad's death was no accident. I think he was gunned down when he stumbled across drug runners and tried to fight them off. I've lost way too much to just run away now."

He cupped her face in his hands and kissed her forehead. "So don't risk anything more. Please."

A premonition of terrible danger and heartache stole through her thoughts, sending a chill deep into her bones.

"So far, I've only had problems in the farthest, outlying areas of the ranch. At the first hint of danger around here at the home place, I'll send Lacey away to her great-aunt Linda's house in Houston," she said. "And I'll make sure Mia gets on the bus for New York. The men here can make their own choices. But I'm staying." She took a deep breath. "I have a bad feeling about all of this. If I leave and something awful happens, I will never forgive myself."

He tilted her chin up with a forefinger, looked into her eyes. Then lowered his mouth to hers.

His kiss was tender, gentle. Reassuring.

It wasn't enough.

She pulled him down into a deeper kiss, needing more than he was giving. Demanding. Wanting the affirmation of life and love amid all the chaos that her life had become.

He held back, his hands trembling. And then he

groaned and swept her tighter into his arms, his mouth seeking, his hands roaming over her spine and then dropping lower, to pull her against the evidence of his desire.

Then suddenly he gripped her arms and stepped away, his gaze burning into hers. "I...should let you go," he said, his voice a hoarse rumble. "This isn't right—you were scared tonight. You aren't really thinking straight."

She gave a seductive laugh, suddenly feeling as free and young as she had at eighteen, before her life had irrevocably changed.

"I am," she said softly, "thinking straight for the first time in years."

SHE DEBATED FOR just a second between her own room and the guest room, then led him down to the room he was using.

"It's quieter over here," she whispered. "And there's no one else we might wake up."

"I still don't think—"

"Then *don't* think."

"You're sure?" He gave her a doubtful look, but already she saw his eyes darken and his skin flush.

She'd been attracted to him from the moment they'd met. She'd watched him ride with a beautifully natural feel for his horse, and that had been an even greater lure. He'd made her feel safe and protected. He'd proven intelligent and honorable, with a sharp wit. Throughout it all, she realized, he had claimed her heart.

Maybe there could be no future with him, but at least they could have this one night.

"I am *sure*," she whispered against his ear. "So what are you going to do about it?"

His eyes glittered. His mouth slanted into a sexy grin. The air between them changed. "I guess," he said slowly, "we'll need to figure it out."

He trailed a finger across her cheek. Down the column of her neck, the buttons of her shirt. He lingered there, slipping them open one, after another…after another. Then he claimed her mouth in a kiss that left her dizzy and disoriented.

And then suddenly, she was standing before him with her clothes in a puddle at her feet, mesmerized by the inexorable progress of his hand as he slowly…oh, so slowly…began unbuttoning his own shirt.

Way, way too slowly.

Taking charge, she swiftly dealt with his buttons and stripped away his shirt, then stopped, entranced by the broad sweep of his muscular chest. The rigid six-pack that jerked beneath her fingertips. The dark line of hair that arrowed downward and disappeared into his unbuttoned jeans.

Ethan had been lean, pale, a little soft, not much more than a boy. Brady was all bronze muscle and leashed power—the stuff of fantasy and the silver screen. "Holy Hannah," she breathed.

In one dizzying motion, he swept her up into his arms and laid her on his bed. In another heartbeat, he'd kicked his jeans aside and joined her. He gave a low chuckle. "My words exactly."

She laughed, then welcomed him into her arms, and reality spun away as she gave herself up to a soul-deep hunger she'd never known existed...a completion that took her breath away.

Brady.

But hours later, when she awoke and wanted to snuggle close, she reached across the rumpled sheet and found only an empty pillow.

His Western hat and boots were gone, too...and she knew he'd left her to go back out into the night and his routine surveillance. Only now, she'd sampled some of the danger he faced, and none of that seemed so routine any more.

And this, she knew, would be his life—long hours, days, maybe even weeks away, facing unknown dangers, while a woman who loved him would be left behind to worry and wait, and wonder if this was the time he wouldn't make it home.

What would it be like to face a lifetime of kissing a man goodbye and wondering if each time might be the last? He wasn't hers. He had said nothing about the future. But it was already too late.

When he left the ranch she might never see him again, but a day wouldn't go by without her wondering if he was still safe and whole. Because sometime during these past few hours, she'd realized that she'd fallen in love weeks ago. And whatever happened, she knew she would never be able to change that fact.

Her heart heavy, Celia made the bed, took a last look around, and shut the door behind her.

"MOM SAYS WE have to stay right here—close to the house," Lacey said. "I think it's *dumb.*"

Mia clutched Frosty's reins and tightened her grip on the saddle horn. "I...um...think it's a good idea."

Sitting on this hard saddle and broad-backed horse felt like straddling a powder keg. Mia had *seen* Lacey kick her horse into a gallop and disappear over the horizon. The thought of thundering after her, but with total lack of control, sent nervous shudders through her midsection.

"Let's jog," Lacey said. "Just kick a little with both heels at the same time."

"What happens if I don't get it right?"

Pursing her lips, Lacey tipped the brim of her hat back with a forefinger. "Well, if you kicked with one heel, he'd ease right into a nice, easy lope."

"Like a g-gallop?"

Lacey rolled her eyes. "Much slower and smoother. And if you kicked him hard with *both* heels, he'd go into a extended trot. Now, that's one thing you probably want to avoid. Frosty's got a fast trot, feels like a jackhammer."

The reins were slippery from the dampness of

Mia's hands. Her thigh muscles were already aching after just twenty minutes of walking Frosty around and around the corral. The dust rising under Frosty's hooves parched her throat and burned her eyes.

Trying to remember which saint she should pray to for safe dealings with a horse, Mia gave Frosty's ribs a gentle nudge. Oblivious, he continued trudging forward at a walk, his head swaying with every step. "Well," she said with relief, "I guess he'd rather go slow, and that's fine with me."

Lacey came up along side them and grinned, then leaned out of her saddle and whomped Frosty's rear end.

Frosty immediately launched into a faster gait, snapping Mia's head back. Bouncing hard in the saddle, she gripped the reins and the horn tighter, and squeezed her eyes shut.

Lacey kept pace with her and nudged Mia's arm with her elbow. "Make your lower spine flex like spaghetti," she urged. "Let your hips just move with the horse, and take up the movement with your back. See?"

Mia shot a nervous glance in her direction. Lacey's butt seemed to be glued to her saddle. Her upper body appeared still and relaxed. And she was *grinning*.

"Easy for you to say," Mia muttered. "Your horse looks smooth as glass."

"Nope. But I take up his motion, I don't fight it. Think soft spaghetti, Mia."

Holding her breath, Mia tried to relax her muscles. Next to her, Lacey gave her a nod of encouragement. "Better—now more."

The first time around the ring, Mia's butt hit the saddle with every stride. The second time was a little better. By the third, she realized just how smooth the old horse was. "Wow—this is really cool," she breathed.

Lacey flashed a wicked grin. "Next, we're gonna lope."

"Oh…please no," Mia begged with renewed alarm. "This is fine. Really it is."

"Frosty is the best loper on the ranch. He's like a big ole furry rocking chair, I promise. And he's so quiet and lazy that his lope isn't much faster than his jog. Now touch his right side with your heel, and he should take off into a left lead around the corral."

Mia tried to remember why she'd thought this was such a good idea. She hadn't, come to think of it—it had been Celia who'd urged her to try. And that had been because of Adan.

Who would probably die laughing if he saw her right now.

Lifting her chin, she gave Frosty's side a nudge… then a stronger one. Almost in slow motion, he lifted into a three-beat lope, rocking gently into it just as Lacey had promised. "Wow!" she called out, delight bubbling through her. "This is, like, incredible!"

Lacey pulled to a halt in the center in the corral and watched her. "Lower your hand. Keep it down by the saddle horn. Give him some more slack."

She'd done this to show Adan that she could. Now, she wondered why she'd ever hesitated. "I can't believe it! I'm galloping!"

"Loping," Lacey called out. "It's *loping*. If we go fast, we just call it a dead run, in these parts. Now, sit deeper in your saddle. Squeeze a little with your thighs and just gently pull on the reins—just a touch."

Frosty slid into a neat, perfect stop.

Mia leaned over and hugged his neck. "I love this, Lacey! I wish I could bring him back to New York in my suitcase!"

She straightened, suddenly feeling a little sad, and saw that Lacey's face echoed her own emotions. "It's been fun, hasn't it? Once we got to know each other a little?"

Lacey nodded. "Out here, it's too far to have friends over much." She brightened. "Hey—I want to show you my favorite place."

She jogged her horse Loco over to the gate, leaned over to unlatch it, and swung it open by sidestepping her horse to one side.

Mia glanced back at the house. "Your mom said we should stay here. Maybe we should do what she says."

"Nah…everyone else is way out, moving cattle down into the south pasture. She probably just wanted us to keep an eye on Jonah. But Vicente is cooking again, so he's in the house. Come on," she wheedled, "this place is sooo cool. No one knows about it but me. Why waste a great Saturday morning just sitting around?"

"Well…"

"Just think—you'll really have a chance to ride, out in the open. It'll be such fun! And we're only going a mile or two. They won't even know we left!"

There'd been something else in Celia's voice this morning besides the usual concern for Jonah. A warning that Mia had heard, loud and clear.

But Lacey was already heading over to the gate leading off into the vast, desolate expanse of sagebrush and grass that stretched to the horizon. And surely it would be better to go with her than to let her go alone.

With a last glance at the house, Mia urged Frosty into a gentle lope and followed her.

Chapter Fourteen

"Young lady, you are *grounded*." Celia held out an arm and pointed toward the kitchen door. "You go to your room, and stay there until supper. While you're in there, you can do your homework and think about what I said this morning before I left."

"Yes, ma'am." Shooting a furtive glance at Mia, Lacey trudged away, looking like someone headed for the gallows.

Celia's frown didn't waver as her gaze settled on Mia. "I don't want to seem rude to a guest, and I know you aren't responsible for Lacey, but I think you might have heard me tell you both to stay here."

Mia bowed her head, embarrassed. Adan and Brady were both over by the coffeepot, their backs turned, but from the dull flush on Adan's neck, she knew he was hearing every word. "I didn't want to go—I can't even ride that well. But Lacey took off, and I figured it was better to go with her than to let her go alone."

"How long were you two gone?"

Mia thought back to the ride through a long, twisting ravine and low-lying hills to Lacey's "secret place"—a cave set high in a craggy rock wall. "An hour, maybe. It started getting pretty hot out there, so we turned around and came home."

Celia studied her. "What all did you see?"

"A lot of rocks and sagebrush, mostly. I think I'm going to have major blisters from riding so long."

"Any livestock—or anything else?"

"I kept thinking I was going to see a rattler behind every rock, but no—nothing."

Celia's expression softened. "I know you're new out here, and I do know Lacey. She's quite a free spirit and often pays the consequences. But please—don't wander far. You two need to stay within sight of the ranch buildings at all times. I just don't want anything to happen, okay?"

Chastened, but also mystified, Mia nodded. This was new, yet Celia was skirting the issue that obviously had her worried. And from the brief glance Celia and Brady had shared a moment ago, it was something *big*.

Excusing herself, Mia wandered to her room, feeling melancholy. Another week, and she'd be on that bus heading for New York, something that should fill her with anticipation.

The new apartment she and her friends planned to share would be available on the first of May, the summer session of school would start in mid-

June. Her life would go on as it had before…and this ranch would be just a memory.

Great-Aunt Dominga was sweet, and Mia had gone into town to see her several times, but Vicente was still surly and would clearly be glad to see her leave. That part of this whole trip still filled her with sadness.

She had exactly one elderly relative left in the world who even cared if she lived or died, and Dominga lived half a continent away. How pathetic was that?

Opening her closet door, she dragged her big suitcase out into the center of the room. Even before Mom died, music had been her escape. Her solace. One consistent thing in a life of moving from one town to the next.

Reaching inside the suitcase, she withdrew her violin case and ran a loving hand over the smooth black surface, then grabbed the handle and headed down the hall.

Somewhere outside—maybe beyond the machine shed, in that little grove of trees, she could pour her heart into her music and let the world just fall away.

ADAN WATCHED MIA leave the room, then he turned to glare at Celia. "That was rude," he said. "She didn't mean anything—and it was Lacey's fault, anyway. What's the big deal about leaving the home place?"

Celia shot a glance at Brady, then cleared her throat. "You're right Adan. I shouldn't have been quite so blunt. It's just that, with the cattle thefts and all, I don't want them roaming too far away. Think about it—what if those thieves came for another load, and came across a couple of teenage girls?"

The image was all too graphic.

Adan felt a warm flush rise up his neck. Celia was right, and he'd jumped to Mia's defense way too fast. The thought of any jerk touching her made his blood pound and his fists clench. That bastard at the bus stop, for instance.

Ducking his head in embarrassment, he grabbed his hat from the hook by the back door. "I—I gotta go check the horses," he mumbled.

"Thanks, Adan," Celia's voice followed him out the door.

She wasn't angry. He heard the friendly tone in her voice. But he was angry at himself, for stepping in where he had no business. For being wrong. And even for caring too much about how Mia felt. Sure, she'd been friendlier, lately, but she'd never once flirted with him, and she endlessly talked about going back to New York.

Despite it all, he'd come to like her a whole lot—but she was leaving and he sure as hell didn't belong in that world of hers.

He tromped over to the barn, but as he stepped inside he heard a sound so foreign, so pure and beautiful that he stopped in his tracks and just closed his eyes to listen.

Then he stepped outside and followed the sound to the far side of the machine shed.

Mia stood under the trees a dozen yards away, a fiddle tucked under her chin and her eyes closed, playing what had to be the most beautiful song he'd ever heard. So sad, so sweet, that it made his heart wrench just to hear her play it. It sounded as if she was laying her soul open—all of her sorrows—to be lifted on each soaring note.

He swallowed hard. Humbled by her talent, he stared at her and realized just how foolish he'd been to think that she might like him, even a little.

Turning to go, he stumbled over a low, wiry sagebrush and sent pebbles skittering like marbles across the ground.

"Adan."

He would have kept going, but she called his name again and sounded so forlorn that he couldn't ignore her. He pivoted and walked down to the grove of trees, where she was already putting her violin into its velvet-lined case, her silky black hair flowing over her hands like a waterfall.

"That was so cool," he said. "How come you never played before now?"

She shrugged, snapped the case shut, and stood up, then scooped her hair behind her shoulders. "Guess I was taking a break. Or maybe I just didn't have the heart for it until now."

"What was that song called?"

"*'Leise flehen meine Lieder.'* It's by Schubert."

"So this is what you do? In school, I mean?" He felt so out of his league that he couldn't even think of the right questions to ask.

She smiled. "Yes, it's what I do. I'm second violin in a community orchestra, which is giving me great experience, and I'm a music major. Someday, I hope to play with the New York Philharmonic."

His mouth dropped open. "What are you doing out here? I mean, I know you help Jonah and wanted to meet Vicente, but why?"

"When my mom died last winter, that was it—I had no one else left. Do you have any idea how lonely it is, knowing there's no one who cares about you?"

Oh, he had a pretty good idea. His mother was dead. During his whole two years in detention, he'd never gotten a single card or letter from anyone except his sisters. And he'd never even met his dad.

"When I came across some papers in Mom's desk, I found out about Dominga and Vicente, and I really wanted to meet them. I hoped," she added quietly, "that I would find lots of relatives out here, and that they might enjoy meeting me, too."

Adan winced, knowing Vicente still hadn't exactly welcomed her with open arms. Even yesterday, the old guy had just grunted yes and no answers when she'd tried to talk to him.

"Instead, I met a grandfather who is a *common laborer* yet is too stuck up to even talk to me." The disdain in her voice grew. "How weird and pathetic is that? I sure won't have any good memories about him after I leave."

Loyalty to the old coot made Adan scramble for the right thing to say, but it also made him careful. "He's not what you think. He's a good man, Mia. He doesn't talk much, but I think there are…um… some really bad things in his past. Celia knows… she once said he could have been famous."

"Ha! For what—being incredibly rude?" she scoffed. "What else could he possibly be good at?"

Adan liked Mia. A *lot*. But she also had the power to make him angrier than anyone he'd ever met. He glared at her, his jaw clenched. "Play for him."

"What?"

"Just do it, Mia. If nothing else, just do it for me."

"Not on your life. If you think he might come around just because of my talent, then that's hardly real love for who I am, is it?" Her lower lip trembled, even as her eyes flashed fire. "A lot of my so-called 'friends' have been like that, and I can't tell you how much it hurts."

She grabbed her case and fled toward the house, leaving him staring after her.

And for the second time that day, he felt lower than dirt.

BRADY PACED THE confines of his bedroom, willing the message to appear on his Internet mail program. Every few minutes he tapped a key and held his breath.

Each time, he stared at a new raft of ridiculous spam messages offering bizarre financial scams and products only a fool would buy. Each time, he deleted the whole mess and then resumed his pacing.

The shipment is expected sometime in the next three or four days, Luis had said on the day Brady got ready to come back to the Triple R.

It had been a week now, without a word.

From out in the kitchen came the familiar sounds of Vicente rattling pots and pans, preparing breakfast. Lacey was rushing around to get ready for school. Adan and Mia were probably out there as well—polite to each other but uncomfortable.

And unless she'd already gone outside, Celia would be there as well, keeping everything on an even keel.

Celia. Brady stopped at a window and pulled a curtain back to stare outside. Early morning light bathed the buildings and corrals in rosy hues, the cloudless sky promising another warm day. Nothing like it would be in a few months, when the thermometer would rarely dip below a hundred during the day.

Hot and desolate and dry, the land here was just about as inhospitable as it came, yet it held its own wild beauty as well. Soon he would be leaving this for the confines of a cityscape, with concrete buildings crowding out the sky, shoulder-to-shoulder crowds, and heat radiating up from the asphalt. The thought filled him with regret.

The thought of leaving Celia behind filled him with far deeper emotions that were better left unspoken.

With each passing day he'd come to admire her more—less for her quiet beauty than for her strength and intelligence, and the streak of pure determination that could be as frustrating as it was admirable.

But since the night in his bed, she'd been distant, clearly letting him know that the most incredible night of his life had been an aberration—just a blip on the radar screen that wouldn't happen again.

But where she seemed to have put that night out of her mind, it replayed constantly through his. The soft scent of her. The smooth satin of her skin. The incredible passion that lay hidden beneath her no-nonsense rancher clothes and practicality. She was, he'd decided, the best-kept secret in this county… and he was thankful for it.

He just wished he had some chance for a future here, with her.

Checking the e-mail program once last time, he waited—then cursed under his breath and shut down his laptop.

Another day lost.

Yet it was a reprieve as well…another day at the Triple R. For what it was worth, he put in a good day's work as a ranch hand, and at night he listened and watched for trouble while dozing. When he finished this job, he was going to need a solid week of sleep just to catch up.

By the time he got out to the kitchen, Lacey had already left for the school bus, Adan was wolfing down his last bite of pancakes and sausage, and Mia was picking at her food, her gaze fastened on the pancakes in front if her. Celia, at the end of the table, had pushed her half-eaten breakfast away and was studying the livestock reports in the paper.

Vicente glanced over his shoulder at Brady and began piling a plate high.

"So, Mia," Brady said as he sat down across from her. "Saturday is the day?"

She nodded without looking up.

"What time does your bus leave?"

"Four."

Celia turned another page of the newspaper and looked up at her. "We'll miss you a lot, Mia. It's been great having you here."

"I appreciate you letting me stay with you. It's been wonderful." Her gaze skated over to Adan, then dropped to her own plate. "I even learned how to ride, a little, so that was sure fun."

Celia gave her a knowing glance. "You know, I don't think you ever got to see much of this ranch, did you? I wonder…Adan, I need to stay around here today, since I'm expecting a buyer to stop in. Could you take Mia out for a good long ride this morning? I won't have time, and I would sure appreciate it."

Adan's fork clattered against his plate. "Um... sure."

"You could maybe check the mother cows and calves up on the ridge, and take along a lunch, if you wanted to. Saddle Frosty for Mia, okay?"

He nodded, and pushed his chair away from the table. "No problem."

Mia flashed Celia a smile of pure gratitude after Adan went out the back door. "I was hoping I'd have a chance to ride again. This is so cool!"

"There's all sorts of food in the refrigerator. Grab whatever looks good and be sure to take some bottled water. There are some ice packs in the freezer. And look in the lower cupboard—there should be some insulated lunch packs that will fit in your saddlebag."

Mia launched to her feet and bustled around the kitchen, and in minutes she was out the door as well.

Brady set aside his plate and braced his elbows on the table, steepling his fingertips in front of his chin. "That was pretty slick, Celia."

Celia's smile turned wistful. "Mia has seemed so forlorn. Giving her a last little adventure was the least I could do. I'm also slipping some money in her luggage. She worked hard, when Vicente was laid up."

At the kitchen sink, his arms buried in sudsy water, Vicente grunted.

"Okay—so you weren't," Celia amended. "But the doc and I just thought you ought to take it easy for a while."

"So what's on tap for us here?"

"I've got to start bringing cows and calves up into the holding pens…it's time to precondition the calves for weaning."

"What's your routine, here?

"We vaccinate, castrate and dehorn while they're still with their moms, then wait a few weeks to wean them. It's just too hard on them if we hit 'em with everything at once, and we've seen a lot less illness this way. Stress weakens the immune system, though some of the older ranchers don't believe it."

"Good plan."

"I'll start tomorrow when everyone is here. Our chute system works really slick, but it still takes a good four people to handle everything."

Brady laughed. "So you don't really have a buyer coming?"

"Honestly, you just never know." She stood and gathered the remaining plates from the table, and took them to the counter next to the sink. "Come on outside—I need to show you something."

Out on the porch, she moved to one end and

leaned a hip against the railing. "You said that you expect this entire operation to be over soon. Have you heard any more?"

Brady shook his head. "Why?"

"I was just thinking…you're going to be gone soon. Is there anything you'd like to do while you're still here? We work darn hard, and the days are never long enough. Maybe there's something fun you'd like to do—some place you'd like to go? I can get along without you for a day, and it ought not affect your other job here—I don't suppose anything dramatic is going to happen in broad daylight."

He could think of quite a few things he'd like to do, but none of them involved being alone. "I'd like to spend the day with you."

"I don't mean ranch work—some people like to go down to the Big Bend area for fishing…or they go rock climbing. Some people—" she gave a little shudder "—like to come out here and hunt for snakes."

"Come with me, then."

Her brow furrowed. "I can't. I mean, I've got cattle to move and colts to ride. I can't just—"

"Yes, you can. What's a single day out of 365?"

She cast a worried glance toward the barns. "I don't know.…"

"Please?" He held out his hands palms up. "Hell, I might get lost out here without you along."

She sputtered, then broke into laughter. "I really

doubt that, but okay—as long as I'm here soon after Lacey gets home. Deal?"

He offered her his hand, but when she shook it, he held on. "Sounds like a good deal to me."

IN AN HOUR, they were on the road with Brady at the wheel. "I'll bet this is your first day off in years," he said, sliding a sideways look at her.

She didn't need long to think about it. "We even have chores on Christmas."

"Then tell me where you want to go. Anywhere is fine with me."

"Hmmm…there's a reservoir about an hour south. It's really pretty—there's pine trees on the north side, and picnic area. I've heard there are some nice little restaurants down there, too."

They made it in less than an hour and followed the narrow, winding road that skirted the lake until they reached the far side, where Brady stopped at a roadside stand to buy cappuccinos and deli sandwiches. Then he continued driving until they reached a dense, cool stand of pines where a few dozen empty picnic tables rimmed the sparkling lake.

"This okay?"

"More than okay. It's wonderful. I was afraid there might be lots of people here." She gazed across the water. "I need to bring Lacey to this place. We just never get away, and she deserves something more than just staying at the ranch all the time."

"Running a ranch by yourself can't be easy." Brady grabbed the sack of food and climbed out of the truck, then headed for a picnic table more secluded than the others. "I'm surprised you haven't found some local rancher and married. Life out here would be a lot easier as a team."

She lifted her sandwich from the sack and perched on the top of the table to watch the gulls swoop and dive over the water. "A team. That sounds wonderfully romantic."

He settled next to her, just a few inches away, and her thoughts drifted to other, far more romantic thoughts. There'd been ranchers who had shown interest in her over the years, but none of them had made her feel any sort of special spark. One kiss, and she'd felt it with Brady.

A man who would soon walk out of her life.

"Tell me what you're looking for."

She chuckled. "There's not much point in looking, because I must already know every last person in this county."

"So you're picky, then." He bumped her shoulder, a teasing glint in his eyes.

"Not picky, just not looking." She took a bite of her turkey and Swiss on rye, considering. "But if I was, I'd say that someone between the ages of thirty and forty would be nice. A good, honest man, who would be a great father to Lacey." She shot a grin at him. "A guy with good bloodlines, good conformation, and a lot of heart."

"Sounds like a race horse."

"And that's my problem—I just keep getting these things mixed up. So how about you?"

The humor in his eyes faded. "Been there, done that—got mighty close."

"You're divorced?"

"Probably would have been, in time. Just before the wedding, my fiancée was injured in a high-speed chase and rolled her squad car. Her physical therapist was good at more things than just helping her heal."

He said it lightly, but there was an edge to his voice that showed he still carried that betrayal close to his heart.

Celia slid her arm through the crook of his elbow and gave him a quick squeeze. "Better to find out sooner than later," she murmured. "I'll bet neither of you would have been happy together."

"True, but it was a bit of a surprise at the time."

They sat hip to hip for the next hour, bantering about nothing, watching the waves and the gulls, and listening to the whisper of the breeze through the pines.

She could have listened to his deep voice for hours longer, but then he glanced at his watch and sighed.

"It's after two o'clock," he said. "Time to head back, I guess."

Disappointment slid through her.

She'd missed so much, not having someone in her life. The friendship. The conversation. And oh, the long, dark and intimate nights. She'd tried to shelve that thought since she and Brady had spent the night together a week ago—a night that still had the power to send a wave of sensation through her.

And now, this brief, innocent break away from the ranch was already at an end.

They gathered their trash and tossed it in a barrel on the way to the parking area. She hesitated at the front bumper of the truck. "Do you want me to drive?"

He looked down at her, and she knew instantly that he wasn't thinking about the truck or driving or getting home to the ranch.

"Let me," he said, brushing her hair back with one hand.

And then he lowered his mouth to hers.

Chapter Fifteen

ONE KISS, and she felt herself melting inside like chocolate warming in the sun. One brush of his gentle hand on her cheek, and hunger swept through her.

Not just for the promise of pleasure or the ultimate joy of satisfaction...but a soul-deep hunger for this man, and all the thoughts and hopes and dreams that came with just being near him.

This man alone had the power to make her feel that way—whether it was just a kiss, or an embrace, or an entire night of exploring the most intimate of relationships.

His hands slid lower and locked behind her hips, pulling her closer as he angled his mouth to deepen the kiss.

When he pulled back, his eyes were dark and searching. "I want you, Celia...but not just this... not just now...."

From down the road came the rumble of a dump truck, and seconds later it pulled to a screeching halt at the far end of the parking lot. The driver waved at them, then gears clanged and he began releasing a load of dusty gravel.

Brady stepped away from her with a rueful smile. "I guess now isn't an option. Should we head back?"

She nodded and tossed him the keys, wishing for things that would never be.

THE BRIEF KISS at the reservoir left Celia feeling restless and empty.

But the trip back to the ranch, sitting within the curve of his arm as he drove, left her wanting more than just the erotic touch of his skin against hers and the satisfaction of physical need.

Being close made her wish for long nights and lazy mornings, and the simple joy of shared lives. The kind of deep and abiding companionship and caring that Jonah had shared with Grandma Grace, and Vicente had shared with his beloved Consuelo. Middle age, old age—the wrinkles and the weary bones had never dimmed the glow of love in their eyes.

"A nickel for your thoughts," Brady said, angling a glance at her. A corner of his mouth tipped up. "You sure are quiet."

"Just thinking." She straightened and pulled away from the comfort of his arm. "You're expecting this big shipment to come through soon—and then what?"

"One night and it will be over as far as the Triple R is concerned. Beyond here—there's a multi-agency task force already in place, and we'll be taking down the big guns every step of the way." His mouth flattened to a grim line. "The Garcia gang will cease to exist."

"And what will you do next?"

"I'm...not sure."

Another drug operation, she supposed. One he'd already been assigned to cover but couldn't discuss. More danger, more intrigue—somewhere far, far away from her ordinary existence at the ranch.

She'd soon be just a case number in a file drawer, and imagining anything else was a foolish waste of time.

At the ranch, Brady gave her hand a quick squeeze, and then headed off to the house to check for e-mails from Luis. Hoping, she supposed, for news that everything was rapidly falling into place. He wanted the action to start. She knew it would be the end of having him here, a part of her world, and the thought left her feeling melancholy.

Slamming her door, she turned for the barn, where Lacey usually headed the moment the school bus dropped her off.

At the breathtaking sound of a violin coming from the grove of trees past the machine shed, she stopped in her tracks. The notes, pure and sweet as an angel's cry, soared, then swept into an intricate, mournful passage that could have been wrenched from a grieving mother's heart.

Mia, surely, though as far as Celia knew, the girl had yet to play in front of anyone here. Her talent and pure emotion were so incredible that Celia simply stood, her eyes closed, and absorbed the music for a few moments before following the sound.

She'd just passed the first cabin when she heard something else…a long, agonized moan, followed by a crash and the shattering of glass.

She pivoted and raced for Vicente's porch, then banged on the door and called his name. When he didn't answer, she opened the door and stepped inside. It took her eyes a second to adjust to the dim light.

A kitchen chair was upended against the wall. Broken glass lay on the floor by the table. And Vicente, his head bowed, stood with his back to the door and his hands braced on the kitchen counter. The framed photograph of his late wife lay on the counter beneath his fingertips.

She started toward him, but he raised a hand in warning, waving her away.

"What's wrong—are you okay?"

The sound of Mia's violin wafted through the open window—this time, something complex and lively, spinning through passages for which her bow was surely a blur of motion.

A deep, guttural sigh rocked through Vicente,

and then Celia knew the stubborn old Mexican was weeping.

"Oh, Vicente…" She went to him and rested a gentle hand on his shoulder.

He jerked away, tipping his head so she couldn't see his face. "Let me be."

"But she's leaving tomorrow. There won't be another chance."

Vicente's head bowed lower.

"Vicente." Celia fought the urge to shake him. "She's your only granddaughter. Don't lose her because of some sort of misplaced pride."

He stood there still and unyielding as granite, until she finally gave a disgusted sigh and withdrew her hand. "So be it. It's your loss, but I thought you were a stronger man than this."

She was at the door before she heard his broken whisper.

"The music…it fills my heart…and tears it into pieces. Hearing her play, I know she is…mine."

Celia paused, one hand on the door, and looked back. "Of course she is. Look at her eyes. Could there be any doubt?"

He turned toward her, his face a ravaged mask of grief. *"Sí.* For all the years since her mother was born…and all the years since my Consuelo died."

"I don't understand."

Waving his hand impatiently, he strode through the kitchen, brushed past her and headed for the barn.

Celia watched him leave, then she shut the door

behind her and headed for the house. It was time for answers, and Jonah might just be the one who had them.

"WHAT'S UP, MOM?" LACEY LOOKED up from her homework strewn across the kitchen table. "Isn't Vicente coming up to make supper?"

Mom swooped in for a quick hug and a kiss on the side of her cheek. "He's feeling a little under the weather. I might make something tonight and give him a break."

Remembering the last time Mom cooked, Lacey grinned. "Or maybe Mia and I could. There's some boxed macaroni and cheese in the cupboard, and we could heat some green beans."

"What a nice offer, honey. I need to talk to Jonah for a while, and then we can come up with something good, okay?"

Lacey shifted uneasily in her chair. "I don't think Grandpa's feeling so good, either. When I came home, Vicente was changing his bed…and when I looked in, he looked awful pale. He didn't even answer when I said 'hi.'"

"Did you see if he was using his oxygen?"

"Even in the chair." Worry slid through her as she struggled to ask the question that had been looming like a black cloud on the horizon for a long, long time. "Is…he gonna die?"

Mom gave her another hug. A tighter one, this time. "He will someday, sweetheart. He's been awfully sick and he isn't going to get any better. We can just hope and pray that we have him as long as we can."

Chewing on her pencil, Lacey watched her mom disappear down the hall, feeling as if a heavy weight had just settled in her stomach. She'd known Jonah wasn't well, of course. The future had been pretty obvious for a long time. But hearing the words made it all so much more *real*.

Maybe this winter, there wouldn't be late night checkers and card games, with everyone betting corn from the canvas bag in the junk drawer by the phone.

And maybe there wouldn't be those good times by the fireplace, either, listening to all the stories from long ago, when Grandpa—great-grandpa, actually—had farmed with a team and struggled to survive through the Great Depression.

Mia was already packing, and Lacey had overheard Brady tell Mom something about his "next job," so he probably wouldn't be around much longer, either. Soon, there'd only be Mom, Vicente and Adan here…and that sounded *sooo* lonely.

Lacey ran a hand over the rubber-band bound stack of mail on the table next to her. Her fingers caught on the ragged edge of a protruding envelope. Curious, she slipped off the band and spread the mail across the table.

Livestock magazine. Auction fliers. Veterinary product catalogs. Bills. Nothing interesting, except the envelope that looked as if the edges had been chewed by a puppy. Lacey lifted it to study the awkwardly printed address.

"Cella Remiton," she read aloud with a smirk. Weird. Who could have trouble with an easy name like Celia Remington? And there wasn't even a postmark, which was even stranger. At the sound of footsteps coming into the kitchen behind her, she lifted the envelope. "Hey, Mom—look at this weird thing that came in the mail!"

When Mom didn't answer, she twisted in her chair. "Did you—" Her words stuck in her throat when she saw her mother's pale face. "Is it Grandpa? Is he okay?"

Celia leaned against the counter, her fingertips pressed to her mouth. She nodded.

"Then what is it?" Alarm skittered through her, because almost nothing ever rattled her mother. Not blood or fire or snakes—not terrible storms or sick cattle or anything else. "What's wrong?"

Celia waved away the question, her eyes closed, but after a few moments she managed a tremulous smile that didn't look very real at all. "It's nothing, honey...just...some things about the past that made me feel sad. What do you have there?"

"Some weird mail, is all." The letter no longer interesting, Lacey handed it to her and then bent over her homework. "The guy doesn't even know your name."

From behind her came the sound of her mom ripping open the envelope, then paper rustling.

A sharp, indrawn breath.

"Lacey. Did you see Brady come in here a little while ago?"

"Sure…" There was an edge to her mom's voice that Lacey had never heard before. "I guess."

"Did he leave?"

"Um…yeah. He said something about the cattle and being out late. Why?"

Celia rushed forward, grabbed her shoulders and leaned down to look her straight in the eye. "You stay in this house, do you understand? I want the doors and windows *locked*. I'm going out to find the others."

Lacey stared at her, frightened. "What is it, Mom? Tell me!"

"Everything will be fine. I promise. It's just a note from someone who thinks he's being funny, but I don't want to take any chances."

But Mom had looked away when she said it—as if she wasn't quite telling the truth—and that envelope hadn't looked like much of a joke to Lacey. The address had been written with the crude, bold slashes of someone who was angry, not someone who was after a few laughs.

Something was horribly wrong.

GIVING THE CINCH a final tug, Brady slipped the tongue of the girth buckle into the latigo strap and flipped the stirrup off the saddle horn. Anticipation buzzed through his veins.

Luis had finally sent word. *Sometime in the next couple days.* The agents down in Mexico had seen the shipment being loaded. They were in position and ready.

When each phase of the operation was in place, the arrests would be nearly simultaneous, from Mexico to El Paso and the connections beyond, to prevent any chance of warnings to the drug traffickers waiting in the Midwest for one of the biggest shipments they'd handled in recent times.

Greed might make some people careless, but these were intelligent, experienced men who'd stopped at nothing to build an empire of corruption.

They'd killed Chuck and the two others—all dedicated and honorable agents—and soon they were going to pay.

Brady slipped the bit into Buck's mouth and slid the headstall over his ears, then checked the rifle scabbard on his saddle and turned to leave.

Celia strode into the barn, blocking his way. "You've got to see this," she said, thrusting an envelope into his hands. "It came with our mail today— no postmark. That means it was dropped off after the mail carrier came by."

Brady withdrew the sheet of paper.

You been trouble enough already. Back off—or someone is going to die.

"It used to be just furtive smugglers crossing my

land. Then it was stolen cattle. *Dead* cattle." Celia's face was pale, but bright flags of anger colored her cheeks. "Now *this*."

He dropped Buck's reins and grasped her shoulders. "These people mean business, Celia. This property has the perfect terrain, isolation, and proximity to a little-used highway and they want to make sure you don't try to interfere. They probably don't have any idea who I am," he added with grim satisfaction, "and figure that since you're a woman, you'll be easily frightened."

"You know what? I never thought I'd say this—but I think I am."

He thought about the night she'd gone riding off into the night to check on a pregnant mare. Her years of struggle to hold this ranch together, almost on her own. The way she'd raised her daughter—alone.

"That's the last way anyone could ever describe you, Celia. You are one of the strongest women I've ever met."

"Which still isn't going to help me, with someone delivering death threats to my door."

Brady thought about his ongoing suspicions about Adan, who could be tipped off by the arrival of a stranger at the ranch, but this operation was close to being over. "I'll have another agent here by tomorrow. He can stay here at the house."

She frowned. "But you said—"

"It's okay. What's important is that you and your

family are safe. You can tell everyone—" he paused for a second, considering "—that he's a childhood friend of mine who just happens to be with the border patrol. That way, they won't think it strange if he calls in extra help or seems to be taking charge. I'll let him know."

"You're still suspicious of Adan?"

Yes, but she didn't need to know that. She had such faith in everyone around her that some things were better left unsaid. Better that than to risk an inadvertent comment that might tip Adan off.

"I still believe in keeping this situation under wraps, as much as possible," he said carefully. "You just never know—the wrong word to the wrong person could jeopardize this entire operation. I won't take that chance."

"I think I'm going to call my Aunt Linda in Houston and see about taking Lacey there for a while. She'll miss some school, but I just don't want her at risk."

"And Mia leaves Saturday, right?"

"Around four o'clock." Celia shook her head. "I hoped everything would turn out so much better for her here, but I guess it just wasn't meant to be."

He studied her, wondering about the weary acceptance in her voice. "When this is over, you and I need to talk, Celia. I've done a lot of thinking these past few days, and—"

"There isn't anything to discuss. I understand completely—believe me, I do." She backed away, shaking her head. "It's been great, but even good things come to an end, right? It's all for the best."

Stunned, he watched her walk down the aisle of the barn.

She was beautiful, true, but she was so much more than that—strong and courageous and absolutely loyal. A woman who could hold her own against adversity and never give up.

Simply holding her made him feel more alive than he'd ever felt before. Kissing her made his blood heat and his imagination go wild. The night they'd made love was the most unforgettable night of his life—and he'd been sure that she felt the same way. He'd seen it in her eyes, felt it in her touch.

The irony of the situation struck hard. She'd walked out of his life just as he was realizing how much he cared.

He had to wrap up this investigation. Nothing was more important than keeping Celia and her family safe. But it wasn't going to be easy staying here, now, and leaving would be the hardest thing of all.

Because now he knew that no one else could ever take her place in his heart.

Chapter Sixteen

MIA FOLDED the rest of her underwear and packed it tightly around her violin case, then tucked in her pajamas, sweaters and jeans. "Guess I'm just about ready," she sighed. "I've only left out what I still need to wear tomorrow and Saturday."

Lacey, sitting cross-legged on the bed with her elbows propped on her thighs, watched with a glum expression. "I wish you didn't have to go."

"The bus only comes through on Mondays and Saturdays, so I'd better be on this one. It takes a long time to get to New York."

"But your apartment isn't ready yet, right?" Lacey pleaded. "Monday would work!"

"This gives me a couple days at a friend's house, and some time to get my things out of storage. What I could keep, anyway," she added sadly. "There was a lot of stuff from my mom's place that I just had to sell because it would have cost too much to move to New York and store."

At a soft rap on the door, she turned and found Celia standing there.

"How was your ride with Adan this morning?"

Mia felt herself blush. "It was great. He…um took me way out to the bluff, and we saw some antelope. He said he saw mule deer, but they were too far away and I couldn't quite tell if they were deer or cacti."

"Hard to tell from a great distance unless you can see them moving," Celia agreed. "Was Frosty good for you?"

"*Super.* I'm going to miss him so much! Oh—and you, too," Mia added hastily.

Laughing, Celia came farther into the room and tousled Lacey's curls. "Well, we'll miss you, too. I hope you'll keep in touch."

Mia felt her smile fade. "Yeah…I will."

"I need to talk with you for a while. Outside." Celia touched Lacey's shoulder. "And you need to get going on your math homework again, now that supper is over. Don't you have a test every Friday?"

Shooting Mia a pained look, Lacey slid off the bed and grumbled on her way out to the kitchen.

Mia eyed Celia, uncertain. "Did I do something wrong?"

"Good heavens, no. But you need to hear something, and then we need to talk."

Mystified, Mia followed her outside and down the lane toward the cabins. When they drew close to Vicente's, Celia touched her lips with a forefinger. *"Listen."*

Mia stilled. All was silent…and then she heard the first, sweet, full-bodied tones of a classical guitar.

"He's been playing for almost an hour," Celia said in a low voice. "Come, take a look."

They moved closer to the cabin where they could just glimpse Vicente through the window. He sat perched at the edge of his recliner, his left foot propped on a footstool, the guitar resting on his left thigh.

He was bent over it, his face contorted with intense concentration as he plucked the strings in a dizzying, rapid-fire sequence of such emotion and beauty that Mia stared, awed and humbled by this man whom she only considered a simple farm worker.

"That's the guitar Lacey found in the storeroom," she whispered. "How can he play so *fast*—and what is he playing?"

Celia listened for a few moments. "I think that's Tárregga's *'Recuerdos de la Alhambra.'*"

"It's incredible!"

"I heard it at an outdoor concert last year in El Paso. The program called the technique *tremolo* and said it involved more than five hundred string plucks a minute. I don't think Vicente is near that fast right now, though. I'm sure he's pretty rusty."

Mia stared at her, open mouthed. "I could *never* do that."

"Ah, but where do you think you got your gift?" Celia asked, reaching over to give her a quick hug. "Musical talent comes in many forms. Maybe it partly depends on what one is exposed to."

"Did you know he could play like that?"

"I've known Vicente since I was around ten years old, but I've never heard him play. Sad, isn't it? All that talent just locked away. So many years lost."

"I don't get it."

"He heard you playing, earlier. I did, too, and I came to watch, but then I heard some noise in Vicente's cabin and went over to check it out. Hearing you opened a lot of old wounds for him, I think."

Embarrassment washed through her. "I—I'm so sorry."

"Don't be, Mia. It's time to work this all out. And maybe now, with a little help, we can get the job done." Celia started for the cabin door and beckoned. "What do you say?"

"Is he…um…going to yell at me again?"

"Not if I can help it." After rapping loudly on the door, Celia led Mia through the kitchen and into the small living room.

Startled out of his deep concentration, Vicente scowled at them both.

"You play beautifully," Mia ventured in a small voice. "I could never do so well."

His scowl darkened as he studied her.

"I think you two need to talk, Vicente. Jonah told me about Consuelo…and Mia's mother. It's unfair to send this child away without telling her the truth."

"I…" His voice faded and he shrugged helplessly. "The words…I cannot."

"Mia, your grandfather had wonderful dreams as a young man. He had musical talent that led him to perform in many places. He saved his money and bought a ranch for his bride, because that was the dream he loved the most. He and Consuelo had a beautiful little daughter…but when she was very young, she was diagnosed with leukemia."

Vicente leaned the guitar against the wall and sat back in his chair, his gaze riveted to the floor.

"They spent every cent they had trying to save her—and during this difficult time he had a brief affair with your grandmother Blanca. Nine months later, your mother was born."

Mia stared at her, as everything started to fall into place.

"Vicente's daughter died, and he and Consuelo never had any more children."

"How sad," she whispered.

"Blanca…your grandmother…demanded a lot of money for child support over the years, with the promise that she would keep her little secret. But when Vicente lost his ranch, he had no more money to give her. She apparently took vengeance by telling Consuelo everything."

"It broke her heart," Vicente said in a voice almost too low to hear. "My beautiful Consuelo, mourning her own child—only to hear that I had another. She did not deserve such pain."

"She died of a heart attack just a month later," Celia murmured. "Vicente wandered from job to job for a few years, and then he came here."

Vicente lifted his gaze to Mia's, his eyes glittering with unshed tears. "But all the time, I thought Blanca had lied—saying her baby was mine when it was not. I could not prove it, not back then. I paid Blanca to keep her from spreading her 'lies,' but anger filled my heart.

"And now—" He broke off. Cleared his throat. "I heard you playing your violin today. It was like I was hearing my own mother—because she, too, had the gift of the angels. Her music touched the soul…and that gift is yours. You even have her beautiful eyes. Why did I not see it?"

He held out a shaking hand. "All these years," he said sadly. "So much lost. Can you forgive an old man?"

She thought about the heartbreak he'd endured— the sorrow over the loss of his little girl. The guilt over his wife's death. The anger that must have eaten at him over the years when he'd imagined that Blanca's lies had turned his life to sorrow.

Mia ignored his hand. Instead, she moved forward and wrapped her arms around him and held him tight. "I love you, Grandpa...I'm so glad I came."

CELIA STRODE BACK to the house, whistling an off-key version of the song Vicente had been playing. *At least they've come together.*

Something moved in the shadows by the barn and she nearly stumbled, her heart in her throat and her pulse racing.

"It's just me, *señora,*" Adan called out. He moved a few steps forward, still silhouetted by the security light overhead.

Curious, she stopped. "What's up?"

"Just restless, I guess." He kicked at a pebble. "Mia's all packed and ready to go?"

Ahhh. "I'm afraid so. She and Vicente are having a talk right now. I expect she'll be there for a while yet, talking about the past. Would you like to take her to the bus tomorrow?"

His Western hat dipped as he nodded.

"This time, she will have to leave, Adan," Celia said gently. "But I'm pretty sure she'll come back again, now that Vicente and she have finally connected. Maybe even this summer—you'll have to ask her for me. Okay?"

"Yeah."

He sounded so disconsolate that she veered from her course toward the house and joined him.

"Mia said she had a great time riding this morning. Thanks for taking her."

"Yeah, well…" He jammed his hands in his back pockets. "It's been nice, but she's got a future. College and all."

"Have you thought about what you might want to do? You're young, bright—you could go to college, or even start with some correspondence classes. Anyone who has the motivation can find a way to chase their dreams."

He snorted. "That all takes money."

"Well…there's a lot of ways to find it—lots of options for financial aid, and some kinds you might not even have to repay. Someday, if you're interested, we could look up these things on the Internet."

When he didn't answer, she folded her arms over her chest and looked up at the waning crescent moon. "Dark night," she said finally. "Well… I guess I'd better get up to the house and do some bookwork. See you in the morning."

She was nearly to the fence surrounding the yard when she heard him call her name.

"Thanks, Celia. You've been real nice to me."

She smiled to herself and went on. It never hurt to plant the seeds, because someday, they might just take root and grow. And after this current trouble was over, maybe she could help him.…

The words of that anonymous, threatening letter came back to her, and her smile faded.

There were escalating risks here—and tomorrow another agent would appear at the ranch. But soon it would all be over, and Brady would be gone. The banter, that breathless flash of attraction when he entered a room, and the pleasure of simply being with him would all be just memories. And then the rest of her life would stretch out like the endless, desolate land around her.

With a sigh, she opened the door of the house and stepped into the light, and accepted what would always be.

"WE'RE GOING WHERE?" Lacey stared at Celia in disbelief. Something was up—she could see it in Mom's eyes.

"After school today, I'm taking you to Great-Aunt Linda's place just outside of Houston," Mom repeated. "Remember? She has a boy just about your age, and two retired greyhounds. Her house has that nice pool."

Lacey remembered the beautiful, queenly dogs, who lounged like royalty on the sofa and love seat in the family room. They were quiet and serene, and she'd liked them a lot, but that *boy* was a jerk. "How long will we be there?"

"I'm actually just taking you there, and then I'll have to come back to the ranch. It'll only be a few days—maybe a week."

"I don't get it. You're just *dumping* me there? For a *week?* Usually, I have to be practically dead before I can ever miss school." Lacey's suspicion grew. "This isn't anything to do with that Brady, is it? You aren't, like, going someplace with him, are you?"

"No. I'm not *dumping* you anywhere. And no, I'm not going anywhere with him."

Mom chewed her lower lip, clearly not sure how much she should say, which concerned Lacey even more.

"I'm not going."

"Honey, it isn't your choice. You have a few minutes before the bus comes, so you can start packing some of your things. Do it now, please."

Scowling, Lacey hesitated just long enough to express her rebellion, then she trudged to her bedroom and jerked the suitcase from beneath her bed. *This sucks.*

Not that missing school was so bad. But something was going on here, and Mom wouldn't say what. What if Mom was in trouble? Or what if this was about Grandpa Jonah—who didn't look so good, and might die? Being sent away was wrong, wrong, wrong.

But maybe…if Mom had a little more time to think about it…

Grinning to herself, Lacey tugged on her boots and slid a sweatshirt over the T-shirt she'd planned to wear to school. Then she opened her bedroom window wide, slid up the screen, and took a careful look outside to see if the coast was clear.

When the bus came, she would call out a quick goodbye and wait until it left. Then she could race to the barn, and no one would know.

Yep—once Mom had time to think things through, she'd be sure to have second thoughts about Great-Aunt Linda and that trip to Houston.

"WHAT DO YOU MEAN, she's not in school?" Celia shot an anxious glance at the clock on the wall of the tack room. "I heard the bus pull in here at seven-fifteen. I heard her say goodbye."

Precious minutes ticked slowly by while she waited near the phone for the school to call the bus driver and do a second search of the rooms.

When the phone rang again, she caught it on the first ring. "She's not? She *didn't?* But she was here—I talked to her this morning. She was ready for school!"

Hanging up the receiver, Celia hurried down the barn aisle, calling Lacey's name. She checked the loft, where the kittens were often a good lure.

Out in the corral behind the barn, she found her answer—Loco was gone. "Girl, you are in such big trouble," she muttered under her breath as she hurried to the house. "Big, *big* trouble."

She made it in time to catch the others just finishing up breakfast—a longer, later affair this morning, because it would be Mia's last at the ranch. Vicente had filled the table with *huevos ranche-*

ros, refried beans, *chorizo,* flour *tortillas* and his specialty, *menudo.*

"Lacey didn't get on the bus this morning," Celia announced. "Apparently she decided to play hooky."

Brady stilled, his coffee cup lifted. "Where is she, do you know?"

"I saw her over by the barn just before the bus came," Adan said around a mouthful of *chorizo.* "I didn't see her afterward, but I was out getting things set up for the calves today, out by the chutes."

"All I know is that she didn't get on the bus, and took her horse out instead. She may have been upset because I told her that I was sending her to my aunt Linda's in Houston for a visit."

Brady's chair screeched against the floor as he pushed away from the table. "We need to find her, now."

Adan gave him a curious look. "She knows the ranch like her own bedroom. She'll be back."

"Brady's right—I want to find her." Celia thought fast for a reasonable explanation. "I heard on the radio that there's a possibility of storms today, with high winds. You never know out here—we can go from dust storms to lightning and tornadoes at the drop of a hat."

"So...we should wait on the calves, then?"

"Absolutely." Celia folded a *tortilla* around a scoop of *huevos rancheros* and a *chorizo,* and balanced it in her hands as she started for the door.

"Lacey could be anywhere on that horse of hers. Vicente—take one of the trucks and drive down the ranch road to the highway, then cover what the pickup can handle in the more level parts of the central pastures. Adan, you head north. Brady and I can start on the two biggest pastures to the east."

"What about me—can I come along?" Mia asked. "Lacey took me riding that one day, and she showed me one of her favorite places. I think it was—" she pursed her lips "—north, I'm almost sure of it."

"I don't know," Celia replied. "You've got that bus to catch tomorrow and you need to get ready."

"But I'm totally packed, and if Adan is still searching, I can come back on my own in plenty of time," Mia said.

"Okay. But watch the time. The usual rifle shot as a signal, everyone. If no one has found her by one o'clock, I want to meet briefly here at the house to discuss it. And when we find her, Lacey is going to be grounded for a *month*."

Celia was halfway out the door when she decided that it was better that everyone knew some of the truth, for their own safety. Avoiding Brady's eyes, she stepped back inside.

"The weather isn't my only concern," she began, making eye contact with each person in turn. "I received some mail yesterday. A threat, directed at me. It's probably from some crackpot…most of these things are, I'm sure. I don't know why it was sent, or by whom."

Mia paled. "Someone who might come here, to this *ranch?*"

"I don't know—probably not. But it has me worried, because I don't know where my daughter is right now. And if there's someone with a grudge against me, I want to find her first."

Chapter Seventeen

By ONE O'CLOCK, they'd all been searching for over four hours without the welcome signal of a rifle shot.

In front of the barn, Celia dismounted and checked her watch as Adan and Mia rode in, followed by Brady, whose face was a grim mask.

His expression worried her far more than any words he could have said.

Vicente scurried out of the house to meet them all. "I came back to care for Jonah," he announced. "I just made a quick lunch—sandwiches to pack if you are going straight out again. There's a man here—he is waiting on the porch and says he needs to talk to Brady."

"Thanks, Vicente." Celia dismounted and tossed a stirrup over her saddle to loosen Duster's girth. "You're right—we'll be leaving as soon as we saddle fresh horses." She looked over the gelding's withers at Mia. "Did you see anything at that special place Lacey showed you?"

Mia shook her head. "I thought that's where she would go—she said she often goes there to be by herself. We found a sweatshirt she must have dropped when she took me there, but nothing else."

Celia's gaze sharpened. "What color was it?"

Adan turned in his saddle and bent down to reach into his saddlebag. "This is it—her Texas A and M."

"It was on her bed this morning." Celia stared at it, her stomach twisting into a cold knot. "My God—she was *there*. So where is she now?"

Brady tied his horse to the rail and drew close enough that only she could hear him. "I'm going to the house to talk this over with Tom. If we have to, we'll bring in a helicopter with a heat imaging system to help find her. She can't have gone too far."

Saying a silent prayer, Celia unsaddled Duster and turned him out into the corral, then roped a fresh horse and had him saddled by the time Brady returned.

"Come with me for a minute," he said. "You need to meet Tom before we all go out again."

Glancing over her shoulder at Adan and Mia, who were busy unsaddling their horses, she followed him up to the porch, where a muscular, middle-aged man in black jeans and a dark-green polo shirt stood ready to shake her hand.

"I understand you have a general idea about what's happening out here," he said, giving her hand a firm shake. "I just thought I should fill you in." He glanced at Brady, who nodded. "We've got bad weather coming—the National Weather Service is predicting high winds, rain and the possibility of substantial hail that will hit here at around nine or ten o'clock."

And Lacey is out there some place, all alone. Celia wrapped her arms around her middle. "We've *got* to find my daughter."

"We'll do our best, ma'am. We've also got other fish to fry—we've received reports that the shipment we've been tracking should be coming through late tonight. We don't know if the traffickers are aware of the weather and are trying to beat it, or if they're oblivious, but we're going to have a number of agents hidden along the river, here, and out along the highway."

Images of gun battles and crazed killers flashed through Celia's thoughts, and suddenly she broke into a cold sweat and felt her knees go weak.

Brady moved closer and took her arm. "We don't expect any violence here, Celia. The arrests will be handled only after the traffickers reach the highway and have sent the shipment off in trucks. There should be just around a half-dozen suspects to arrest, and that will occur beyond your property."

"But Lacey…" Celia caught the exchange of glances between Brady and Tom, and her anxiety escalated. Weather wouldn't be the only risk her daughter could face this night. "We've *got* to find her."

"We're calling for a tracker dog, Ms. Remington," Tom said quietly. "He can be here in an hour or so. Just hang on tight. We'll find your daughter and bring her home."

But the grim look in his eyes told her that he was thinking the same thing she was—the weather was changing, and soon heavy rains could wash away every trace of scent.

And with it, the chance to find her daughter.

Numb, Celia moved to a window and leaned her forehead against the glass.

And prayed.

AFTER LEAVING LACEY'S sweatshirt and one of Loco's extra saddle blankets for the dog handler, Celia, Adan and Brady rode out again, leaving Mia behind with Vicente.

Pushing the horses hard, they made it out to where they'd been before and fanned out, checking arroyos and canyons, searching for any sign that Lacey had passed by.

Three o'clock. Four o'clock. Five-thirty. With every passing minute Celia's fear grew and her hands shook more—and every little sound made her heart skip a beat.

The sun had been setting at around seven-thirty these past few weeks. And when it did, the balmy seventy-degree daytime temps would plummet into the forties.

Lacey had left her sweatshirt behind.

If she was injured…or had been bitten by a rock rattler sunning itself…or was in shock, and unable to call for help…

Tears burned beneath Celia's eyelids as she reined her gelding up yet another ravine and prayed that this time, she would find Lacey safe and whole and eager to come home.

At the distant, faint crack of a rifle, she nearly jumped out of her skin.

Spinning her horse around, she spurred him into a dead run toward the sound and prayed even harder that Lacey had been found.

Her horse was lathered, its sides heaving, when she topped the last low rise and saw a pickup parked by a gully, a number of strangers, and a golden lab lying at their feet. *But where was Lacey?*

From her right came the sound of thundering hoofbeats. Seconds later, Brady rode up alongside her and reached out to squeeze her arm as they rode down the slope side by side.

"You're shaking," he murmured. "Listen to me. That dog has earned a number of commendations—he's one of the best. If he can't track her, they'll radio for a helicopter."

Alarmed, she gripped her reins tighter and swiveled in her saddle to face him. "But what if those drug runners have her…and they see all this happening and they panic, and…"

"We've got access to an EC-120B copter—it's super quiet and if it's flying high, they aren't going to hear a thing. It has a FLIR system that will even pick up the body heat of a rabbit and show it as a white image on a screen. If she's out here, the pilot will find her, Celia."

"If?"

"Let's see what these guys say. Don't worry— we'll have your daughter home and tucked in bed before this day is over."

Celia dismounted, her knees nearly buckling, and she had to take a deep breath before she could leave her horse ground-tied and approach the agents talking by the truck.

When they all turned toward her, fear shot through her at their identical, grim expressions. No one spoke until Brady walked up beside her.

A woman with a silver badge at her hip offered her a gentle smile. "We were able to track your daughter and her horse until we got here," she said. "After this point, the dog couldn't pick up her scent." She motioned toward a stand of blooming yucca next to a rocky outcropping. "Her horse is over there…but there's no sign that she walked anywhere else."

"But there are tire tracks—from a four-wheeler," one of the taller men said. "They look fairly fresh, though the ground is so hard that it's difficult to set a time frame. We believe she was picked up here. There's a good chance she could have been taken much farther than we thought."

Celia glanced wildly between the sympathetic

expressions of the woman and the three men standing before her. "Now what? Why aren't you all searching? She's got to be out here somewhere!"

"Celia." Brady slid an arm around her shoulders. "We'll find her. I promise."

But a dark, cold night was fast approaching. Her heart was ripping into a thousand pieces. And his promises just weren't good enough.

BACK AT THE HOUSE, Brady settled down at the kitchen table with his cell phone while Celia briefly checked in on Jonah and Mia.

Impatient to get on with the search, she grabbed a jacket hanging from one of the hooks and put it on. Guilt lanced through her over this simple act. *Lacey doesn't have a jacket. Maybe she's cold, and shaking....*

Setting her jaw, Celia jammed her hands deep into the pockets and started for the door. Her fingertips curved around something angular and hard at the bottom of one of the pockets. Pulling it out, she stared at the Dallas key ring she'd found out by the loading chutes after the cattle were stolen.

Some clue. How many thousands of these key rings existed? The day they'd gone to Gil's for hay, Brady had sauntered over to "admire" the pickup with dealer stickers in its windows, but returned with the report that the new vehicle had come from a lot in El Paso, not Dallas.

She hadn't been able to think of any other locals

with newer vehicles, much less one that hadn't been sitting on the dusty little used car lot in Saguaro Springs. And God knew her own junk drawer in the kitchen could probably yield a half-dozen key rings and other logo-imprinted items from places she'd never been.

But now…she fingered the small square of plastic, remembering a visit to Gil's place years ago. She'd been just a teenager, but she still recalled him preening over the purchase of a new, top-of-the-line dually crew cab. *Oyster shell white,* he'd said, with the air of someone who'd just picked up a bauble at Tiffany's. *Fully loaded. We bought it from a dealer in Fort Worth.*

She looked over her shoulder at Brady, who still sat studying a map spread out on the table and had his cell phone at his ear. "I need to run over to Gil's place. It's important."

"Hold on." His brow furrowed as he listened to someone on the line. After a couple of seconds, he responded in a voice too low to catch, then he disconnected the call. "What's up?"

She tossed the key chain on the table in front of him. "I need to talk to Gil."

"This dealer name doesn't match the source of that new pickup of his. I checked."

"Yes—but Gil has had a *lot* of new trucks over the years." Celia's words poured out in a desperate rush. "And I just keep thinking of all the times he's warned me to 'be safe' and just ignore what happens along the border. Why would he be so insistent?"

"Because he knows—as you do—that it *is* safer for the average person to just stay clear?"

"Maybe he's seen or heard something that will help me get Lacey back," she retorted. "Maybe some of his men were out fixing fence...or overheard something in town."

"I'll come with you. But let me make one more call." Brady punched in a speed-dial number. "Marcy—Brady here. I need a history on a 2004 white Ford 3500 pickup registered to Gilberto Banuelos, Gelman County." He recited the license plate number, drumming his fingers on the table. "Yeah—I know you tried once before. Give it another shot. Maybe under another name...yes, in Gelman County."

Celia fidgeted at the door, fear and impatience spinning through her mind. "Come *on*," she urged.

He held up a hand. "I could lose reception. Wait..."

Grabbing a pencil, he braced the phone against his ear with his shoulder and started writing. As soon as he ended the call, he was on his feet. "There is no truck by that description registered to your uncle, Celia, and the plates don't match the vehicle—they were stolen from a Dodge Ram. The police in Dallas recently filed a report on a stolen truck that may match the one at Gil's place."

Stunned, she turned to face him. "He'd never do anything like that."

"But he has at least one new employee, Jose Nieto. He was out by the barn when we were there."

"A guy who didn't exactly look like Mr. Personality, come to think of it."

Brady pulled on his jacket. "You stay here, and I'll go over there to check things out. I want to get the VIN number off that truck to make sure we have a match."

"No. I'm coming along."

He sighed heavily. "It's safer for you here, Celia. Please."

"You don't know his place like I do. You need me—and I need to do everything I can to find my daughter." She raised a brow as she fished for the truck keys in the pocket of her jeans. "If you go by yourself, I'll just follow."

In fifteen minutes they were speeding down the highway with Brady at the wheel. In another ten, they'd turned off onto the Rocking B ranch road and were pulling to a stop in front of Gil's house.

The yard was oddly still and silent. The little hairs at the back of Celia's neck prickled. "This is weird," she said in a low voice. "His blue truck is here, but not his housekeeper's Chevy...and that German shepherd of his usually raises a ruckus."

"*Stay here.*" Brady stepped out of the car, scanned the area, then started for the house.

He circled the perimeter, and when he came into

view, she could see that he'd drawn a handgun. He knocked on the door, standing well to one side of it. He knocked louder...then tried the handle.

The door swung open and he eased inside.

A few endless minutes later he appeared at the door with his cell phone at his ear, gesturing for her to hurry inside.

"I'm calling 911," he said as she stepped past him. "He's in the kitchen—and he doesn't look good. I've been through the house—there's no one else here. Just be careful—his dog is closed in a bedroom, and it's trying to tear the door down."

Alarmed, Celia rushed down the hallway—then drew in a sharp breath.

Gil lay on the floor, his face pale and sweaty, his arms doubled over his stomach. Blood stained the front of his white polo shirt and blossomed across the tile beneath him. *So much blood.*

Fighting her sudden nausea, she grabbed a stack of clean kitchen towels from a drawer and knelt beside him, slid a few under his head and tried to staunch the flow of blood with the rest. "What happened? Who did this?"

Gil coughed weakly, then moaned.

"It's me, *Celia*. Tell me what happened!"

"Gunshot." Brady knelt beside her and lifted Gil's wrist to check his pulse. "Help is on the way. Just hang in there a while longer and you'll be good as new." He gave Gil a reassuring smile. "Hell, this is just a scratch."

Gil raised his head a few inches and reached for Celia's hand, his shaking fingers cold and sticky with blood. "I…I'm sorry…." His voice was barely audible. "Before…I have to tell you…Ray…"

He fell back, his head lolling to one side and his breathing rapid and shallow, his skin ashen.

"You can tell me later," she assured him, struggling to keep her voice steady. "After we get you patched up." She looked up and met Brady's gaze, and felt her heart tumble out of place when he gave an almost imperceptible shake of his head.

The minutes ticked by. One…and then another. The bleeding had slowed beneath her steady pressure with the towels, but Gil had already lost a great deal. And given the vast area covered by the county's small EMT crew, his chances for quick medical attention were slim to none.

"Where is that ambulance?" she whispered urgently. "Should we try to transport him ourselves?"

Brady lifted his cell phone from his pocket, dialed 911 again, then dropped his phone into his shirt pocket. "We're in luck, because they've been at a call in this part of the county." He leaned down closer to Gil. "They'll be here within twenty minutes, max. You're going to be fine."

Gil rolled his head toward Celia. "My fault… Ray died. Never meant…"

She stared at him, stunned. *"You?"*

"The…others…" His brow furrowed in concentration as he tried to speak. "Be careful…." Then he gave a low groan and his contorted expression went slack.

"Oh, my God—*Brady*—is he gone?" Celia grabbed Gil's hand and chafed it, trying to elicit a response.

Brady rested two fingertips at the corner of Gil's jaw. "He still has a pulse—but it's weak and thready. He's lost a lot of blood."

From outside came the distant sounds of approaching sirens, and in minutes the room was filled with EMTs and deputies. Celia stood in a corner, feeling dazed and cold, her hand at her mouth as she watched the EMTs work feverishly on Gil, stabilizing him and preparing him for transport. Over in the breakfast alcove just off the kitchen, Brady gave the deputies his identification and talked to them while they stood taking notes.

Until today her life had been challenging and physically demanding. There'd always been risks during her private war with the drug traffickers who tried crossing her land. Still, she'd met each day with determination, and she'd managed to carry on.

But this—the enormity of her daughter's disappearance and Gil's wounds—felt like an iron fist crushing her heart. If she hadn't called in the DEA, would things have been different? Would Lacey be safe at home, grumbling about homework and bedtime?

In minutes, the EMTs were rolling the gurney

out the door, and seconds later, the ambulance roared away with its siren wailing.

Celia stared out of the window, feeling as if a leaden weight had settled on her chest.

Whether Gil lived or died, one inescapable fact remained—someone had shot him and left him for dead. And if this shooting and Lacey's disappearance were related, Celia might never again see her beloved daughter again.

CELIA STOOD ON her front porch with her arms wrapped tightly around herself, feeling as rigid and cold as a metal post.

Hushed voices rose and fell from within the house.

Brady had gone out—to wherever he was conducting his surveillance, she supposed, though she didn't know or care. All she could think about was Lacey—was she warm? Was she scared and crying for help? Anxiety gnawed relentlessly at Celia's stomach as she tried not to think of other, far more horrific possibilities.

More agents had come in the last hour. People she didn't recognize—faces she couldn't focus on. All of it was a dim blur of motion just beyond the emptiness of despair that surrounded her.

Mia, who'd cancelled her Greyhound ticket for tomorrow and was bustling around the kitchen with Vicente, had tearfully approached her a few minutes ago with a steaming cup of coffee, but Celia had waved it away, unable to even think of holding that hot, comforting cup when Lacey might be outside somewhere, crying, and hurt and frightened.

The alternative—that she might already be dead—was so overwhelming that it had skated into Celia's thoughts only once. *Lacey—where are you?*

And the wind—Celia raised her eyes to the darkening sky and prayed as she never had before. If it rose to thirty miles an hour, the helicopter would be grounded. The ceaseless, back-and-forth sweeps of her ranch would cease, along with any chances of finding Lacey before daylight tomorrow.

Watching the American flag whipping from its pole out in the yard, Celia knew those chances were just about to end.

A blinding lightning bolt hit a willow just beyond the cabins and confirmed it.

Her fist at her mouth, Celia listened to thunder rumble and echo across the empty landscape. *Please God, let them find her.*

A touch at her elbow broke into her ongoing litany of prayers. "Ma'am, the pilot has radioed. He's encountering high winds and hail, so he has to go back to El Paso."

She closed her eyes and clenched her jaw against the sound of the young agent's voice. He was whisking away her hopes with just a few words. "He can't leave. Not yet. *Please.*"

"He'll return when the storm passes. Don't worry—these storms don't usually last long."

Don't worry? Celia fought the urge to smack him. What did he know about fear and worry and the wrenching grief of not knowing where her sweet, innocent little girl was—or even if she was still alive?

A sharp gust of wind blasted across the porch, bringing pellets of hail and stinging sheets of rain. Celia stood still, unwilling to move, until someone pushed her under the lee of the porch roof.

It was Vicente, who took her hand in his gnarled fingers and held his other hand over his chest. "I know Lacey will be all right," he said. "I feel it *here*. Just *believe*."

He stood with her as the lightning crashed and thunder shook the earth, and her tears mingled with the windblown rain.

By midnight the storm had passed, leaving the rare, fresh scent of rain-washed earth in its wake. Vicente, mumbling about his arthritis, had limped into the house, and Celia had gone back out on her horse, searching.

At four o'clock in the morning, she came back to check for any news, then started out the door again. When Brady walked out of the shadows with his hair slicked back and his wet clothes plastered to his skin, she blinked, momentarily at a loss.

"Stay inside," he urged. "There's no sense going out here—you must be freezing."

Was she? Numb from fatigue and anxiety, she

couldn't tell, but after a moment's hesitation, she allowed him to take her hand and lead her into the bright warmth of the kitchen. *But only to hear if he has any news, and then I've got to leave.*

Tom sat at her table with a coffee cup in one hand and a cell phone in the other. Vicente dozed at the far end of the table, while Mia and Adan sat shoulder to shoulder next to him, their eyes downcast.

Tom held up a forefinger, listened to his phone intently, then pressed a button to turn it off.

"Local sheriff's office just took a call—traceable only to a pay phone a hundred miles from here." His gaze skated to Celia, then to Brady. "We've got good news and bad."

Time narrowed down to a second.

Then another, slowly, inexorably stretching out the fear of what this man was about to say.

Her heart pounding in her ears and blood turning to ice, Celia held her shaking hands at her mouth.

"We think we know who has your daughter, ma'am."

The man's eyes were so gentle and sympathetic that Celia wanted to scream. *"Tell me."*

He expelled a deep breath. "She's been taken—by the Garcia gang, we think. And if we cooperate, they might just give her back."

"I should have sent her to Houston weeks ago, before this all started. Now, her life and this entire investigation are in danger." Celia blinked hard, holding back her tears. She swayed on her feet. "What do we have to do? I'll do anything."

"They want to make a trade…her, for the four men we arrested on the border tonight. We figure three of them are just mules, but the fourth is higher up in the chain. The bosses are apparently worried about him being interrogated. If we let them go tonight, they'll release her in the morning and let us know where she is."

Brady gripped Celia's elbow, steadying her, but she heard the meaning behind Tom's words.

These were ruthless killers, motivated by powerful greed. They'd killed before, and now her daughter was in their hands.

"There's not much chance this will work out, is there," she said, trying to hold back her tears. "Not much at all."

CELIA SAT AT her kitchen table, feeling numb and cold, then launched herself to her feet and began pacing again.

Staying home was driving her crazy—but both Brady and Tom had insisted that she stay here while they worked on a rescue plan, rather than risk having her inadvertently get in the way. "How far could these people get with her?" she asked no one in particular.

"Not far," Brady said. He looked up from the topographical map he'd been studying. "We have so many agencies involved in this operation that someone would have noticed travel on that highway—especially since it's usually deserted."

Hope flooded through her. "You think she could still be somewhere on the ranch?"

"With twenty thousand acres here, yes, it's possible. You've got several thousand acres of almost impassable land in the northeast quadrant."

She jumped up and stood next to him, her forearms braced on the table. "Someone could at least get to the base of those mountains with a four-wheeler. After that, it's either horses or hiking. The trails are too narrow and rugged for anything else."

When a cell phone on the table jangled, she jumped.

Tom lifted it to his ear and listened, giving Brady a small thumbs-up. When he ended the call, he gave Brady and Celia a grim smile. "Our 'copter pilot has been up in the air and searching for the last half hour. He picked up four heat images in the far northeast quadrant of your ranch. Could be wildlife, but he's guessing they're human, from the type of movement he's seen. They seem to be in a very rocky, hilly section, several miles from that sharp, right-angled bend in the highway."

"Which is damned convenient, if they think they're going to be collecting their buddies tomorrow. Well hidden, with good access for escape. Or so they think," Brady said.

Celia shot out of her chair. "I know the place—big cliffs, with caves the Native Americans once used. I used to go there to hunt for artifacts when I was a kid. Some of the drop-offs are a good five hundred feet."

"Tom and I will head out at first light. If these are the kidnappers, we'll—"

"Now! Why can't we go now? I know this ranch like the back of my hand."

Brady rested a hand on hers. "It's treacherous going, Celia, and these guys mean business. We don't even know for sure that these images are the people we're looking for."

Celia stalked across the room, grabbed a rifle from the rack and jerked a set of keys from the hooks by the door. "You stay here. That's fine. But I can trailer a horse out onto the highway near there and ride in—I could do it blindfolded. If my daughter is there, I'm getting her back."

Tom shook his head. "You need to stay here."

"And I don't think you can stop me." She glared at him. "If these are the guys who have my daughter, they won't be expecting visitors this soon. Maybe they'll even be asleep by the time I get there."

Brady and Tom looked at each other.

"It's going to take more than one person," Brady said. "If we go, promise that you'll stay here."

"I've got the keys," she said. "I've got the truck, trailer and horses. I'm *going*. There's no way that I can sit here and worry—and there's no way that you'd ever find your way around in the dark out there."

Brady sighed. "Okay. Then promise that you'll stay in the truck, with the doors locked. Maybe you know the way, but you don't have the training to do this. Understand? You—or someone else— could get hurt."

"I'm riding," she retorted. "But I'm not a fool. I'll stay well out of your way."

"I think we should wait," Tom said to Brady, tipping his head in her direction.

His condescension rankled. "And what happens if these *suspects* get spooked tomorrow and decide to kill my daughter no matter what? She can probably identify them by now, and that sure presents a risk." Celia met Brady's gaze with a steely one of her own. "I'm not willing to take that chance."

Chapter Eighteen

WITHIN TWENTY MINUTES, one of the pickups was hitched to the stock trailer, and four horses were saddled and loaded.

Brady slammed the gate shut and rounded the back of the trailer, his nerves humming and senses sharpened, ready for whatever lay ahead.

Until the moment Lacey disappeared, he'd been driven by the need to take down Garcia's organization and avenge Chuck's death. Now all that mattered was finding Lacey alive—and that hope dimmed with every passing hour.

Adan stepped in his way, his face pale and drawn. "I want to come along. I *need* to."

"Look, kid. You're safer here."

"But I can help." Adan swallowed hard. "I… might know someone who's involved."

"That new guy at the Rocking B?"

Adan's eyes widened. "You know about him?"

"He sure seemed to know you."

"Nieto is big trouble. I know of him from back

home…back when I used to get in trouble with the law, too. But that's over, I swear." Adan gripped Brady's forearm. "Please—you might need someone else with you who can handle a horse."

If he'd ever had doubts about the boy, the raw emotion in Adan's eyes swept them all away.

"I can't put you in danger, kid. You're better off here."

"Celia and Lacey are like family to me, now." Adan's voice broke. "Don't leave me behind."

Brady hesitated. "You could help Celia with the horses, when Tom and I go ahead on foot…as long as you stay put, well out of sight. No heroics, got it? Get in the way, and you could jeopardize everything—and you could get hurt."

Relief filled the boy's eyes. "Promise."

Tom stood by the cab of the truck, his face creased in a frown. "This isn't going to be easy," he muttered. "After all the rain, the footing will be slick. We won't know where we're going. We don't even know if the objects Joe sees on the FLIR screen are our suspects."

"But in daylight, they'd see us coming, and I'm confident Celia can help us get to where we have to be." Brady clapped him on the shoulder. "Come on, we need to get moving."

They all climbed into the truck, and Brady took off with the headlights dimmed. For the first six miles of ranch road he drove fast and hard. The truck flew over the bumps, its engine roaring. For the last two miles, he slowed down and switched off the headlights.

Once he hit the highway, he kept it steady and quiet at an even thirty miles an hour.

"Please—we've got to hurry. Lacey must be so scared!" Celia cried as he pulled to a stop well off the highway.

"But we can't chance alerting anyone to our arrival, either." He studied the landscape, then pulled forward and parked between two towering piles of fragmented rock. "Any more word from the pilot, Tom?"

Tom spoke into his cell phone as Celia, Adan and Brady began unloading the horses. "Wind's picking up again," he said after a moment. "Joe says he'll stay in the sky as long as he can to direct us, but he'll have to leave if the gusts get any worse."

Brady handed Tom the reins for a small mare. "Tell him not to take any chances. Where do we start?"

"He has us on his screen—says we should head two miles due west of where we're parked. When we get there, he'll guide us in for the last half mile or so. He thinks the suspects are in some sort of shallow cave or are beneath an overhang—a while back, one of the figures stepped out and the image intensified."

"I can't stop thinking about what those bastards could do to her. Being kidnapped is terrifying enough." Celia's face was ghost-white as she led her horse across the highway and pulled open the gate, then closed it behind her when everyone had ridden through. "If they so much as lay a hand on her..."

"These guys aren't the brains behind this trafficking setup," Brady said, wishing he felt as confident as his words. "They're probably too nervous to think about anything beyond making the trade and running for safety."

But being armed and nervous could be a very bad thing if Lacey could identify them. Given too much time to sweat over the prospect of prison—or worse—there was no telling what they might do.

The sliver of moon overhead offered pale illumination as the horses rounded sharp-edged boulders and picked their way over the rocky ground.

"Damn," Tom muttered when his horse stumbled and went down on its knees. "I think I'd be better off on foot."

Celia looked over her shoulder. "Any word from the pilot?"

Tom talked into his phone, then dropped it into in his shirt pocket. "Still another good mile and a half west, and it's gonna get rougher...we've got a climb ahead of us."

"Maybe the pilot sees the overall distance from up there, but that doesn't mean we can take such a straight route." Brady touched his watch to illuminate the dial. "I just hope we can get there well before dawn, or we won't have much of an element of surprise."

Forty-five minutes later, Brady signaled a halt. The wind gusts were picking up now, tossing the horses' manes and tails and making them skittish. Far to the west, lightning crackled across the horizon.

Tom pulled out his phone again. "'Copter's gotta take off," he said after a minute. "He's got twenty-eight-mile-an-hour gusts up there."

"But he can't leave! We'll never find my daughter. *Please*—tell him to stay."

Her face was a mask of fear, and Brady knew how she felt. Without air support, finding anything out here in the dark would be impossible. "He won't do us any good if he ends up crashing that bird into the side of a hill. But don't worry. I'm not leaving without finding her. I promise."

"We're almost there," Tom announced. "Joe says we turn along this ridge and go another hundred yards or so. He thinks the cave is up maybe sixty feet or so, on the west face of a cliff."

Brady dismounted and handed his reins to Celia. "You and Adan stay here—maybe in that little draw, a quarter-mile behind us. Just keep the horses quiet. We should be back with Lacey in an hour or less." He dropped a swift kiss on her forehead, then gave her a hug. "I promise."

"Please—I've *got* to come along. My daughter is out here. *Please*."

She'd been all business and ready for action when hitching up the trailer and getting the horses ready. But now that she faced the prospect of staying behind, her hands were shaking.

"I need you to stay here. If you got in the way, things could go wrong. You've got your rifle, right?"

"There's a scabbard on every saddle."

"Don't worry—the pilot said there were no other infrared images on his screen. The only people within a several-mile radius are the four of us and four up in that cave, so we'll have everything under control in no time. You and Adan will be safe here while we're gone."

"I don't care about me. I just want my little girl. *Hurry.*"

FIVE MINUTES STRETCHED into ten. Twenty. Thirty.

Adan, clearly exhausted, sat on his horse with one leg cocked over the saddle horn, his chin dropped to his chest and his hat pulled down over his eyes.

Celia could barely sit still. An owl hooted from some distant place, but otherwise the night was eerily quiet—all the more so because somewhere, not too far away, Brady and Tom were seeking some hidden cave and getting into position to rescue her daughter.

The magnitude of that act—and her roiling emotions—made her desperate to rush after them to help. What if just one more person, one more weapon, could make all the difference? How could she ever forgive herself if Lacey was hurt during this attempted rescue?

A lifetime of taking charge and being in control warred against Brady's warning to stay put and out of the way.

The path Brady and Tom had followed led up into the rocks, beckoning her. Maybe the other guys had heard a noise or seen some motion. Maybe they were lying in wait this very moment, ready to pick off Brady and Tom when they least expected it.

And nothing—certainly not the three bastards who might be holding her daughter hostage—was going to keep her from bringing Lacey home.

Her pulse thrumming through her veins, Celia slid silently off her horse and tied the reins to a waist-high sagebrush. Slowly, careful to avoid making any sound, she slipped her rifle from the scabbard, then turned toward the path, taking care with each step.

At the top of the path, she looked back and found Adan still dozing. *Thank you, God,* she whispered. He was better off with the horses, out of harm's way.

One false move—one unnecessary noise—and the kidnappers could panic. And Lacey might be the one to pay the price.

At a skittering of pebbles across the rocks ahead, her heart stopped for a moment. It could be Brady

or Tom. It could be one of the smugglers. But whoever it was, she wasn't going to stand out in the
open and take any chances.

Crouching low, she moved behind some boulders
and continued on, running parallel to the trail, taking care with every step. Just ahead, she caught a
flash of white and the furtive movements of someone moving in the same direction Brady had gone.

Both Tom and Brady were dressed in *black* from
head to foot.

Releasing the safety on her rifle, she picked up
her pace and slipped behind the guy ahead of her
on the trail.

Four images had shown on the helicopter's FLIR
screen. If Lacey was one of them and this guy was
the second, then there were two more ahead. And
this one must have seen or heard something and
decided to circle around for a closer look.

Which meant Brady and Tom were in danger.

Up ahead, the loud crack of a rifle resounded
through the hills like cannon fire, then another.

The figure in front of her stood taller and raised
his rifle to his shoulder. Took aim at some object
ahead. *Brady?*

Celia moved closer. "I wouldn't do that if I were
you," she announced. "Drop your rifle or I fire."

"Now why," he snarled, "would you want to do
a thing like that?"

He spun around and dropped low, his rifle instantly raised to his cheekbone. Even in the darkness, his face was strangely familiar. Nieto?

If I don't fire, I'm going to die...and maybe Lacey, too.

Panic slammed through her as she curled her finger around the trigger.

The deafening crack of a rifle exploded into the night air. The man screamed, doubled over, then crumpled to the ground.

She stared, horror and deep regret swamping her senses.

Then Adan stepped past her and lowered his own rifle, the stunned expression on his young face surely matching her own. "I had to, Celia—it was either you, or him."

"*Y-you* shot him?"

The man on the ground moaned and clutched his thigh as he struggled to pull himself up enough to lean against a rock. He glared at Celia, then Adan. "Calaveras." His mouth curled into a sneer. "We meet again, eh? Only now, I would not want to be in your shoes. Efrain does not ignore betrayal."

Not Adan. Not the kid she'd been hoping to "rescue" from his troubled past. Stunned, Celia glanced between Adan and the Nieto. "What does he mean, Adan? *Betrayal?*"

"Efrain is going to be singing to the Feds if he knows what's good for him—and Nieto will, too, if he has any sense." Brady appeared out of the darkness, on the other side of the fallen man, with a rifle in his hand. He swooped down to pick up Nieto's weapon and set it out of reach, then slipped a pair of handcuffs out of his pocket, pulled the guy's wrists behind his back, and snapped on the cuffs.

He bent down to take a look at the gunshot wound on the man's thigh. "You're damn lucky—looks like it went through the muscle and didn't hit any arteries. It isn't even bleeding all that much right now."

The man spewed out a litany of curses in Spanish and jerked at his cuffs, then winced and sat still, eyeing his leg. He gave Celia a venomous glare. "You and your girl should be dead—just like your neighbor."

"What?"

"You couldn't just leave things alone. And for that, you deserved to pay."

"Brady—"

"I heard." Brady shifted his attention to Adan. "Now, you don't have any plans to do anything stupid, do you?"

His eyes wide, Adan shook his head.

"Then put your rifle down on the ground, son, and take five steps back. Nice and easy. I just don't want to take any chances."

"What about Lacey? Where is she—is she okay?" Celia searched the shadows, then skirted Brady and started up the trail. "Where's Tom?"

"Two of these dudes tried to ambush us not

twenty yards from here. We've got 'em cuffed and ready to haul out of here. Tom is going after Lacey."

Almost on cue, Lacey raced up the path and flung herself into Celia's arms, sobbing and laughing until she was out of breath.

"Mom! I'm so sorry! I just went riding, but these guys were there—and one grabbed my reins—it was awful! They kept saying that I'd die if something didn't happen…and then when they heard someone coming, they divided up and I just knew it had to be you out here—" She gulped and scrubbed her tears away with the back of her hand. "I was so scared!"

Celia stroked her face, then held her close. "It's all right, sweetheart. Everything will be okay."

But looking over the top of her head at Brady cuffing Adan, she knew that wasn't so.

Chapter Nineteen

A HALF-DOZEN law enforcement cruisers, unmarked DEA and Border Patrol cars had converged on the highway by the time they made it back to Celia's truck.

Celia and Lacey unsaddled the horses and loaded them into the trailer while Adan and the others were taken to the waiting patrol cars and whisked away.

After another twenty minutes of answering questions, Celia felt weak-kneed and relieved when Tom finally closed his notebook. But Lacey was next.

"Could you both come with me, please?" the female agent asked. "This won't take long—I just want to get some notes down before she has time to forget, or get a little confused about the details. I'll come back tomorrow as well."

Celia gave Lacey a big hug, reveling in the pure joy of that soft, warm contact and the familiar scent of Lacey's honeysuckle shampoo. "Are you okay with this interview, honey?"

Lacey nodded and leaned into her. "I—I *have* to make sure I get this right. I want those guys sent far, far away. For *good.*"

The agent gave her an encouraging smile. "Kidnapping means life imprisonment—and these guys have a lot more charges against them as well, including a previous murder charge. If they don't receive the death penalty, you can still be sure they will never, ever be on the street again. Your testimony can make sure that happens."

She led them to a more private spot away from the others, where Lacey cuddled next to Celia on the tailgate of a pickup, and the agent stood next to them with a notebook in her hand.

Celia curved an arm around Lacey's shoulders and held her tight as Lacey told them about the all-terrain vehicle that had come up from the shore of the river and sped off to the east. It had then done a high-speed donut and come straight after her.

The images were terrifying.

Lacey's horse had been no match for the speed and unlimited endurance of the four-wheeler. Two men had grabbed her out of Loco's saddle, tied her hands, and thrown her onto a pile of slippery plastic-wrapped packages in the back of the vehicle.

The one with the scarred face had wanted to kill her. Nieto had insisted that it would only make things worse—she only had to be kept quiet about seeing them until some sort of deal was over.

They'd held her in a cold, dark cave where a third

guy was guarding stacks of boxes and packages. She'd had nothing to eat or drink but, praise God, none of them had touched her.

They had, however, started arguing again about the risk of her identifying them later. Then one of them heard footsteps approaching.

"Oh, honey—" Imagining what could have happened, Celia turned and pulled her beloved daughter into a closer embrace, with Lacey's head nestled beneath her chin. At the damp warmth of tears falling against her shirt, Celia's guilt and sorrow grew. *How close I came to losing you, sweetheart.*

Since coming home from college to take over the ranch, she'd been forced to be strong. She'd had to stand on her own two feet despite all odds, or risk losing the ranch. But those very qualities had made Brady's job here more difficult…and had nearly cost Lacey her life. The enormity of her failure was overwhelming.

"This is all my fault," Celia murmured, unable to hold back the tremble in her voice. "Brady told me yesterday that I should take you someplace safe. I should have listened to him and done it right away. I am so, so sorry."

Lacey wrapped her arms around Celia. "But I'm the one who ran off—I didn't *want* to go to Aunt Linda's. I figured you wouldn't make me go if you had time to think about it."

"I guess we're just a little bit alike—bullheaded Remington women who think they need to be right." Tears burning beneath her eyelids, Celia smiled down at her, her heart overflowing as she studied each precious feature of her daughter's face. "Maybe we both need to change—just a little."

The agent asked more questions, until Brady broke away from a trio of grim-faced agents and walked over. "I think she's had enough for this morning, don't you? Why don't we let these people go home?"

Celia gave him a smile of pure gratitude. "We're ready, believe me. What about Adan? What will happen to him?"

"He was planted out here, Celia. He was supposed to keep an eye on things for Garcia, and pass the word if anyone seemed to be getting too suspicious."

Celia thought about the teenager's shy smile. His acute embarrassment over dealing with Mia when she first arrived. "But he *shot* that man when I hesitated too long. I could be dead, if it wasn't for him."

"It sounds like he was having second thoughts about his life of crime before he ever got here. Prior to his stay at the detention center, he ran with a gang that developed an association with Garcia's drug trafficking ring."

Celia drew in a sharp breath. "I knew he'd been in trouble, but not that much."

"Apparently, he wanted no part of the drug organization, but there were threats against his sisters to 'encourage' his cooperation."

"The poor kid. He probably figured he had no choice." Celia reached out and laid a hand on Brady's arm. "Can you help him?"

"I'll do what I can, but the decision on any charges will be up to the District Attorney, not me."

She nodded. "I'll never forget what you did tonight. You and Tom gave me my daughter back."

"It ended well. We've identified the major players in this organization clear to Minneapolis and Chicago, and the Mexican government has already arrested Garcia and his key associates."

"I'm so sorry I didn't listen to you better—I guess I was busy trying to stay in control, and you were always just trying to do your job. I've been too stubborn for my own good."

His mouth lifted in a faint smile that didn't reach the sadness in his eyes. "I wouldn't change a thing about you."

"Now that I've had a hint of what your life is like, I wish I could change one thing about you—and find you a safer career. How can you deal with this, day after day? The lies, the greed, the people who'd do anything to make a score?" She shook her head. "You could lose your life over this, yet the drugs just keep coming across that border and the traffickers just multiply."

"It's what I do," he said. His thumbs jammed in his back pockets, he stood looking out over the landscape to the first blush of dawn, his face etched with exhaustion. "Or have done, anyway. I'm not sure what tomorrow will bring."

"Please—just keep safe." *Please decide to stay.*

But she already knew that the Triple R had nothing to offer a man like him. The sweat, the dust, the hard work and endless heat would hold no excitement for a man who'd spent his life as a special agent. Neither would a woman like her, with calluses on her hands and ranching in her blood, and too many responsibilities to even name. A man looking to enjoy life would never land here.

"I've got a meeting with the other agents in the morning," he said. "After that, I'll stop at your ranch to say goodbye to everyone."

This was it, she realized. Already, she felt emptiness seeping into her bones. "So now, you'll go on...though I guess you can't say where, right?" She stiffened her spine and offered her hand in farewell. It was one of the hardest things she'd ever managed. "Thank you...for everything you've done."

She held her breath as his gaze settled on her, his eyes weary and accepting, and infinitely sad.

And then he shook her hand and walked away.

WHEN THE PHONE RANG at midnight three days later, Celia knew it meant trouble.

"Ms. Remington? Mr. Banuelos is asking for you. If you want to see him, you'd better come soon. He's still in intensive care, second floor, but he's not doing well."

Thankful that Mia was still at the ranch to watch over Jonah and Lacey, Celia ran for her truck and floored the accelerator.

Three days after his emergency surgery, Gil was still drifting in and out of consciousness, and had yet to acknowledge Celia when she came to see him. With damage to his liver, small intestines, and spleen, he'd been close to death when he hit the operating table. Since then, he'd been fighting a raging infection that wasn't responding to antibiotics.

She had so many questions. And there was so little time.

After reaching the hospital parking lot, she raced for the emergency room entrance, and took the stairs rather than waiting for an elevator.

At the expression of alarm on a nurse's face, she glanced down at herself and realized that she'd rushed to El Paso in her work boots, jeans and a faded sweatshirt—the clothes she'd worn this afternoon and evening when Vicente, the veterinarian, and she had preconditioned a hundred calves.

Chute work was never easy, and it was never, ever clean.

Darting into a ladies' room just outside intensive care, she splashed water on her face and ran her fingers through her hair, then scrubbed her hands.

When she came out, the nurse at the station eyed

her dubiously. "Maybe you should leave those boots here," she said, waving a hand toward the door.

"Gladly. How is Gil doing?" Celia toed off her boots and crossed the aisle in stocking feet. "Any change?"

The brunette behind the desk ran a forefinger down a clipboard and viewed the monitors in front of her. "No worse, no better—he's holding his own. The only time he has said anything was when he asked for you. You can go in for a few minutes right now, if you'd like—he hasn't had anyone here for an hour or more."

"He had *visitors?*"

"A man came earlier. Tall, dark hair, broad shoulders. He stayed the full ten minutes and left." She gave a sigh of pure admiration. "*Real* nice guy, but he seemed distracted."

Brady, maybe, hoping to get some answers, too. She hadn't seen him since the morning he left the ranch, and she'd felt melancholy ever since. Lost dreams were poor company during the long and lonely nights when there was too much time to think.

And Brady hadn't called. Not even once.

It was for the best, she knew—a quick, absolute resolution, with no uncertainty to drag out any hopes or useless efforts on either side.

Celia nodded to the nurse and strode to the cubicle just opposite the station. Gil lay there as he had before, on his back, the head of his bed raised, tubes and wires and IV stands crowded shoulder to shoulder with monitor screens and equipment she couldn't begin to name. The whoosh of a ventilator in the next cubicle sounded like the respirations of some prehistoric beast. Monitors beeped, machines hummed, the phone rang, and a gurney rattled past, accompanied by several sets of footsteps.

If the poor guy wasn't practically comatose, he surely wouldn't have gotten any rest here.

"Hey, Uncle Gil…you're looking mighty fine," she murmured, reaching over the network of tubes to brush his hair away from his forehead. "I hear you had a visitor."

He lay still as granite, his eyes closed. Only the reassuring lines squiggling across his monitors and the almost imperceptible rise and fall of his chest reassured her that he was still alive.

She settled in a chair close to the head of his bed. "I just want you to know that we're worried about you. They said prayers for you at church on Sunday. I talked to your foreman Alvarez yesterday—he's doing okay, even with Jose Nieto gone. I went over and helped him brand and vaccinate yesterday, and your calves are looking good."

The lines on the monitor gave an extra little blip, and she wondered if maybe he was hearing her, even though he seemed so still. Encouraged, she reached over and rubbed his hand. "I hear Brady Coleman was here to see you…I suppose he hoped to get some answers, but I'd guess you weren't up to much conversation. Did he tell you that he's a DEA special agent, and that the guys who shot you have been arrested? It's been pretty wild at our place. A big 'operation,' they called it—and now it's been on the national news."

She glanced up at the big clock on the wall above his bed. Just eight minutes…and then it would be another hour before she could come back in. "Let's see…Lacey was missing for a while, but she's home, now. Mia left for New York on the bus this morning, but she and Vicente are getting along so I'll bet she'll come for a visit again."

Adan would have been a big draw as well, but there'd been no further word about the boy since he had been arrested with the others early Saturday morning.

"You know, you and Jonah were right," she murmured, her thoughts drifting back to the emotional roller coaster of the past few weeks. "You both were always saying I should find some nice guy and settle down—that I would be happier and life would be so much better. I never really thought about it because I never really found the right guy. Know something funny?" She reached over and tucked the blankets a little higher over Gil's chest. "I found the one who truly does make me happy—and he left with barely a goodbye. Ironic, right?"

Behind her, someone rustled the curtain and cleared his throat.

She turned—and the moment she saw Brady, a

warm flush of embarrassment flooded her cheeks. Dressed in a black polo shirt and black slacks, he looked muscular, trim and as handsome as sin.

"I…um…didn't know you were here," she stammered.

"Just got here. The nurse was sweet—she said I could come in for a minute, even though Gil had another visitor."

"I think she has a crush on you, actually."

"No, she's way too young." He nodded toward the double doors leading out into the waiting room. "I thought I'd stop here to check on Gil before going out to your ranch. I have a present for you."

"Adan?"

Brady smiled. "He's been questioned extensively but not charged. He was allegedly planted at your ranch as a lookout, but he wasn't exactly a model Garcia employee. He stayed to protect his sisters, but once he settled in and found he really liked all of you, he never did do what he was told."

Celia felt a flash of almost motherly pride. "From the beginning, I was sure he had potential to make something of himself. I've even been talking to him about college, so we'll see."

"I'd better talk fast, I guess, before I get booted out of here." Brady looked over his shoulder at the nurse behind the nurses' station. "The local interrogations have been successful. With kidnapping, attempted murder and dozens of counts against them related to drug trafficking, these guys have been singing their hearts out."

"That's good, then." Celia dredged up a faint smile. "You must be thrilled."

"You might be, too. We've discovered that Nieto was behind your cattle thefts—probably as retaliation for your stand against drug shipments crossing your land. We have some people hauling them home for you, right now."

At that, she could smile for real. "One of my young Brangus bulls went missing, and he was a $20,000 investment. I would have been paying on that note for years, with no return. Where were they?"

He glanced at Gil, who still lay motionless in the bed with his eyes closed, then he lowered his voice. "A remote area of Gil's ranch. We think Gil has known about the trafficking situation for years. We found barns on his more distant properties that are being used as stash houses for accumulating drug shipments."

She wanted to deny the possibility, but too many pieces fell into place with just those simple words. The new trucks. The expensive home and fences, and the new barns. Gil had always appreciated luxury, but he'd never been particularly adept at ranching. "Then why would someone shoot him?"

"We're guessing he might have found out about the cattle, or have gotten edgy about the whole deal and threatened to call the sheriff, so Nieto shot him and left him for dead."

Celia felt Gil's hand barely squeeze hers. Surprised, she turned and leaned closer. "Gil—it's me. Celia. Can you hear me?"

"I…got…what I deserved." His voice was rusty and faint, but he cracked his eyes open and met her gaze. "I—I'm so sorry…for everything.…"

"You don't deserve to be here like this," she retorted. "That bastard nearly took your life."

Gil winced and shut his eyes tight. He took several shaky breaths. "Your dad…was no accident. I n-never told—they would…have killed me, too."

All the years of anger, grief, and frustration coalesced into this one moment as she stared at Gil, willing him to continue. "What happened? *Tell me* what happened."

A faint smile played across Gil's features. "Such…a strong one, your father. He was a… fighter…like you. He tried to stop them, and he was shot. I knew then to…cooperate was the…wise thing."

Celia released his hand and sat back in her chair. In her heart, she'd known all along, no matter what the official reports said. But hearing the words, from the man who'd kept the truth from her all these years, made her heart wrench in her chest.

Her father had chosen honor and had died for it…alone, in a distant part of the ranch, where he hadn't even been found for days. Gil had chosen weakness and had enjoyed the last decade in financial security. The unfairness of it all tasted so bitter she could barely speak.

"I think I'd better be going," she mumbled, rising from her chair. "It's a long drive home."

She brushed past Brady, her head bowed, but he caught her arm.

"Listen," he said in a low voice. "He's an old man, now. He knows he's made mistakes and probably wishes like hell he'd never seen a penny of the money he's gotten from these people. As sick as he is, he might not last long. If you ever want to make peace with him, this is the time."

He was right, of course…again. Even tomorrow could be too late. She took a deep breath and went back to Gil's bedside, where she took his hand once again. "I understand why you did what you did, and I'm sorry for all that you've been through. You've tried to be a good uncle all these years. My father would have appreciated that."

Gil rolled his head toward her. "I owed him—" he gave a wheezy cough "—that much."

They were just past the nurses' station when the alarms went off and nurses came running from every direction.

Celia didn't have to go back inside to know that he was gone.

Chapter Twenty

AN HOUR LATER, Celia, Adan and Brady stood out in the hospital parking lot, where Celia gave Adan a quick hug. "I'm glad you're here, Adan. We've missed you."

He ducked his head in obvious embarrassment. "If you don't want me to work for you again, I'll understand."

"From what I hear, you did nothing wrong. Maybe your reasons for showing up at our ranch were shady, but you never betrayed my trust."

He gave her a shy grin. "Is...um...Mia still there?"

"I'm sorry. She had to leave today or she couldn't have helped her roommates move into their new place." He appeared so crestfallen that Celia almost gave into the temptation to give him another hug. "She left her e-mail address, though. *And* she plans to come for a visit in August."

Brady clapped him on the back. "August will be here in no time, son. Do you have a laptop?"

He shook his head.

"Well, I've got an older one—it works fine for e-mail, and you're welcome to it. Celia could help you learn how to use it, if you don't know already. It's a good skill to have if you ever decide to go on to school."

Adan looked up at the stars. "I'd like that, *amigo*. Thanks."

"Hey, could you go on over to Celia's truck for a minute? I need to talk to her." Brady winked at him. "Alone."

He waited until Adan crossed the parking lot, then he turned to Celia and rested a hand at the small of her back, guiding her toward a bench set in the shadows. "How are you holding up?"

She perched on the edge of the bench, her hands curved over the front of the seat. "It's been quite a week, hasn't it? Losing Lacey was the worst thing that has ever happened to me. Getting her back was my greatest joy. And Gil…despite everything, I'm going to miss him. Soon, Jonah will be gone too, and life is going to be empty without those two. So how about you?"

Brady leaned forward to brace his elbows on his thighs and loosely clasp his hands. "Things change," he said.

Leaning over to him, she gave his shoulder a small, playful bump with her own. "A good thing, right? You spearheaded the investigation here in Saguaro Springs, and that sure turned out well.

You've probably got assignments scheduled to kingdom come."

He lifted a shoulder. "I would if I still worked there."

"You *quit?*"

"It was my life for almost ten years, Celia. But nothing was ever the same after Chuck and the others were killed in that ambush. I knew that once their killers and the rest of the Garcia gang were in jail, it would be time to leave."

"And that time has come?"

He nodded. "In ways I didn't expect. For years, I'd planned on starting an investigation firm. During the past two, I'd resolved to start it close to where Chuck's widow lives, because she needed help."

"And she doesn't?"

"For the past two years, she did. But this week she was actually rather blunt. 'I know you feel bad about my husband,' she said, 'but I'm building a new life, and so should you.' She also said she'd found a boyfriend who's wonderful with my godson Tyler."

"Well…that's good for her and Tyler. Right?"

He studied his folded hands. "Really good."

"So now what?"

"All this time, I was focusing on what I could do for Melissa. I knew she needed a lot of help to get by. She needed someone to be a father for her son. And since I was responsible for the DEA operation that took her husband's life, that person had to be me."

Celia had seen Brady walk out of her life. Given who she was and where she had to be, she'd accepted that he wouldn't return. But now, an ember of hope flickered to life inside her. "And now?"

"And now, I'm free to follow my heart." He looked down at her, his eyes grave. "Leaving here was the hardest thing I've ever done until this moment, because now you hold my entire life in your hands. I love you, Celia. I tried to stay away, because I know you deserve better than someone like me. But I'm hoping that what you said to Gil is true."

"I did find someone who made me truly happy." She reached up to rest her hand against his cheek. "Someone I will love the rest of my days, no matter what happens. And that someone is you."

* * * * *

YES! Please send me the *Cowboy at Heart* collection in Larger Print. This collection begins with 3 FREE books and 2 FREE gifts in the first shipment, and more free gifts will follow! My books will arrive in 8 monthly shipments until I have the entire 51-book *Cowboy at Heart* collection. I will receive 2 or 3 FREE books in each shipment and I will pay just $4.99 U.S./ $5.89 CDN. for each of the other four books in each shipment, plus $2.99 for shipping and handling.* If I decide to keep the entire collection, I'll have paid for only 32 books because 19 books are FREE! I understand that by accepting the 3 free books and gifts places me under no obligation to buy anything. I can always return a shipment and cancel at any time. My free books and gifts are mine to keep no matter what I decide.

256 HCN 0779   456 HCN 0779

Name	(PLEASE PRINT)	
Address		Apt. #
City	State/Prov.	Zip/Postal Code

Signature (if under 18, a parent or guardian must sign)

Mail to the **Harlequin® Reader Service:**
IN U.S.A.: P.O. Box 1867, Buffalo, NY 14240-1867
IN CANADA: P.O. Box 609, Fort Erie, Ontario L2A 5X3

* Terms and prices subject to change without notice. Prices do not include applicable taxes. Sales tax applicable in N.Y. Canadian residents will be charged applicable taxes. This offer is limited to one order per household. All orders subject to approval. Credit or debit balances in a customer's account(s) may be offset by any other outstanding balance owed by or to the customer. Please allow 4 to 6 weeks for delivery. Offer available while quantities last. Offer not available to Quebec residents.

ReaderService.com

Manage your account online!

- Review your order history
- Manage your payments
- Update your address

---

*We've designed
the Harlequin® Reader Service
website just for you.*

Enjoy all the features!

- Reader excerpts from any series
- Respond to mailings and special monthly offers
- Discover new series available to you
- Browse the Bonus Bucks catalog
- Share your feedback

Visit us at:
ReaderService.com